Storm-Star
By
I.N. Morgan

Storm-Star by I.N. Morgan
Published by Heavy Rush Media LLC
www.heavyrushmediallc.com[1]
ISBN: 978-1-7328765-1-4

---

1. http://www.heavyrushmediallc.com

Special thanks to:

Dave and Allanah for editing

RJ for the cover art

Steven for German translations

Friends and Family for support

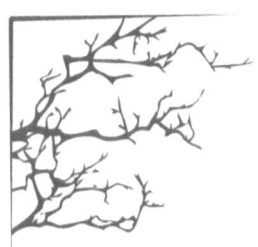

Prologue

"It's getting chilly out here." Jason pulled his jacket tighter around his body. His girlfriend sniggered at the comment.

"Well, duh, it's fall." Amy said, smirking. "It's supposed to be cold."

"Man, I wanna be by the bonfire." Jason complained as the two moved deeper into the woods. "Why did you drag me out here?"

He and Amy were hanging out with their friends at the Rust Springs State Park, drinking alcohol and smoking weed at the secluded location. A lot of kids from their high school liked to use the area for different activities, usually those they did not want their parents or authorities to know about.

"Because I have something special I don't want to share with the others." Amy replied. Jason perked up a little.

"Like what?"

Amy pulled out a sandwich bag filled with blunts from under her sweater.

"What's this?"

He manipulated the green buds through the plastic with his chilled hands.

"What do you think, doofus?"

"I know what it is, but where did you get it?"

"Got it from some women near the farms." Amy took one of them out of the bag. "I spent all night rolling these. Do you have your lighter?"

"Sure." Jason passed his shinny Zippo to her, eager to consume the stash. Amy quickly lit the blunt, taking a long drag. Relish lit up her face as she offered it to Jason.

"Have some, baby."

Jason took it in his fingers and took a drag himself. He smiled at the sweet, earthy taste.

"Damn, that's good." he coughed. Amy grinned, kissing him on the cheek.

"That's why I'm keeping these to myself. You're the exception of course."

Jason chuckled lightly as they continued to walk in the nighttime forest. The moon was bright and the young couple soaked up the milky rays on their journey. Jason and Amy came to a clearing where a couple of rocks were piled on top of each other. A pentagram marked the stone structure in bright red. A rainbow of melted wax candles littered the forest floor around the altar.

"What the hell?" Amy inspected the remains of a messy ritual.

"Hey, I think we found the little meeting area of those "teen witches"!" Jason laughed.

"Those dweebs? Well, I did hear something from Vanessa about them conducting rituals at night."

Jason already climbed on the altar, sending rocks tumbling down.

"What are you doing?"

Jason struck a regal pose, joint still in his mouth, and pulled his jacket's hood over his head.

"Lord Satan demands a sacrifice." he growled, "Give your weed and body to me, Amy. Satan commands you!"

The girl giggled at her boyfriend's antics. A snap of twigs caught her attention. She looked around but could not see anyone or anything beyond the clearing. Amy would normally chalk it up to a deer or some other animal making those sounds. Uncertainty snuck into her heart. Even through the mellow high, she had a strong urge to get back to the bonfire.

"Jason, we should go back…"

"Don't tell me you're scared!"

"I'm not! I-!"

Jason fell, tackled off the altar by a large shadow.

The high school junior hit the ground with such force his body gave a sickening crack. Amy gazed upon his motionless body, bloodied and clawed, for a split second. Another figure rushed at her from the side. She never had a chance to scream again as her throat was ripped out.

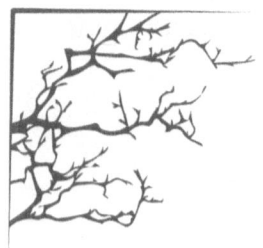

Chapter 1

C leveland, Ohio
November 1997

ASH APPROACHED THE dead deer, nose wrinkling at the horrible stench. Cars raced past him on the busy highway leading into the city. He saw the innards spilling out of the deer's abdomen and maggots accumulating on the festering body. Ash deduced it to a standard hit-and-run. The car hit the deer so fast its internal organs ruptured.

Road-kill collection was not a glamorous or interesting job. Ash would often pass the time by investigating the bodies of carcasses; determining what did the furry creatures in. He was only a few weeks into the job, but he could already deduce the cause of death based on various signs. Ash grabbed the buck by the antlers, pulling with all his strength. The upper half of the carcass was pulled away from the rest of the body with a wet rip. The disgusting smell became even more prominent. It made him reconsider why he liked eating meat in the first place. He regretted eating that leftover hamburger from earlier this morning.

HHHHOOONNKKK!!!

"Hey, fuck-tard! Move your ass! We ain't got all day!"

Ash rolled his eyes at Johnny, who was yelling behind him in the truck. Usually Johnny did not work with him, but the boss assigned them together for the day. Groaning over the weight of the dead animal and his rotten luck, Ash managed to haul both parts of the deer to the back of the truck himself.

"What took you so fuckin' long?" Johnny questioned rudely as Ash got in the truck. Johnny, a sloppy pudgy man with blond corn-rows on his head, was the epitome of white trash and would have never gotten anywhere in life if it was not for his father. Ash ignored him, removing his orange hard-hat and gingerly removing some guts off his reflective vest. He was not in the mood for a fight with his boss's son.

"Whatever. Fuckin' faggot." Johnny snorted when he did not get a response. The truck tore off down the road to the compost plant where the animals would be disposed of. Johnny pressed one of his pudgy fingers on the console and the radio came to life.

"Last night, the body of a Rust Springs High School boy was found in Rust Springs State Park. Police said it looked like a vicious animal attack based on the wounds found on the body. At the site of the slayings, a makeshift stone altar with a pentagram was found -"

Ash listened passively to the gory news details, trying to block out Johnny's one-sided conversations.

"There was this one time when I was with this chick and we were getting high..."

Ash continued to listen to the news.

"Authorities are searching for Amy Bryant in the area surrounding the park. Friends and family remain hopeful for her safe return. Meanwhile, Rust Springs police are looking into possible suspects -"

Johnny turned the radio off.

"I was listening to that -"

"Shut up, dick, unless you want me to write a report to dad."

Ash groaned as Johnny continued with his inane "high school glory days" stories. The man found the need to brag about his exploits although no one cared to hear them.

"Man, those were the days." Johnny concluded a tale of a hedonistic frat house party. Ash never had a great school experience, little to any friends and lots of fights. Sometimes he won, sometimes he lost. His foster parents, whoever they were at the time, would get a call from the principal and punishments would follow afterwards. Most people were afraid of him after they saw him fight. Ash was a ball of rage in the heat of the battle. He remembered names of "psycho" and "freak" in the back of his mind. It was not a way to make connections with his peers. Not that he cared; he was fine being on his own.

A dirt road marked where the compost plant was located. Mud and rainwater kicked up on the truck, splattering the white vehicle a dark brown color. They parked and Johnny waddled next to a particularly large pile of mulch where they would dispose of the dead animals for the day. Ash would have to do all the work, but he was relieved that his shift would be over soon.

"Hurry up! I wanna go to lunch!"

Ash shot Johnny a dirty look for his outburst as he threw the dead bodies in the pile.

"Damn, you're so slow." Johnny groaned in frustration and hunger.

"You could help you know. I mean, it's a lot of work carrying some of these bastards." A hand landed on Ash's shoulder.

"Don't touch me, Johnny." he warned, whirling around to face the obese jerk.

"You don't get to tell me what to do." Johnny pushed Ash, who lost his footing on the wet ground and fell into the mulch pile face first. Old blood and maggots covered his head. Ash tried to get up, but Johnny's heavy elephant foot pressed on his spine like a cinderblock.

"You should know better than to mouth off to me, foster trash. Yeah, I know about your little sob story. I looked at dad's files. You're just a sad little shit who's mommy left him. You comfy down there? Kiss the little raccoons for me." Johnny ground his foot into Ash's back.

Ash gave a pained grunt beneath him, an ember of anger glowing inside him while Johnny laughed. He was suffocating in the filthy fur, scrambling for any purchase with his hands. Johnny could kill him if he didn't get off. The god-awful smell of the carcasses sent him back in time.

A filthy little boy sitting in squalor. He was so hungry. The smell of blood, piss, and shit permeated the small house. He had eaten everything until only the raw meat in the fridge was left. And he ate that too. He did what he needed, to survive.

Johnny stopped laughing when he noticed Ash's muffled growling and thrashing underneath him.

"Hey, man. Be cool - " he stuttered fearfully. Ash shook as he stood up, shivering with rage. Johnny almost messed himself when he got a look of Ash's face. Lips pulled back in a snarl and eyes dark with hatred, Ash leapt onto Johnny. The two were fighting on the ground. Johnny was desperately trying to flee but Ash kept punching and clawing him like a feral beast.

"Get off me, freak!" Johnny yelled trying to push Ash back with his hand. Ash promptly bit the extended appendage and punched Johnny in his fat face. The men's loud struggle brought the attention of the plant workers. Five men were apprehending Ash and helping Johnny to his feet. Ash was still struggling wildly until a well-placed blow to his midsection knocked the wind out of him.

"You're done, freak! You hear me!"

Ash came to his senses, not realizing what had transpired. His back and upper abdomen were sore. Johnny cursed him from a safe distance, holding his injured hand tenderly and sporting a shiner on his left eye. Ash cursed himself, realizing he blew it with this job.

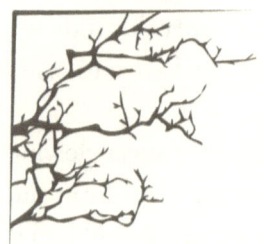

Chapter 2

The mailbox was filled with bills and junk mail. He wasn't looking forward to reviewing it all tonight. Ash opened the door to his small apartment. The sparsely furnished home was a welcome respite after the hellish day he experienced. Collapsing on the musty couch, Ash curled up in a fetal position. He considered his options. He was relieved there were no charges pressed. It was hard enough job hunting without having a criminal record attached. The grey walls of the living room seemed much smaller to Ash. He had to find something soon. The holiday season was starting; he could find a seasonal job to get by. Not like he had any plans anyway. First, he needed a shower.

He had no known family and his "friends" were hardly worth mentioning. At twenty-three, Asher Jagerhund's life was bleak with few options. Stripping off his clothes and standing under the water stream, he reflected on what happened at the plant. He did not have a lot of memories of his mother after she abandoned him. They came in brief flashes, usually if he was asleep or triggered by sensory input. Some were pleasant but most of them were terrifying and surreal. They always had a creature of sorts in them; unseen but present in the room where he hid. His caseworkers chalked it up to PTSD from the trauma of parental abandonment and being left alone to fend for himself. Out of the shower, he dried off quickly and put on a pair of sweatpants.

Ash's stomach gave a hungry gurgle. Time to eat. Ash walked into the dingy kitchen and opened the fridge. A half-gallon of milk, a carton of eggs, some moldy cheese, and some wilted salad mix. He desperately needed to go shopping, hoping his last paycheck would be enough. Something simple for now would do. After fixing a bowl of cereal, Ash went back into the living room and looked through his mail. Rent notice, junk mail, grocery store discounts...what was this? A white envelope with blue ink written on it:

From: Jasper Jagerhund 25 Yellow River Road, Rust Springs, OH 45426

Ash's mind started racing. Rust Springs? Where the killings took place? Jagerhund? Was this Jasper a relative? With a quivering hand, he ripped open the envelope and pulled out the letter. Typed on a word processor, it read:

DEAR ASHER,

Let me introduce myself. I am your uncle: Jasper Jagerhund. I can't believe I have found you after all these years. Your mother, Naomi, fell out of contact with me years ago. After months spent string-pulling and researching, I am elated to have finally found you. I feel terrible for what happened to you and your mother. I wish I was there. Anyways, I wrote this letter in hope we could meet in person. Unfortunately, I am in no condition to travel. In the case you are not interested, you do not have to see me. I know it must be disorientating to know you have a blood relative suddenly contacting you out of the blue and I would not force you to do something you don't want to.

It would be nice to talk to a Jagerhund again since we are the last of our bloodline. I will leave my telephone number in case you wish to communicate further. I hope you come visit at least.

Thank you.

Best regards,

Jasper

Ash could not believe what he was reading. He had family out there? This Jasper could have the answers to the questions he had carried with him all these years. Still, he was unsure. How did Jasper find him and why now? He was torn between hopeful curiosity and reluctant suspicion. Walking toward the kitchen phone, he considered his options. What did he have left to lose? At the worst, Jasper could be a hoax. In the best possible situation, Jasper could be family. Ash punched the numbers, anxiously determined to get to the bottom of the mystery. The ring tone clipped through the receiver.

A click and a pause.

"Hello?" A man's voice answered on the other side, clear but slightly raspy.

"Uh, Jasper Jagerhund?"

"This is him speaking."

"My name is Asher, or Ash, Jagerhund. I received your letter today-"

"Ah! Yes!" the voice was elated. "I was hoping you were going to call or respond but, how are you doing?"

"Uh, fine." Ash didn't know what to make of the situation. He was talking to a complete stranger about his background. It was best to tread lightly.

"Good, Good. Well, how is Cleveland?"

"Better yet, how did you find me?" Ash heard a sigh on the line.

"It took some research. The last time I spoke with your mother she was in the Cleveland area. At the time, she told me she was pregnant with you. After I heard of her disappearance, I launched my own investigation to see what became of you. And here we are after a month of research."

"Why not sooner?"

"I assumed your mother wanted to be left alone so I didn't bother her. Therefore, her disappearance was quite a shock. It was a while before I exhausted the resources at my disposal to find her. So I searched for you instead." Jasper explained. Silence followed, Ash not knowing how to continue with the conversation.

"So have you considered coming to Rust Springs?"

"I'll think about it."

"Well, let me know what you desire, if you wish to be in touch. Have a good evening, Ash."

The line went dead. His sweaty hand placed the phone on its resting place. He walked into the living room, seeking to slump on the couch again. A knock at the door diverted his intentions. Opening the door, he found his landlord on the other side.

"Do you have the month's rent?"

Ash scratched the side of his face and looked at the floor. This was not a good day. It was downright shitty.

"That was due today?"

"Ash, this is the second time you've done this..."

"I'm sorry, Mr. Ralston. I-I've run into some difficulties - "

A yellow slip appeared before his face, interrupting him.

"You have 90 days. I'm sorry but this can't go on." Ralston told him, leaving his tenant in the doorway. Ash slammed the door. The day could not get any worse. Ash returned to the couch, staring at the paper. He balled it up and threw it in a dusty corner of the room. Grabbing the remote, the TV came alive to provide its escapist offerings. The news was on at this hour.

"Brutal killings send shockwaves through Ohio town. Tonight, we discuss the latest set of bizarre murders by the alleged Rust Springs Ripper - "

Rust Springs. It was a city in southwestern Ohio, known for its namesake waters, which were a popular tourist attraction. The documentary he remembered talked about the orange waters, caused by large iron deposits in the ground. Other than that, it was another struggling post-industrial city in the Midwest. Major manufacturing had moved out, sending employment to faraway areas.

"Joining me is Pastor Calvin Clarkson, televangelist and resident of Rust Springs." the newscaster announced. The image of a clean-cut man appeared on screen. "Pastor Clarkson, what do you take from these recent slayings? Any insight?"

"I have stated this time and time again. We are dealing with possible occult ties. Rust Springs, and America in general, are embracing these so called "post-Christian" ways of living and spirituality. It's not a mere coincidence those kids were killed at a Satanic ritual site – "

Jasper's offer lingered on his mind. There was the issue of the recent killings. Occultists or not, Cleveland streets were more dangerous. It could have been a freak animal attack. He walked back into the kitchen, TV still blaring in the background. He didn't have much choice, without a job and a place to live. Maybe Rust Springs was his ticket out of here. If not, he could always leave for another part of the world. He might as well try. He dialed the number from the letter again. After a few minutes, Jasper answered.

"Hello?"

"It's Ash again."

"Have you made a decision?"

"Uh, yeah, I have no place to live now. Just got the notice from my landlord."

"Sorry to hear that. "Ya'know, I have room at my place. It's a big farmhouse. I wouldn't mind if you decided to crash here for a while."

"I wouldn't want to impose - "

"Believe me. You're not imposing on anyone. It's been a long time since I've had any company, let alone family. It would be a welcome change."

"Uh, okay. Thanks. I'm gonna head out soon. Maybe tomorrow."

"You sure?"

"Yeah, I don't have much and the furniture practically came with the place. I'm ready to move on, I guess."

"Ok, I'll see you soon, Ash."

"Ok, thanks. Bye."

Ash hung up the phone and prepared to pack up his belongings. Clothes and personal effects were packed in a large duffel bag, which had served Ash all his years in the foster system. He could pack light, having moved so much in his young life. Exhaustion draped over him like a heavy blanket. This stressful day ended with a fresh start at least. Ready to put it behind him, he took off his clothes and got into bed. Sleep settled into his bones as his mind faded away to the dark sea of unconsciousness.

Rupture

A fissure opens further.

F ar above the Midwestern sky, stars shined ever so brightly, unpolluted by the city lights. White, blue, yellow, red; if ever there was a black star. He knew it was here. He often held communion with it, not wanting to leave the abyss from which it imparted him with great wisdom.

The dark light shines brighter.

Carve the runes into the flesh of the wall. Meditate on the feeling and impose the force into this world. Separate from all distractions; do not let them get in the way of the goal. Nothing in the world motivates him more.

He couldn't remember the last time he saw another soul. Was it a week? A month? Speak the ancient songs of which know no origin. Feed it. Make it real. Let the voice be strong and bold.

A cosmic maelstrom is coming.

The dead star shines now even brighter than its brethren; the dark rays soaking into his bones. He could sense it becoming a part of him. Rejoice! A major breakthrough. He knew he came to the right place. *"It rises above Ohio."*

Traveling through the aeons.

He remembered telling someone that, or at least he thought. It did not matter.

The dead one they fear.

Their Aion was upon them now.

A black star shall rise.

When the end time draws near.

14

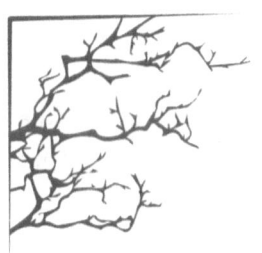

Chapter 3

Farmlands and fields rushed passed Ash's vision as he continued on the interstate to his destination. With only his used Volvo and belongings in tow, a sense of freedom mixed with uncertainty weighed on him. He could not shake internal reenactments of potential encounters with Jasper. What would happen? Would Jasper be friendly? He seemed amicable, based on their brief phone conversations. There are always risks. What if he was crazy or lying? Ash drummed his fingers on the steering wheel. He had to see it through; it was the only way he could know for sure.

A truck-stop off the road gave him a chance to relax and stretch his legs. He walked over to the store, interested in finding some snacks for the final leg of the journey. A trio rushed passed him out of the double doors, almost running him over.

"Watch it, asshole!" a tow-headed man barked at him, "Unless you want some of this!"

Ash looked at the man and his companions, two unremarkable and frumpy women. They looked unfriendly. Ash shook his head.

"I'm gonna head in..." He didn't want any trouble. The man glared, unhinged.

"That's what I thought." the man growled, making his way to the pale blue truck where the women were waiting. Ash gripped the door knob, pushing effortlessly. A frazzled clerk greeted him.

"You're not with them are you?" the older man adjusted his glasses.

"No. I just got here."

"Good, good. Anything I can help you with?"

Over-turned display stands and merchandise littered the floor. "What happened?"

"Eh, I caught some punks soliciting out in my lot. Looked like they were waiting for someone - selling drugs or whoring. It happens at places like these. They didn't take well to me telling them to take their business elsewhere."

Ash looked back outside through the store's tall dirty windows. Rows of trucks were lined up in the lot; parked as the drivers rested. He could understand some of the loneliness the truckers might feel, being on the road and far from their families. Drugs and intimate company were a welcome, if not temporary, remedy.

"Do you need help?" He normally wouldn't put himself out there but he felt sorry for the old man.

"No, thanks. I'll get someone to clean it up. I would prefer you to purchase something instead." the clerk replied good-naturedly. Ash browsed the various isles looking for some salt-and-vinegar chips.

"We are at Fulston High School, the same school the two teenage victims attended. Here, rumors of a "teen witch" cult operating in the school-"

The TV screen on the corner wall of the shop played a news clip. A female news reporter was standing in front of a stately building as teenagers walked around her in the background.

"One that is of interest to law enforcement concerning the case." she continued.

"Ain't that something?" the clerk asked, "Now, we got kids killing each other in the woods over some devil. World's crazy now-a-days. You'd think with computer games and cable TV, people would have something to entertain themselves with."

Ash placed his bag of chips and on the counter, trying to listen to the reporter. The whole thing looked to him like the doing of a serial killer; a twisted mind. The clerk bagged the chips quickly.

"Are you heading to Rust Springs?"

"Yeah." Ash replied, wondering where the clerk was going with the question.

"Good luck. The place is a cavalcade of crazy. That would be $2.50." Ash forked over the change and was on his way out.

"Police are hesitant to release any names. To local students, the occult group has attracted ridicule and suspicion - " the reporter continued. The story was interesting to Ash but he had to get back on the road. What would he find in Rust Springs? With any luck, answers and not meeting a grisly end. He restarted his journey, the sun settling in the middle of the sky.

"Rust Springs Welcomes You!"

The gradient, painted sign depicted the signature orange waters that give the town its namesake. Empty and anemic industrial plants came into view as Ash entered into the outskirts of the city. Dead cornfields and barren land lots created a sense of quiet gloom. The sun was lower now, around late afternoon, which cast a dim look upon the land. Ash took the appropriate exit off the highway in order to proceed to his uncle's house. It took him to an old country road as he was diverted from the city limits. The barren trees were like gnarled hands reaching up towards the darkest part of the sky. Ash was enjoying the isolated drive, unconcerned by other motorists. A pale blue truck came into view ahead. Ash lifted his foot off the brakes, letting himself coast. It was, undoubtedly, the truck of the rude man at the rest stop. He did not want to come into his line of sight. Ash trailed the truck slightly behind. The surrounding trees gave way to a clearing. Ash looked to his left and saw an old white two-story farmhouse surrounded by rosebushes.

"25 Yellow River Road? This must be it." he concluded from a quick glance at the address on the protruding mailbox. The truck continued forward, oblivious of Ash's presence. He turned into the gravel drive-way. Two cars were parked there already, one shiny black BMW and the other a worn Buick LeSabre. Ash parked his own

Volvo in behind the other vehicles. Turning off the ignition, two large spotted dogs barreled towards him. Their pricked ears and brushy tails wagged as they surrounded the car and barked.

"Raini! Stormi! Get in here!" a familiar raspy voice cried from the house. A thin-looking man wearing a knitted sweater and acid-washed jeans stood on the screen door stoop. His visage a tired, yet pleasant expression. Was it Jasper Jagerhund? The dogs immediately returned to the house, out of sight. Ash exited his car and walked towards the house hesitantly. He was at a complete stranger's house, miles away from familiar territory. The oddity of the situation was not lost on him. The man watched from the stoop, giving a sly smile.

"Are you Ash?" the man asked kindly.

"Yes, and I assume you're Jasper?"

"Indeed I am. Please come inside. We can get your bags later."

Ash took the invitation and followed him inside. The creaky screen door led to a porch littered with various nick-nacks and spare parts.

"Pardon the mess. Some leftovers from junk and different projects."

Ash ignored it and walked into the foyer. He marveled at the interior of the old house. The woodwork was truly a relic of the past, left behind by modern housing. The interior of the house was austere, as if Jasper did not bother decorating. Bare white walls were lined with more boxes and a few antiques. To his left was the small dining room. There, a tall black man with long dreadlocks sat at the cloth-covered table. He was wearing an olive green tank top, black jeans, combat boots, and a pair of amber-tinted aviators.

"Ash meet my friend, Attila Gadsden." The man got up from his seat to shake Ash's hand.

"Nice to meet you, Ash." Attila greeted. Attila was tall compared to Ash. He had to be around six feet at least.

"We were just having some drinks and wings. Attila got engaged today." Jasper explained, inviting Ash to help himself to the feast. A cold beer sounded good but he decided to skip the wings and head to the veggie platter first.

"Congratulations." Ash picked up a plate. Attila grinned.

"We decided to make it official. It'll be easier for Daize and I to conduct our business. An' to think, years ago I wanted nothing to do with gettin' hitched."

"It happens to the best of us." Jasper commented. "I still have my wedding ring somewhere..."

Attila, seemingly saddened by the comment, focused his attention on opening anther beer.

"So, Ash, what did you do for a job? Jasper told me you were let go recently."

"Road-kill clean up." Ash grimaced inwardly at the bad memories.

"Damn! Talk about shit work..."

"The pay was decent. The dead animals didn't bother me much but the people did."

"Yup, crappy co-workers are a bitch." Attila attested. Jasper looked at his nephew with genuine concern. At least it wasn't pity.

"What do you wish to do with your life, Ash? I mean, I can't imagine seeing you waste your youth and energy on menial jobs." Jasper asked.

Ash had not given his future much thought. Honestly, he was content to merely survive. That's all he had done since he was five: survive. He only loved one girl in his whole twenty-three years of existence. She was long gone, though. No hopes, no aspirations beyond sustenance.

"I don't know." He disliked being put on the spot.

"Don't worry, kid. You're still young. You got plenty of time to work things out compared to us geezers." Jasper teased, trying to make Ash feel better.

"Geezer?" Attila scoffed playfully. "Speak for yourself. I was fine as hell in my 20's and I still am to this day."

"Sure, sure..."

Ash nibbled on a carrot, savoring the ranch dressing it was dipped in. Content his nervous stomach would hold out, he added some wings to his plate. He took a sip of the rich lager in his hand. The sublime sensation of the frothy drink washed his taste buds with a bitter but pleasant wheat taste. Jasper and Attila partook of their share of the meal as well. The dogs gazed at the feast above their heads, longing for a bite. Ash was enjoying himself so far. Jasper was hospitable and Attila seemed like a nice guy.

"Getting ready for the big show?" Jasper asked Attila.

"Yeah, I got to pick up a few things still. I got the posters today from the print shop. They look great."

"Big show?" Ash asked, sucking his fingers clean of Buffalo sauce.

"Attila here owns a night-club. A gothic-industrial one, to be precise."

"This band called *Eldritch Enema* is coming into town and they'll be performing at my club."

"*Eldritch Enema*! I love those guys!" Ash exclaimed.

"Really, now?" Attila smiled, "That's cool. Hey! If you're looking for a job, come by and see me downtown sometime this week. I'm sure I can find something for you."

"Thanks. I appreciate it." Ash was elated about the offer. Night fell as the sun set in the west.

"Damn, I need to get going." Attila mumbled, "Shouldn't be out this late. Especially with that animal or whatever on the loose."

"It's dangerous at night." Jasper petted one of the dog's heads. "I doubt those "witches" were responsible, regardless of what Clarkson says."

"Don't get me started on him!" Attila slammed down his beer in frustration. "He called my place up today saying I was to blame for the deaths, partially anyway."

"What? That's insane."

"No, that's Calvin."

"I heard about it in Cleveland." Ash interrupted, "What's this thing about teen witches?"

"Some local high school Satanists or what not. Apparently, Calvin believes they are responsible." Jasper said.

"No way! How the hell could a couple of kids do something like this?" Attila asked.

"Who knows?"

They dropped the subject.

"Ash, come outside. I got something to show you." Attila called as he walked out the door.

Ash promptly followed. Attila opened the trunk of his car, allowing Ash to look inside. Various promotional materials for a live band performance filled the interior.

"Wow! Sweet posters!" Ash marveled at the twisted and macabre artwork on the posters and flyers associated with the *Eldritch Enema* brand.

"You think so? I was hoping you would say that. It's going to be a great show." Attila closed the trunk and walked to the driver's side. "I'll be seeing you around, kid. Watch Jasper for me, alright? He hasn't been doing so well lately."

"What's wrong?" Ash was confused by Attila's words.

"He's been very sick. The doctors are not sure what it is and Jasper ain't saying a peep. I respect his privacy either way but watch out for the man, okay?"

Ash nodded, trying to alleviate Attila's concern.

"Where's your club located?"

"Down on West Main Street. Look for a sign that says "The Grotto". It's near an old factory. You can't miss it!"

He did not know Jasper had a chronic illness but it did explain his physique and complexion. Attila got in his car, bidding Ash and Jasper farewell. He pulled out of the driveway and on to the road, disappearing around a bend of dormant trees. Ash went back inside to find Jasper beginning to clean up.

"Hey, I can help with that." he offered.

"Very kind of you. Are you finished?"

"Still working on it."

"No problem. I'll put away the other stuff." It did not take long to clean up the dining area. Raini and Stormi were treated to a few scraps.

"Come, I will show you to your room." Ash got up to grab his bag as Jasper joined him shortly. Going up the wooden stairs, they were led into a narrow hallway.

"The room first to your right is yours. Feel free to get comfortable and relax. There's a small television in there and you can hang your clothes in the closet. The guest bathroom is on your left." Jasper pointed to an open door across from his room.

"Where's your room?" Ash asked.

"At the end of the hall. You can knock if there is an emergency. Mind Raini and Stormi, though. They get a little protective of where I sleep."

"Who?"

"Oh, I forgot to introduce you to them." Jasper turned to face the two spotted, prick-eared dogs. "The male with the blue collar is Raini and the female with the purple collar is Stormi."

The tall dogs were sitting on the floor, panting and seemingly not acknowledging their existence.

"Beautiful dogs. Where did you get them?" Ash marveled at the creatures.

"They were littermates I got off some old woman who couldn't care for them anymore. She gave them to me a week before she died."

Ash noticed the female, Stormi, was giving him an intense glare. Eye contact was a no-no in the animal world unless there was a potential for violence. He couldn't help but stare back into the light blue eyes. Stormi pulled back her lips and snarled. Raini looked unsure and walked away nervously. Jasper snapped at Stormi with his fingers and she immediately backed off and went to follow her brother.

"Strange dogs. Stormi is the temperamental one, but she never seems to follow through on threats. Raini is more friendly but can be skittish." Jasper continued.

Ash had never stayed with a family that had pets. There was a mangy stray he befriended one time. Mr. Whitaker ended up shooting it. He said it was best to "put it out of its misery." The Jenkins had a cat but it mostly stayed outdoors and wandered the neighborhood until it was time to eat.

"Good night, Ash. I'm gonna turn in myself." Jasper walked down the hall towards his bedroom; his dogs at his heels.

"Same. Good night."

Ash was interested in getting unpacked and resting. After unloading his clothes and putting them in the closet, he looked over the few treasured possessions he had. Besides his CD binder, Ash unearthed his *Eldritch Enema* album collection. He ran his index finger over their debut album from 1992, *Killer Kilauea*. The name was an allusion to the band's Hawaiian origins. He placed the CD inside his portable CD player, placing the earphones over his head. Pressing the play button, the ominous album intro funneled into his ears. Sliding underneath the clean sheets, Ash closed his eyes and drifted off into the darkness.

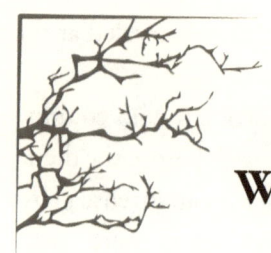

Wolf and Serpent

Terrible harbingers swallowing the world
Inside, something festers
Fangs gnashing against bone and flesh
Deeper in the blood destiny entwines in catastrophe
Bastards of the Fenris-kin
They hunger in the shadows
Their brilliant glow betraying them in the night

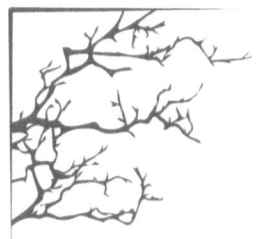

Chapter 4

The smell of bacon filled Ash's nostrils as he walked down the stairs into the sitting area. Across from him, he saw the dining table filled with fresh fruit, bacon, eggs, and hotcakes. Two empty plates were set aside one another with silverware. He wasn't comfortable with his new surroundings and co-habitants yet. A walk would do him some good.

Opening the squeaky screen door, cool morning air provided a polarizing but welcome sensation compared to the stuffy warmth of the house. The sky was overcast and a thick fog settled on the ground like a large blanket. Ash walked barefoot on the grass, disturbing the fog and coating his feet in icy dew. He took a left into the woods. The trees were bare with the fiery remnants of leaves surrounding their bases. The woods were fairly unremarkable in the Midwest, especially Ohio. Without mountains and few water features, there was nothing that captivated a sense of peace and wonder besides the occasional pure meadow. He had to make a pilgrimage to see the rusty waters of the town one day.

Ash found some disturbed leaves and shrubbery, along with some hoof and boot-prints. Jasper didn't mention any neighbors around. A ravaged deer on a felled log lay near a small fire patch. Tracks in the damp earth and trash indicated the signs of poachers.

Ash had dealings with them before when it came to getting rid of deer illegally hunted. Most landowners let the corpses decompose at a safer location on the property, but others would call the fish and game authorities and have it disposed of after investigations.

He checked to make sure there wasn't anyone following him. Poachers could range from the ignorant and lazy hunters, to drug addicts looking to trade meat and trophies.

He noticed Raini and Stormi playing by the rose bushes. They seemed content to chase each other around, tongues lolling in excitement. The two didn't notice Ash going back inside the house. Ash was once again greeted with the scent of delicious breakfast. He had to tell Jasper what he saw.

"Hey, uh, looks like you got a poaching problem on your land."

"Why am I not surprised?" Jasper sat and took a sip of hot tea. "They start up this time of year. Raini and Stormi usually deter them but every now and then, they slip through."

"Do you know who they might be?"

"I have a suspicion they are most likely some poor souls looking for a way to get their next fix. Other times, I think they are connected with some drug gang or something."

"Gang?"

"There's been rumors of a white supremacy group setting up shop over the past year. They are assumed to be responsible for more aggressive drug dealing in the area."

Jasper laid a newspaper in front of him. *The Rust Springs Current* had a back article concerning the increased drug activity in the city. There was reference to the front-page article, concerning the recent killings.

"And the police have nothing?"

"No. Not a thing."

The article suspects that drugs linked the murders, possibly between rival dealers. It was an unusual phenomenon for a small town. Ash took a bite of the eggs on his plate.

"It's indeed odd. Rust Springs is not a big city and has never been a huge drug area. But times are changing and people are looking for ways to make ends meet. It's not the big manufacturing hot-spot it used to be."

"So I've heard."

"There's nothing anyone can do. Everything is speculation and heresy." Jasper droned, seemingly growing bored of the conversation. Ash finished off the rest of his food and headed into the small kitchen to clean his dish.

"Got any plans for today?" Jasper asked, picking at some bacon.

"Thinking about exploring downtown, possibly find some places that are hiring." Ash rinsed the warm water over his plate.

"Don't forget to follow up with Attila."

Ash ran upstairs to clean up and put on the nicest clothes he could find from the closet. He grabbed his wallet and hurried back down stairs.

"Need any money for gas or food?"

"I should be fine." Ash patted his pocket.

"Okay then. Good luck!"

Ash walked out to his car. The dogs followed him out, giving his backside a sniff.

"Stop! I can't have dog drool on myself while I look for jobs."

The dogs stopped in their tracks, watching him get in his car and drive away. Ash followed the road back to the interstate where he headed straight for downtown into greater Rust Springs. The business district was fairly empty for a Saturday morning. The remains of old industrial mills and factories lingered around like memories of another time. Newer skyscrapers and complexes overshadowed their predecessors. Ash parked on the street, a few blocks where he remembered Attila's club was located.

"*Coming soon! The future home of the Rust Springs Technology Initiative Center.*" a sign read on a fairly new looking office building.

Ash looked inside the modern concrete and glass structure. It was vacant sans a few furnishings. He found another banner on the pane promoting Rust Springs as "a city for the 21st Century". The transference of a former manufacturing power into a new-fangled technology hotspot was understandable to Ash. The Internet was becoming a big deal for communications and commerce; it would make sense for a local government to attract such prospects in a poor economy.

Ash continued to walk Main Street, looking for hiring opportunities. Although Attila offered him a job, Ash decided it was best to widen his application pool. Within two hours, he received three applications from stores looking for help. Ash found a little coffee shop, *Fine Grinds*, which would be an ideal place to fill out the paperwork and get a caffeine fix. After finding a table and ordering a Reuben sandwich, he got to work.

"Did you hear about the developments concerning the murders?" a woman gossiped to her friend at a small table across from him. Ash listened to the local chatter.

"Yes, I heard about the forensics. Rumor is they found both human and animal DNA at the scene. Is the killer using animals for killings?" the friend, another middle-aged woman asked.

Ash grit his teeth, twirling his pencil in his hands. He had to list his former employer as a reference. Considering what he had done to get fired in the first place, he could not imagine having that discussion with a potential employer. Ash crumpled the paper, taking himself out of the applicant pool. He sighed and took a sip of his dark drip coffee.

"Who knows? This town hasn't been the same. Everyone I know is scared to go out at night."

"Let's not talk about it. Do you have any plans for-?"

"Can I get you anything, Sir?" a waitress asked Ash, carrying a carafe of fresh-brewed coffee.

"No, thanks. Can I get the check?"

"Here, I can take that for you." she offered, taking up his empty sandwich plate and laying a receipt on the table. Ash paid his bill and walked out of the café. Man and beast slaying together, the nature of the killer. It sounded a little beyond the ability of teenagers. Conceptually, it was out of this world. He did not know too much about serial killers but the most infamous ones often worked alone. He continued down Main Street. Ash could see the great, unlit neon sign of "The Grotto" up ahead. A sudden impact jarred his bones. He staggered backwards, unsure of who he ran into.

"Sorry." a low voice said. A blonde kid bowed his head in front of him. He could have been no older than Ash. The stranger looked nervous and shifty.

"It's fine." Ash replied, "I should have been more careful."

The young man walked off, headed in the opposite direction and ducked into an alley. He brushed off the encounter and continued on his way. At the intersection, the familiar blue pickup pulled to a stop. Ash crossed the street, not wanting to draw any attention to himself. In the corner of his eye, he could see the man from the truck stop in the driver's seat. He was able to cross the street before the driver became impatient and ran through the red light.

What is he doing downtown? He thought of the kid. Was it related? He shook it off. He had to meet Attila today.

The Grotto was located in a large brick building. Vivid graffiti art covered the fading logos of the extinct company who used to own the building. Technicolor demons, skulls, and assorted hell beasts conquered the dying presence of American industry. Ash knocked on the black-painted double doors. When he did not receive a response, he gingerly opened one of the doors. The inside of the club was dimly lit, setting an intimate atmosphere. The interior was overall industrial with an Art Deco flair, giving it a sense of class and refinement.

"Hello? Is anyone here?" Ash called out.

"In the back, kiddo!" Attila shouted back. Ash followed the source of the voice to a back office at the end of a hallway. A Baphomet sigil dangled from the middle of the red door. Was Attila into devil worship? He turned the brass knob and stepped through the door.

"Ash, my man! Welcome to my humble abode." Attila greeted him warmly from behind an elaborate Oriental-style desk. The room was filled with various obscure nick-nacks, taxidermy animals, and bound documents.

"So, what brings you here today?"

"Following up on that job offer."

"Right. Well, we open around six p.m. and stay open till three a.m. I am in serious need of a janitor of sorts and someone who can run errands occasionally. Not the most glamorous job but I will make it worth your while; I promise."

"Not an issue for me, Mr. Gadsden. I've picked up road kill for most of my life. Being on cleanup duty and an errand boy is no big deal...really."

"I take that as a "yes" then?"

"Most definitely."

"Congrats! You got the job!" Attila clapped.

The door slammed open and hit a filing cabinet behind it. The noise was loud enough to startle the two men. A tall, flustered looking redhead was clutching a phone. She was wearing jeans and a tank top but still managed to look stunning to Ash. Who was she?

"Can't you knock, Daize? I'm in the middle of a meeting here." Attila yelled at her, startled by the sudden intrusion.

"Sorry, but this is an emergency. It's my brother, Devon." Attila groaned upon hearing the name.

"Dammit, Daize. I love you an' all but you can't keep bailing out him out every time he gets into trouble. He's a tweaker for Christ's sake!"

"Hey, he's still my brother! This isn't jail or anything. Some bad people are after him, or so he says. He's actually in town right now!"

She noticed another person was in their company, looking a little shy and composing herself.

"Oh, hello. My name is Daisy Grayhart but people call me Daize. I'm the head bartender - "

"Along with being my business partner and fiancé." Attila interrupted.

Ash noticed the beauty of Daisy. She was dressed in jeans and a tank top but her radiance showed through her "plain Jane" appearance.

"Anyways, he's always paranoid. He cooks meth and is cracked out of his skull half the time. People get up to strange stuff on that shit. You know that, girl." Attila continued.

"I don't care. This has been going on for some time. It's those damn bikers! He left the scene years ago and they are still fucking with him. He might be in real danger this time."

Attila leaned back in his chair and rubbed his temples.

"Please, Attila. I just want to get him out of there for a few days. If he stays at that place, who knows what will happen."

"Fine. I'll go with you to make sure you're alright. I don't trust your brother or any of those friends of his." Daisy walked over and hugged Attila in his chair. He kissed her on the cheek.

"Sorry we had to cut this short, Ash, but I gotta take care of some personal things. Now, where's my gun?"

"Uh, I can come too if you want." Ash offered. Attila gave him a wary look.

"It's better that you don't. I can't guarantee your safety."

"Don't worry about me. I can handle myself. Besides, three is better than two. I can stay in the car for a quick getaway if need be."

He was curious about this Devon character but he also did not want Daisy and Attila to find themselves in a dangerous situation.

He had encountered numerous crazies of all sorts in Cleveland. Safety in numbers was key.

"Okay, if that's what you want. Don't come crying to me if things go south." Attila warned.

Chapter 5

Cracked pavement and mounds of trash waiting outside for collection accentuated the drab and dreary atmosphere of the Valdosta Trailer Park. Devon's trailer was the last one on the left, situated distantly from the rest of the homes. Ash's gut lurched. A familiar pale blue truck parked in front of Devon's trailer. What business did the owners have here? The lingering smell of cat urine emanated from the dwelling.

"Looks like he has company." Attila warned, "Let's proceed with caution."

"I've seen that truck before. I think it belongs to some drug dealers." Ash admitted. Attila muttered something about "shitbag tweakers". He parked the car and the trio made their way towards the home. Daisy knocked on the thin wooden door, making a hollow sound.

"Devon! It's Daize. Please open the door." Ash's eyes were watering. His sensitive nose was becoming irritated by the trailer's odors. Devon had to be cooking something foul inside. Thundering footsteps approached the front door. A woman answered, pale blonde hair and a rough demeanor. There was no compassion in those cold eyes of hers.

"Who are you?" The woman gave a stern look to Attila.

"I'm Devon's sister. Is he home?" Daisy stared down the strange woman.

"Who's there, Collie?" a male voice hollered from back in the trailer.

"It's Devon's sister, with two men." the woman answered.

"Tell them visiting hours are over!" the voice yelled. Daisy pushed her out of the way and went into the back before the blonde woman could block her.

"Keep an eye on her, Ash." Attila followed suit. Ash brought up the rear, keeping the woman from getting too close to his boss and co-worker.

"Heads up, Wylie! They're coming in!" the woman warned. A filthy bedroom with trash, clothes, and bottles thrown around the place. A buzz-cut man wearing a red muscle shirt was holding another man who was pinned on the bed. The man on the bed was half-dressed, wearing only a *Slayer* t-shirt and some underwear.

"Get off my brother, asshole!" Daisy screamed at the man. Ash noticed the man was short and his shirt had a snarling black wolf wearing a German cross around its neck. He gave Daisy a dirty look. Ash gave a sharp breath, eyes widening. He had seen the man before; at the gas station!

"You heard her. It's probably best you leave." Attila told the attacker.

"A fucking nigger telling me what to do? That's rich. Who are these *fine* people, Collie?" The man stepped off the mattress where Devon lay.

"You're telling me you didn't hear me?" the woman replied in a bored tone.

"See! This is what I am talking about! I can't get any respect around here thanks to Monty and Ida!" The man landed a kick to Devon's side. "Now, I have this sad-sack telling me he doesn't have the item he stole!"

Devon was quivering, his breath coming out in uneasy shakes.

"It's three against two, man. I suggest you leave." Attila crossed his arms, standing firm. The intruder looked annoyed at the suggestion.

"Name's Wyoming and that's all you need to know, you black son-of-a-bitch. Over there is Colorado."

"We should leave." Colorado hissed to Wyoming.

Wyoming growled and spit on Devon's face. Colorado was fairly calm, but underneath Ash could sense a suppressed rage brewing in Wyoming. The man was tense when he walked, commanding a sense of authority despite his short stature. Colorado turned tail with Wyoming on her heels. Attila was close behind them.

"Bitch, tell your ape to get off my back!" Wyoming addressed Daisy, "I don't like people too close to me, let alone niggers!" With all of the racial slurs being spewed by Wyoming, Ash was surprised by Attila's quietness.

"This ain't over, cunts!" Colorado and Wyoming were back in their truck and speeding down the road. Devon moaned and wheezed on the bed. He slowly sat up, looking disoriented and tired.

"Jesus Christ, Dev! What the hell was that?" Daisy checked her brother for injuries.

"Some assholes I used to know..." Devon rubbed his aching throat.

"What did they want? – God this place is a mess - don't tell me you've been cooking again! I thought you left that shit back in Kansas."

"What do you think? I mostly cook for myself though."

"Still keeping good company I see." Attila leaned against the broken doorframe, looking wholly unamused by the situation. "Tell me who did you piss off this time? Your biker buddies or some drug dealers?" Devon shot Attila a dirty look and turned his attention to Ash.

"Who's that?"

"My new employee at the bar." Attila answered.

"How long have you been in town? Weren't you in Oklahoma or something?" Daisy asked. Devon shook his head.

"Bad shit went down. I had to move. I went to Utah on a hunch and...met some people."

"What kind of people?"

"Can we take this conversation outside now? I'm getting a goddamn migraine in this dump!" Attila covered his nose with this t-shirt, eyes watering. Ash agreed, having covered his mouth and nose with his own shirt. Devon winced due to his injuries and fatigue, putting on a pair of jeans and a worn black leather jacket. Ash noticed the signs of drug use as he followed the group through the living area. Needles and some makeshift pipes littered the floor. Peering in the kitchen he could see evidence of a poorly structured drug lab. A slight hiss told him it was best to leave. Outside, Devon smoked a cigarette Attila had offered him.

"So I had gone to Utah. I heard there was a group offering protection of sorts for folks like me. It was a ranch. Lots of different families living there. I met a guy named Washington Loupcroix. He recruited me for a job. He offered me a new life for my skills. We moved up here a couple of months ago." Devon took another drag, letting the smoke flow out of his mouth and nostrils. He fidgeted, eyes widening.

"I thought it would give me some life purpose. I hated hanging with damn junkies all the time. It was pretty good but the meth got the best of me. They tried to kill me but I escaped. They think I have something of theirs-Thank fuck you came when you did! My ass would have been grass! Shit! They'll come back tonight! I'm not safe here!" Devon panicked while Daisy tried to calm him.

"Did you know what you took? Where is it now? What did they do that has you so scared?"

"Shit, man...I don't know...fuck." Devon paced. "So many people have been in and out of here - THOSE BASTARDS STOLE MY TV; I JUST KNOW IT! - But I don't remember anything from the compound." He chewed his dirty fingernails.

"It's okay, Devon." Daisy reassured him, "We can — " Devon ran back into the trailer as if suddenly possessed by some insane notion. He searched frantically for something in the kitchen drawers.

"I remember Justin was here last time. He had come in here looking for drugs - I was so fucking high at the time to do anything-an' I remember he found this weird leather bundle. Had a stone or something in it. I think Justin has what Wyoming was looking for. It looked valuable - "

"Great! Now the mystery has been solved. Where is your buddy?" Attila asked with an edge of sarcasm.

"He is a drifter, never stays in the same place for too long. But he likes to hang out by the springs." Devon scratched his head. "There's a bum camp there."

"Let's go! The sooner Wyoming gets what he wants, the sooner he will stop pestering Devon." Daisy offered, sounding relieved. Attila wasn't so optimistic.

"It's going to be dark soon and I don't like the idea of walking through the woods to meet one of your pals."

"You brought your gun, right? I don't think Devon's acquaintances will give us much trouble." Daisy reasoned. Devon shook his head rapidly.

"No, no. These boys are harmless. Justin is a little sketchy but I can talk to him."

"A 'little sketchy'. Way to boost my confidence, son." Attila sneered, annoying Daisy.

"Stop fussing, Attila. We need to get that package."

Devon was dysfunctional and that was putting it lightly. The man was a career criminal who had run-ins with the dregs of society. The man's fidgeted and paranoid behavior could be attributed to drugs, but Ash's instinct told him otherwise.

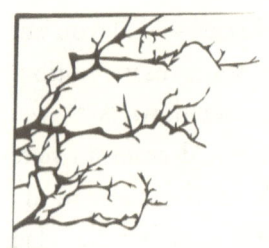

Chapter 6

It was dusk by the time Ash and his companions left Valdosta Park and night was growing fast. The sky had an eerie blue-black color to it. Attila parked his car outside the entrance to the forest surrounding the city: Rust Springs State Park.

"I'm pissed we even have to be here right now. The killer could be out here!" Attila parked the BMW in the deserted parking lot, prompting the passengers to exit.

"Let's get this over with." Daisy sighed. A sign warned visitors to proceed at their own risk inside the park. It was nice to know their safety was not guaranteed. Daisy held a flashlight and Attila kept his gun close. Devon took the lead as he tried to remember the location to the homeless camp. Having slept for three days straight, he was not well, his body craving for another fix.

"Shit, what I wouldn't do for a hit right now." Devon moaned.

"We're going to get you a bite to eat and lots of water. You're starving and dehydrated. You don't need any more shit in your system." Daisy scolded her brother. Ash could see how scrawny Devon was. It was a miracle he didn't keel over and die. Ash remembered the rangy frame of his uncle and how miserable his existence must be. The group traveled the main pathway, diverting after a half-mile into the forest. It was quiet, only a soft breeze rustling what little leaves remained on the tree branches.

"Damn!" Ash exclaimed.

"What? What is it?" Attila responded, jumpy from the sudden outburst.

"I forgot to tell Jasper about all of this. I told him I would be back around five. This little side adventure threw me off." Ash was worried and felt guilty about Jasper waiting for him; not knowing where he was.

"Uh, we're here." Devon announced. The flashlight illuminated the camp's demolished state. Tents were ripped, foodstuffs were strewn across the ground, and various items were damaged. Most disturbingly, there was a large amount of blood spilled on the scene. Trees, soil, and clothing were covered with it.

"What the hell?" Attila stepped back. There were three dead bodies with their entrails ripped and torn. Some parts were missing. It smelled like a slaughterhouse. Devon promptly vomited. Panic settled among the group.

"We gotta call the cops!" Daisy placed herself behind Attila.

"Wait! What about the stone-thing?" Devon screamed.

"Screw that! Getting the hell outta here should be our top priority!"

Ash froze. The dead homeless reminded him of the animals he used to collect. There was a scent. Something familiar yet foreign spoke to the core of his being. He heard a stirring in the woods. Someone was moving away from the scene and fast. Ash bolted. Despite the protest of his companions, his legs propelled him forward. He did not understand why he was compelled to move towards certain danger. Something burned deep inside himself. Was it fear or realization? His rational mind told him this was crazy, foolish even. However, his instincts told him different: this was right and natural.

He lost sight of the person he was pursuing. He could not make out much in the dusk light but the silhouettes of trees. A creek babbled nearby. A low growl behind him. A flash of white as he was knocked backwards by a hard blow. He looked in the direction of his attacker. They were in a hunched position like an animal. They slowly rose to two legs, looking slightly humanoid. He could make out sharp protrusions on the form, like horns or spikes. Ash's heart raced. He cried; a sharp pain in his back. Warm wetness told him he was injured and bleeding. When he looked up again, the being was gone.

"Ash! Ash!" Attila called, shuffling leaves with his hurried pace.

"Over here!" Ash hissed through his teeth in pain. His back was on fire. Attila came closer.

"Jesus, Ash! What happened to your back?" Attila pocketed his handgun.

"I was attacked by...something or someone. I couldn't get a good look at them."

"Goddamn! Were they a fucking bear or something?" Attila helped Ash to his feet. "We need to take you to a hospital. You got some bad wounds."

"Are the others okay?"

"Yeah but they are freaked out. Hell, I am too. Who could have done something like that?"

Based on the nature of the carnage and what he encountered, Ash was sure the killer was not entirely animal or human.

...

Ash awoke to the smell of sterilized hospital room. He remembered passing out in the back of Attila's car after leaving the park. The bed was comfortable but the cool air in the room made him pull the covers tighter around himself.

"Welcome back, kid." Attila looked tired and uncomfortable sitting in his chair. Ash sat up only to ignite the burning pain on his back.

"Easy. They had to stitch you up. Fortunately, the wounds weren't too bad. Your clothes must have protected you somehow."

Indeed. Ash was wearing a hospital gown and his boxers.

"Daize and Devon are being questioned by the police. Devon's not too happy. He hates cops. Jasper is on his way. I gave him a call when we got in. He told me he would arrive soon as he could. It's hard for him to get going sometimes."

Ash tuned out Attila. This was all too much to process upon waking. What connected the campsite and the killer to Devon's dealings with the Loupcroix? He did not remember retrieving the stone they were looking for.

"*Breaking news. Three dead bodies recovered from Rust Springs State Park. The unidentified men, presumed to be homeless, were attacked and killed by an unknown assailant.*" a voice from the TV barked. His reflections were interrupted by news broadcast on the room's television set.

"*Could this batch of killings be related to the Rust Springs Ripper? We now go to on-scene correspondent...*" the pretty blonde anchorwoman trailed on.

There was a knock at the door. Two men dressed in trench coats marched over to Ash. Attila stood to greet them.

"Can I help you, gentlemen?" Attila turned down the volume on the TV. The men reached into their pockets to pull out two badges. They were cops, more likely, detectives.

"My name is Detective John Mullen." the man on the right introduced himself. He was average looking, tall, some-what out of shape, and had greying red hair. He seemed tired but his eyes were vigilant.

"This is my partner, Detective Antonio Vasquez." Mullen introduced his partner. Unlike the middle-aged detective, Mullen's partner was youthful with tanned skin and dark eyes. His more relaxed expression offset his partner's tense demeanor.

"Names?" Mullen asked.

"Attila Gadsden. This is my friend and new employee, Ash Jagerhund."

"Mr. Gadsden. I am going to have to ask you to leave while we question Mr. Jagerhund." Mullen stated. Attila was reluctant to leave but obeyed the detective's order.

"Why were you at the campsite?" Mullen asked, closing the door. "Mr. Grayhart mentioned he was looking for something but wouldn't say what."

"I don't know." Ash replied, "I was pretty much just along for the ride. Devon told us we were looking for some sort of stone or something. He said it was important to this group he was a part of and he needed to give it back to them."

"Two people named Wyoming and Colorado Loupcroix were allegedly threatening Devon. Is this true?" Vasquez probed.

"Yeah. I've met Wyoming before. I didn't think he recognized me."

"Where?" Mullen asked.

"At a truck stop outside of town. I believe he was dealing drugs there. He tried to pick a fight when I bumped into him."

Mullen and Vasquez gave a quick look to each other.

"Your friends said you were attacked by a possible suspect. Do you know whom? Can you provide a description?" Mullen whipped out a notepad. Ash shook his head.

"The only thing I know for sure is that it definitely wasn't human...or wholly an animal." Ash choked on the words, trying to block the mental image of the dead bodies. Mullen and Vasquez whispered amongst themselves. Vasquez leaned over to give Ash a card.

"Thank you for your time. Don't hesitate to call us if you remember anything more." Vasquez said in a friendly tone. The door busted open, exposing an imposing policeman. The man clad in the trademark navy blue uniform of the Rust Springs police force was beet red in the face.

"Shit." Vasquez murmured. What was the young detective was nervous about?

"Mullen! Vasquez! Get out here now!" the man barked. The detectives paused, as if questioning if they should obey the order or not. The policeman left with Mullen and Vasquez following him. Attila moved around them to re-enter the room.

"What was that all about?" Ash asked.

"That was Brock Traynor, chief of police. He has a reputation of being a hard ass." Attila told him.

Jasper ran in the room before Ash could ask him to elaborate.

"Jesus Christ, Ash." His uncle hugged him. "I was so worried, especially when you didn't call me. And what Attila told me about the woods..." Jasper checked him over, giving him a soft pat on top of his shoulders.

"I'm fine. I've been through worse." Ash reassured Jasper, sounding hollowed and humorless. He just wanted to sleep. His nerves were shot and he hadn't eaten anything since lunch. Food and rest sounded heavenly at the moment.

"The cops got their work cut out for them." Attila commented. "I'll be curious to what they find on the Ripper."

"You and me both." Ash whispered, still shaken by his experience in the woods.

"I find Traynor to be unpleasant." Jasper said, "However, aside from his attitude, he does have an impressive track record of getting things done. If anyone has a chance of cracking the case, it would be him."

Daisy entered the room to join the conversation.

"Boy, Traynor seems to have a mean stick up his ass this time. This case must be getting to him. I heard him berating those detectives in the waiting room."

"Figures. Where's Devon?" asked Attila.

"He's downstairs getting some snacks from the vending machine." Ash could see the worry on Daisy's face. Being the relative of a drug addict is not easy, especially when they are on bad terms with their former partners. Ash could see a perfect view of the Rust Springs skyline out the room window. The sky was pitch black, illuminated by the vibrant city lights. Ash came here to look for answers only to find more questions. His experience so far in the small city was bizarre. Not even the bustle of Cleveland had anything on the oddities in Rust Springs.

"I'll see you tomorrow, Ash." Attila put a hand on Ash's shoulder. "I gotta get back to the Grotto and see what's going on. Arrive around noon so I can get you acquainted with the staff and the facilities."

Ash nodded and Jasper bid his friend goodbye.

"I hope you feel better, Ash." Daisy followed her fiancé out of the room. Jasper checked Ash's stitches.

"They don't look too bad. By my estimation, you should be able to go to work tomorrow as long as you don't do anything strenuous." Jasper told him. He was barely aware of his uncle's words. Aside from the minor sting of his wounds, there was a dull ache in his chest. Ash could not shake the impression that something was about to change.

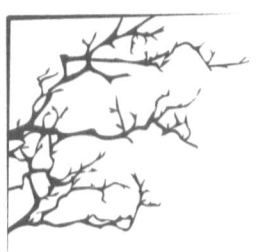

Chapter 7

"**I**'m telling you! I don't know anything!" the voice of a teenage male crackled through the tape recorder.

"You mean to tell me you have no knowledge of the ritual site?" Vasquez inquired on the recording.

"Well, yeah. It's something our coven created two years ago but I – we had nothing to do with the killings. I don't even know Jason or Amy - "

Mullen turned off the recorder. He waited in the parking lot for his partner to return from the convenience store. After the chewing-out Traynor gave them, Mullen contemplated his next steps. The chief of police's behavior was unusual. Traynor usually pursued a case as doggedly as a bloodhound and now he is bullying anyone getting too close to the Ripper case, to the extent that no one wanted to compare notes. What was it about this case that had him so spooked? He didn't chalk it up to witches, teenage or otherwise. Regardless of those who are hanging on to the occult panic of the past decade, a settlement outside of Rust Springs cropped up recently. Highly secretive and nameless, the inhabitants did not draw much attention to themselves besides the occasional accusations of drug-related activities. Traynor usually ignored the calls of the concerned, refused to look deeply into matters, and discouraged anyone who did. Did the compound have anything to do with the so-called *Ripper* killings? What was Traynor trying to hide? He did not notice Vasquez dropping a box of donuts in his lap. The 1980's Chevy Caprice was filled with the smells of hot dogs, spicy nachos, and warm coffee. Mullen's stomach rumbled. He was starved but not too thrilled about the dining options. Mullen strived to watch his weight and cholesterol among other things.

"Tony, would it kill you to eat a salad or something?" Vasquez did not take offense to his older partner's remark. Instead, he laughed as he took a bite out of a cheese and jalapeño-laden corn chip.

"Don't worry, gramps." he teased, waving a plastic container in Mullen's face, "I got a chicken salad sandwich for you." Mullen grabbed the container and consumed the contents. Vasquez retrieved a worn leather briefcase from the backseat. He flipped open the bronze clasps, revealing an assortment of papers and photographs inside.

"I obtained some information on our compound friends. You'll find it interesting to say the least." Vasquez passed some papers to Mullen.

Most of them were print outs from a website, the URL listed as *stormstarrising.com*. The pages were plain and filled mostly with text. Mullen skimmed through Vasquez's highlighted notes, absorbing chunks of information quickly. One page in particular provided an overview of a mythology of sorts:

The Storm-Star will bring about a new age for our people. The Folkvagnr will allow our race to thrive and be free of the shackles of this oppressive government and society that hates and shuns us.

We can reunite with our destiny as a race. The Thule called it Hypoborea, but I look to the sign of the Black Sun. There, I knew it to be the representation of the Storm-Star in this world.

Mullen did not know what to make of the morbid prophecy other than the minds who generated it were not well. He noticed the anti-government rhetoric, something popular amongst white separatists and those involved in the survivalist movement. A photograph taken outside of the compound showed an American flag hanging upside down on a flagpole. The rest of the web pages detailed rants against the American government, Christianity, and "inferior races" along with a lengthy statement, summarizing the cult's dedication to ensuring the life and freedoms of whites.

"This is some *Turner Files* shit. Who comes up with this stuff?"

"Apparently, the friends of a Mr. Devon Grayhart." Vasquez answered, crunching on a nacho chip.

"How did you gather that? Grayhart was so tight-lipped."

"Not his sister."

"Oh?"

"I asked for her interpretation of events. Devon Grayhart has a long history with criminal dealings. She says he left that all behind. He didn't tell her about these Loupcroix characters. Ash confirms the same pickup truck has been seen at the compound and the owners may be involved in drug dealing."

Mullen reclined his chair a bit, re-sealing the files. For those living on the edge of society, unconventional and illegal means of revenue provided an opportunity.

"Interestingly, they brought Devon Grayhart aboard at one time for meth production." Vasquez commented. "I think it's safe to say why they let him go."

Mullen saw the emaciated and paranoid state Devon was in. Allusions to his failed relationships to other criminal groups, demonstrated a lack of trust or inability to form strong ties. Devon, himself, did not say much about his time with the cult; likely afraid he would incriminate himself. As if the obfuscation mattered to him or Vasquez. They were more interested in a potential standoff or terrorist situation on their hands, not a self-destructive meth head.

"Daisy Grayhart mentioned some valuable stone the Loupcroix were looking for." Mullen noted, "If Devon's acquaintances took it, did the Loupcroix do the killings in retaliation?"

"Unlikely. Devon didn't reveal who took the stone to them directly. And unless the Loupcroix are werewolves, I doubt they could pull off something like this."

"Be serious, Tony. Jagerhund is in shock."

"I don't know. He seemed pretty collected to me." Mullen took another bite of his sandwich.

"How far down does this rabbit hole go, John?"

"What?"

"I mean this whole case feels...bigger. Like there is more to this than what meets the eye."

There was no telling what they will find when they overturn those stones. His estranged wife and daughter would be fine without him. He made reconciliation long ago. He was more concerned for Vasquez, who still had a good life ahead of him with his fiancé. Regardless, he was aware of Vasquez's dedication to the job and would not insult him with petty concern. He was a grown man with his own convictions and is more than capable of making his own decisions. If he wasn't, Vasquez wouldn't be sitting with him in this car.

"You may be right, Tony." Mullen stretched out his sore body in the driver's seat. He needed to get up and walk soon or his legs will get numb. He hated sitting in one place for too long.

"We need to be careful and plan for anything. This place is a powder keg waiting for a fuse."

The sun split the darkness as a new dawn came to Rust Springs.

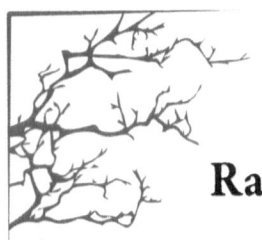

Racing through his mind.

24-7-365
It was all he focused on.
He had to or it wouldn't come to pass.
The wolf and serpent needed his input.
Without him, they were limp puppets.
Servitors of his will; they worked tirelessly through his workings as he slept.
Tearing through the boundaries separating this plane from which lay beyond.

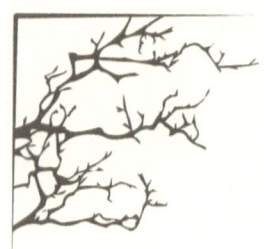

Chapter 8

Traynor waited at the dam for Washington to show up. The stars glimmered like broken bits of sparkling glass on the night sky. If Washington was coming, it must be a big deal.

Damn Ripper. The force was as clueless as he was. Whoever the Rust Springs Ripper was, it slaughtered like a wild beast. The power and damage reminded Traynor of pictures of animal attack victims, injured by the rending maws of large predators. Unlike the chance meetings of such encounters, these killings seemed targeted. The victims consisted of either Lodge members or their clients.

If he could not figure it out soon, the Lodge would be at his doorstep. Sure enough, a tan Suburban drove up the top of the dam bridge. Four men along with Washington piled out. The other four were packing, no doubt as a means to intimidate.

Traynor rolled his eyes. He wasn't impressed. He's dealt with his fair share of crazy in the past. The Lodge was nothing to him.

"Why the hell haven't you found the Ripper?" Washington grumbled, voice low and menacing.

The tone annoyed Traynor.

"Well hello to you too, sunshine. What did I tell you about staying in the designated areas?"

"Are you telling me you have no leads?"

"Look, I'm afraid the department is a little out of their depth with this. This isn't like anything I've ever experienced. We can't tell if it's human or animal...or even both."

Traynor and Washington looked over each other as if searching for a tell, a sign of deception. They were both dead serious.

"That's too bad." Washington sighed, "It has killed our own and our clients, which fucks with business. And here I thought you were supposed to protect and serve."

"Don't get fresh with me! Especially, considering your position. You're lucky I'm doing anything for you."

Washington eyes widened slightly, surprised Traynor would say such a thing.

"At least I am what I am. What are you? A piggy playing wolf. I'm sure the citizens of Rust Springs would like to know their chief of police is a dirty cop."

"You don't dare." Traynor threatened evenly, "If I go, I'm taking you down with me."

Washington laughed.

"Oh?" Washington got in Traynor's face, "You're mistaken. You're on your own with this one, little piggy. Rat on us and you'll be finding yourself twenty miles out in a deep grave. You need our fee more than we need your services."

Traynor was pissed yet unnerved by Washington's steely resolve.

"Catch the ripper, for your sake. If we have to bury another Lodge member, it'll be on your head."

Washington and his entourage left, leaving Traynor at the dam. He cursed his predicament. Deep down, he knew the Lodge would deliver their promise if he failed.

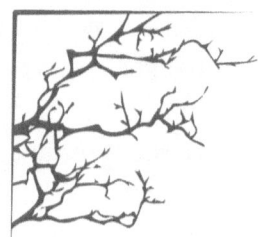

Chapter 9

Ash awoke with a start. It was his first day on the job and he had to be ready. He was careful to wash around his stitches in the shower. They were sore and itchy but he managed. Fortunately, Jasper was a former vet tech and knew about proper stitch maintenance. Breakfast was quiet. Stormi lay contently on the floor next to Jasper after eating her eggs and rice while Raini sat close to Ash. He was uncomfortable with the silence as the dog watched him eat. Jasper, while cordial, seemed agitated and distracted reading the morning edition of the *Rust Springs Dispatch*.

"So..." Ash compelled to the break the silence. "Why do you feed the dogs people food?"

Jasper looked up at him from behind the wall of paper.

"It's healthier for them. Some may disagree, but I despise the pet food industry with its by-products and fillers. With some exceptions, I wouldn't feed the dogs something I wouldn't eat myself. They're family after all." Jasper returned to reading the paper. Ash toyed with the blue-yellow tablecloth, trying to ease into another conversation topic.

"Can you tell me about our family?" Ash asked. Jasper smiled as he recalled memories of the past.

"Our family hails from the Blue Ridge Mountains of Virginia. In those days, there was your grandfather, grandmother, your mother, and me. We were a family of humble laborers, nothing special. I grew up and moved to Philadelphia to study veterinary medicine. I loved animals and your mother did too. But she moved away for opportunities in Ohio and I lost touch with her."

Jasper noticed Ash's sullen look.

"She was a wonderful person. I am sorry you lost her. I couldn't imagine what could have happened for you to be abandoned. I am sure she loved you dearly." Jasper told his nephew.

"Yeah. I don't remember much of her but I remember her warmth. What happened with you?"

"Well, when I was receiving my license, I fell in love with a fellow student. We started a family together. She worked at a vet clinic and I was at a testing facility as a vet tech. It was a difficult job, but it was money while I worked to receive my license. Unfortunately, she died trying to give birth to our twins who passed as well."

"Shit, I'm sorry."

"I became severely ill as well shortly after her passing. I continued to work but I wasn't able to obtain my license. It was too painful."

"What do you do now?"

"I took leave a year ago from work. My sickness got too severe to keep a job. Disability checks, savings, and pills keep me afloat, now." Jasper looked down at Raini and Stormi. "But these two keep me company. Some days it's good, others are worse but the dogs keep me alert."

"Ya'know, if there's anything I can do..." Ash could relate to Jasper's struggles. It seemed misfortune ran in his family. Depressing as it was, he was still comforted by the information he gained about his mother.

"No, no. You got your whole life ahead of you. Don't worry over a sick old man like me." Jasper waved his hand dismissively. "Are you ready for your first day?"

"I'd better get going." Ash got up from the table and walked out to his car. Raini and Stormi sat on the porch and watched him pull out of the dirt driveway. The two canines were as stone lions or gargoyles, standing guard over a sacred place.

The midday sun was hidden in a blanket of overcast weather. Ash parked in The Grotto's side parking lot. Opening the sturdy doors, Ash could see Attila and Daisy arguing on the stage. The velvet black and red curtains created a tense scene around them. The two looked like a pair of actors playing out their emotions for an audience.

"Damn it, Daze! I am telling you right now, Dev is going to stay in a hotel!" Attila hollered as he set up some sound equipment. Daisy was exasperated.

"Look, he will only stay with us for a while. He has nowhere to go and he is the only family I have. Well, at least the family he's on good speaking terms with."

Attila paused at her last sentence, shaking his head and giving a deep groan.

"Babe, I know how much you care for him and what he means to you. But, he can't stay with us. I cannot have a dysfunctional person living under the same roof as me. He needs to be independent." Attila was speaking out of love and concern for his fiancé. Daisy shrugged her shoulders, despondent.

"However, I can set up an apartment for the time being. I'll even pay for the first month. We can check on him and invite him to dinner every once in a while, but that's as far as I will go. I can't indulge - "

Attila was cut off by Daisy enthusiastically running up and hugging him from behind. With her smaller frame, she only came to his middle.

"Thanks, 'Tila."

Attila touched her hand around his abdomen. Ash witnessed a tender and intimate moment between the two. It reminded him of his first girlfriend whom he shared adventures with, along with some of the pain from foster care.

"*Psst.*"

He heard someone beckon from the direction of the bar. A man in a black t-shirt with a red devil figure on it. Dark slicked-back hair gave him a sophisticated look in the mist of his surroundings.

"Are you the new worker?" the man asked in a heavy Eastern European accent. Ash nodded.

"Name's Radimir, but some call me Rasha." the man said in a cool manner.

"Nice to meet you. My name is Ash." The bartender did not acknowledge him as he continued to stock and organize behind the bar. His behavior was off-putting to Ash.

"Don't mind him, sweetie." a woman's voice piped up behind him. "Rasha is shy around strangers. He'll warm-up once he gets used to you."

Ash turned around to see an elderly woman behind him. Her eyes were bright and full of life along with the rest of her body. She looked like someone's grandmother, but was way livelier than any senior Ash had seen in his short lifetime. Her hands were soft and slightly wrinkled as she shook his hand.

"Name's Lucinda Ledbetter, but people call me Lucy." she introduced herself. "I'm the head chef around here."

"My name is Ash Jagerhund."

Needless to say, Lucinda was way friendlier than her co-worker.

"Oh, you must be the new cleanup crew. Attila told me about how nice of a kid you are. You have beautiful eyes - and hair too."

"You're not so bad looking yourself." Ash complemented. He had never been told he was particularly handsome or good-looking by anyone. It was weird, but good all the same.

"I can give you a tour of the kitchen later if you want, but you better check with the boss first. It's your first day after all."

"You're right. I'll get back to you on that. It's nice meeting you."

"Same here, Ash." Lucinda responded as he walked away.

Attila gave Ash a tour of the club and oriented him on his duties. Ash would be responsible for cleaning up before and after hours along with any "spot-checks" and mess-management performed behind staff and customers. If necessary, he might have to do other small errands or assist co-workers with tasks. It was fair enough. They ended up in Attila's office as he typed away at some documents on the computer.

"Orientation is over. Go get yourself something to eat and come back to start working. Again, welcome to the family." Attila told him.

Ash exited though a side entrance leading to an alleyway and the garbage disposal. There, the same stranger from yesterday he ran into was talking with two men. One was tall and the other was a tad shorter but they both had dirty blonde hair. One had brown eyes and the other hazel. Ash hid behind a dumpster, picking up on the conversation.

"Monty wants you back. He misses his little brother, Ida." The shorter of the two men said. The young stranger shook his head.

"No, Ori. I'm fucking fed up with the whole nomadic compound lifestyle. You know how I feel about this shit."

"Please, Ida. Monty is getting worse and worse as the Storm-Star grows stronger here. He needs you to be at his side. He can't face this alone. Dad would - "

The taller man remained silent; his vivid hazel eyes staring at "Ida" like a brooding hawk.

"Fuck Dad!" the kid shouted in the man's face. "You know what? He didn't do jack shit for us! Always moving, living in shitty hole after shitty hole, no friends. All he cared about was this fucking retarded prophecy! If that's what you want, you can have it!"

The tall man swung his fist at the young man, hitting him with such a force that he was knocked out. The other man stared at the kid's crumpled form, stunned.

"What you do that for, Wash?" the man rushed to carry "Ida".

"The brat needs to show some gratitude and know his place, Oregon. We've all had to make sacrifices to get us to this point. We can't afford to turn back now."

They carried the unconscious boy around the corner. Ash snuck around the corner, watching them load the youth into a black paneled van and drive off.

What did he see? What should he do? Should he tell Attila? It was better to keep the incident to himself. It had nothing to do with him, and Attila had bigger things to worry about at the moment. Switching gears, his hunger decided the deli on the corner would be the best course of action for lunch.

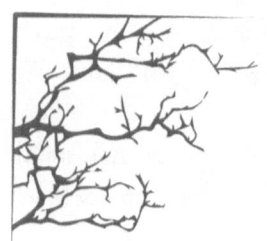

Chapter 10

"I knew nothing about what happened that night. Me and my friends were out by the mall." Forester Jones recounted to Mullen and Vasquez. The interview room was small and bare except for a cheap wooden-laminate table and three chairs. Forester picked at his nose piercing nervously. Considering the circumstances, he had every right to be. The high school student was clad in black and wearing various silver jewelry; the leader of the "teen witches" of Rust Springs High.

"I thought those woods were your hangout area?" Vasquez questioned, "At least from what I've heard from your classmates."

"Well, yeah, but we like to have some variety. Besides, if the "in-crowd" was there, we would have stayed away."

"Why's that?"

"Well, our cliques don't get along for one. Second, we like some privacy out there."

"For sacrifices? We've heard the rumors around town." Mullen said.

"No! No! That's a stupid myth perpetuated by a bunch of close-minded morons. Us "teen witches" don't sacrifice anyone, animals or otherwise."

"Witnesses didn't report seeing you or your vehicles there, but there seems to be motivation if you guys didn't get along - "

"No way! I hate the jocks and cheerleaders, but I wouldn't want to see any of them dead! From what I've heard, the killer might not be even human."

The gruesome pictures from the murder scene spilled slightly out of the folder. Forester was right. If the slayings were done by human hands, it would have to take immense strength and odd, possibly customized weapons. There was also the issue of the marijuana found at the scene.

"Do you and your little friends know where you can score some pot?" Mullen asked. Forester's eyes darted around the room.

"Uh, no...I mean, I wouldn't personally, but I know Amy was bragging about getting some from a group of rednecks or something at school."

"Rednecks?"

"Well, I remember at lunch we could overhear her talking about a group of "trailer trash" that had some good bud. I haven't seen them around personally, so I don't have a clue what they look like or where they may be. Apparently, they are kind of anti-establishment; white power types. She mentioned one of them had a swastika tattoo on his arm."

"Noted. We'll look into it."

"Am I free to go?"

"Yes." Vasquez told him, "Make sure to call someone to give you a ride home."

Forrester left the room quickly, not wanting to stay any longer than he had to.

"Have you heard of any white supremacist gangs dealing here?"

"Not really." Mullen responded, "They're probably referring to some of the run-of-the-mill locals."

Mullen stopped in the middle of the hallway.

"I just remembered something."

"What?"

"Jones mentioned a swastika tattoo?"

"Yes..."

"We recently arrested someone with the same tattoo last night for disorderly conduct and public drinking. He had an out of state driver's license and a gram of weed on him."

"Well where is he?"

"Traynor let him go."

"He's probably long gone by now." Vasquez groaned.

Mullen bit his tongue. Vic Traynor, the chief of police, was acting suspiciously recently when it came to certain drug related arrests. Traynor was an ass, but now he had the inkling there was more to the behavior.

"Know anyone we can talk to?" Vasquez asked.

"I might...Vinnie."

"Him?"

"He knows all about the criminal elements in this town; being an ex-dealer himself."

"Well, we know where to look then."

Mullen and Vasquez drove to the seedier east side of Rust Springs: Pike Valley. A large number of old Victorian houses in the area were boarded up or torched by arsonist activities. There was a particular house at the end of the block that was once a known nuisance. A red sedan told him their contact was already here.

"He must be inside." Mullen knew they would be in trouble if they were caught talking to an informant without permission. Up the cracked concrete steps, they saw their informant at the top waiting.

"Hello, Vinnie." Mullen said.

"Long time no see, detective." the Guido-looking man greeted, wary due to the informal circumstances. Vinnie looked like a Mafioso wanna-be tough guy.

"We need to talk with you about some recent movement." Mullen was ready to get down to business.

"Man, I got contacts from Seattle to Indiana. You're going to have to be more specific." Vinnie told Mullen, who was rubbing his temples. A migraine was incoming and he needed some coffee soon.

"You said you know Devon Grayhart." Vasquez commented.

"Devon. Sounds familiar..." the drug dealer rolled the words around on his tongue, as if his memory was trying to recall the taste.

"Oh, yeah! Devon. Crazy kid, liked meth and into white power shit. Well, I guess you have to be a tweaker to buy into that crap...Anyways, he was part of the Kansas Outfit, those brilliant boys who make those trippy products. Devon was working in creating meth with them but ya'know, his habit and company make for a rocky relationship."

"What happened?" Vasquez asked.

"Long story short, Dev's biker friends, The Devil's Thunder MC, decided to storm the place and take what they wanted. However, the Kansas boys weren't ready for such an occasion and got their ass handed to them. Dev escaped and was on his own. After that, never heard from him again."

"Anything else?" asked Mullen.

"No, not to my knowledge. Just thinking of all the craziness going on in this town. Oh, one more thing. From what a customer has told me, a big group has moved in. Allegedly, from back west. They're the ones slinging pot. Kinda got skinhead vibes from them."

"You think they may be responsible?"

"Maybe. 'Cuz from what I hear, they been pretty aggressive. Most of us don't have much manpower to do anything with them, not that some have tried."

Vasquez took notes. They got a good lead on the group but how exactly they were connected had yet to be seen.

"Honestly, I don't blame those of the profession. I mean, it's a dog eat dog type of world now." Vinnie professed.

"Doesn't excuse their crimes." Mullen retorted.

"People gotta feed their kids."

"And you say this as an informant?" Vasquez asked. Vinnie gave a harsh laugh.

"What can I say? I picked the option that was best for me. I give people the benefit of the doubt that they operate on the same pretenses."

The two detectives left the decrepit dwelling and went back to their car to discuss what they had heard.

"Could Devon's "cult" and the new dealers be connected?" Mullen asked.

"Maybe but I checked and couldn't find anything on those Loupcroix characters, besides a few crooks and cons who endorsed them or who are allegedly associated." Vasquez reported.

"Loupcroix? Assumed names? Fake identities? They sound like the type of people who want to live off the grid. If what Vinnie says is true about the separatist notion, this is likely."

"Probably. We need to do more digging in regard to cult formation and membership. Got any leads as to who is associated or has been associated?"

"A few around the state. As we've noticed, most of the cult is made up of out-of-towners."

"Well, let's get started. We need to create a profile on the suspect and decide our best course of action moving forward."

Their car took off down the empty city street. The weather was grey and overcast for November.

"You think snow is gonna come early?" Mullen asked.

The sky seemed to give a vague answer as snow flurries descended on the road.

"Got any plans for Thanksgiving?" he asked his partner.

"Me and Claudia are having a little get-together. You?" Vasquez responded. Mullen clutched the steering wheel a little tighter.

"No. Me and the old lady are not on the best of terms right now."

"Oh. Well, you want to join us? We got room for one more at the table." Vasquez had tried to include Mullen in holiday plans since he would not see his family. He didn't want to impose because he couldn't keep a relationship together.

"No. I'm fine. I got business to take care of anyway. Besides, I wouldn't want to intrude on time spent with your fiancé."

"John, please. It's no big deal."

Touring on the highway out of Rust Springs, he reconsidered the offer.

"I'll think about it. Just for you, Tony."

It's preferable to spending Thanksgiving alone. Dead cornfields saluted the pair as they left town with their drab-colored stripped stalks. Vinnie was right. As factories closed, drug houses sprung up. Families who could leave Rust Springs did. While those left in the fallout, struggle for sustenance. International business and technology are king and they had no room to share the throne with the modest, industrial Midwest. With Rust Springs in an economical slump and nearing a new millennium, Mullen did not know what to expect. Now, this cult was stirring up trouble. Why would they kill their own customers, if the dealers and the cult were one and the same? He suspected outsiders were involved, but unsure as to whom. Has the whole town gone mad?

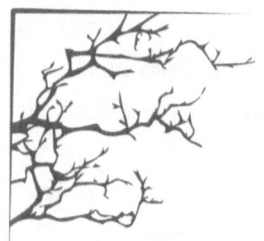

Chapter 11

"**R**ight now, I need these bathrooms spick-and-span for tonight. It's Metal Mondays so we are expecting a huge crowd tonight." Attila ordered. Ash chewed anxiously on his lip. It was his first night on the job and he was eager to do well.

"How's your back doing? Make sure you don't push yourself too much. Don't want you breaking your stitches."

"I should be fine. Took a pain pill earlier. I feel good."

"Anyways, fix the bathrooms and you can go on spot-clean duty as the night goes on. Now if you excuse me, I have to get the sound-mixing fixed for the band tonight."

Ash and Attila rose to their feet and walked out of the office. Ash turned into the men's bathroom. The white porcelain urinals contrasted the black marble bathroom with the green lights; casting a sickly hue. He gathered his cleaning supplies and got to work. Ash heard death metal music roaring through the sound system while replacing urinal cakes. It must be 5:00 p.m., the time when patrons start lining up outside. Ash, having completed his task, was about to leave when he heard a loud commotion.

"Mr. Gadsden! I implore you to put a stop to this reckless incitement to violence and blasphemy!" a shrill male voice yelled over the music.

"Goddamn it, not you again! I told you this is a private establishment and I will do whatever the hell I please!" Attila shouted.

Ash ran out of the restroom into the main area where he saw a slight, bookish looking man with sandy hair. Clad in a tweed suit with a violet tie and clutching a bible was Pastor Calvin Clarkson.

"Don't you take the lord's name in vain! I hear your satanic establishment beckoning people of this town like a demonic Pied Piper! With all of the perversions inside, you are corrupting the nation with your filth! Stop paying lip-service to Lucifer and get right with God!"

"You must have lost your damn mind! First, as I told you last year, this is not a "satanic" establishment. It's occult-themed. It's a gothic-industrial nightclub for crying out loud!" Attila told the man.

Daisy walked into the fray.

"Calvin, what are you doing here?"

Calvin turned his attention to her.

"Well, well, if it isn't the harlot. Living in sin with her lover I see." Calvin sneered and shook his bible at her. Daisy's demeanor changed. Her saucy expression changing to one of cold indifference.

"Watch your mouth, Calvin. You of all people should know not to cast judgment, lest you be judged in turn." she threatened.

"I know what is in store for people like you. I see the demons of lust and iniquity clinging to you if you do not repent."

"At least, I don't deny mine, Calvin. How about you? We all have demons, shortcomings, and crosses to bare. I see yours on display every day. They're on the news, on the radio, and amongst your congregation. Pride and greed are your masters, not God. Now, get your sensationalist crap out of our club."

Attila and Calvin looked at her with slightly astonished expressions. Calvin turned his back to them, opening the double doors.

"We'll be praying for you." Calvin said over his shoulder. Outside, crowds of metal fans were waiting to get in. It was getting close to opening time.

"Ash, did you finish the restrooms?" Attila asked.

"I finished the men's, moving on to the women's next."

"Get cracking. We have to get this show on the road soon."

"What was that all about?"

"I'll tell you later." Daisy told Ash as she joined Radimir behind the bar. Attila muttered something about finding bouncers and restraining orders. Ash returned to the restrooms to finish his last tasks, curious about the controversy between The Grotto and the local televangelist personality.

The Man in Red and the Woman in White

"I hate doing this. Why can't they get some of the men to do the dealing?" Cindy resisted the urge to crush the bag of buds in her sweater pocket. It was one of her mother's old clothes she happened to take the day she left home with Blake; her boyfriend turned common law husband.

"You're so high maintenance." Blake was wearing his trusty red hoodie. He wore it the day Cindy met him, hardly ever taking it off unless the weather was hot.

"They do." he continued to chastise her, "It's just that some of the non-moms need to pull their weight is all."

"Seriously?" Cindy confronted him. "We don't have a shortage of work at the compound as it is already. Cooking and cleaning, not to mention baby-sitting when the moms need a break."

Cindy hated kids. Although it was encouraged, she would be damned if she gave birth to a bunch of mini-Blakes. To be honest, she wanted out of the Lodge. She'd been convincing Blake to leave with her, but he wouldn't budge. He threatened to chain her up if she ever tried to leave. It scared her. After she caught wind of the violence the Loupcroix are capable of, she developed a negative outlook on her current situation. Cindy especially didn't like that jerk, Wyoming. She had to keep these things to herself. She didn't want to know what would happen to her if she did voice them.

"Didn't I tell you to wear something dark?" Blake asked harshly.

"This is all I had that was clean. You know, from being busy washing y'all's dirty drawers."

She wasn't in the mood to fight. She wanted to go back to the compound. She didn't sign up for this. Blake growled at her complaining.

"Shut up. We need to keep quiet."

Cindy and Blake found the street corner where the deal was going to go down.

"Well, why are you wearing red, mister?"

"It's dark red at least, bitch."

Cindy wanted to slap him. She hated when he called her that. But getting into a fight at eleven PM at the corner of Auburn and 3rd wasn't a good time or place. Thirty minutes later and still no client. She was getting paranoid.

"Is this a set-up?"

"Be cool. They'll be here."

It wasn't the cops they were worried about. They both heard about the Ripper and prayed they would never meet him. It was protocol to leave if the client didn't show. However, Blake was desperate to get on the leadership's good side. Five minutes later, the client arrived.

"Sorry about that." the young man apologized.

"You know how dangerous it is to be fucking around like that? Why are you late?" Blake was tense, trying to put on a tough front. Cindy knew he was as nervous as she was.

"I'm sorry! You got the stuff?"

Blake's fists tightened, wanting to pummel the client but resisted the urge. He motioned Cindy for the weed. She quickly fished it out.

"You good on the dough?" Blake waved the bag in the guy's face. The client pulled out a bundle of cash; green for green. A rattling noise from the adjacent alley.

"What was that?"

The client ran but didn't get far. He was tackled by a large humanoid figure a few feet way. Blake pushed Cindy.

"Run!" he yelled. Blood and viscera burst from his abdomen as a clawed fist ripped through.

She ran, crying and terrified. The terrible bark came closer to her. Jaws jumped around and through her, brutally snuffing her life.

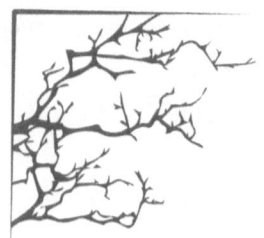

Chapter 12

"How are sales coming?"

Wyoming was busy chewing on some jerky, playing around with a pocket knife.

"Fine, Ori. Just fucking peachy." Wyoming growled at his brother. Oregon Loupcroix frowned at the tone in his younger sibling's voice.

"Don't sound like it." Oregon muttered. "Did you help Colorado with the trimming today?"

Wyoming stabbed the knife through the wooden table.

"No! That was supposed to be Idaho's fucking job. Remember? Yet, I had to go and run around chasing after a fucking rock all day!"

"You know Monty is not going to be happy. He needs those things."

"Like I give a shit! Maybe the little shit is right. You guys are taking his whole mystical crap way too seriously."

Oregon looked at him, a placid expression on his face.

"Go see Collie. She needs you at the greenhouse."

Wyoming pulled his knife out of the table, folding it quickly and placing it in his side pocket.

"Whatever." he groaned, exiting the house.

He traversed the large property, passing by the trailers. His destination was a large, unkempt greenhouse in the wooded area of the land. The smell of the plants growing inside as he approached made him want to smoke a large bowl of the stuff. The Loupcroix made it a rule to never dip in their own stash, but Wyoming would occasionally break it. Incidents often ended with Washington giving him a sound beating, but he still violated the rule anyway. He was craving for a smoke since what happened yesterday with Devon. The ominous warning about Montana's attitude weighed on his mind and marijuana had the magical ability to lighten his load.

He opened the unlocked door to the warm grow house. His sister trimmed away at the buds along with some of the other women that lived on the compound. While the men provided the security to the compound, the women usually helped with: upkeep, watching the children, caring for the plants and occasionally doing drug runs. He would rather watch paint dry than babysit plants all day. At Wyoming's presence, Colorado excused the women.

"Thanks for helping, ladies, but I have to talk to my brother."

The five women rose from their seats and placed the trimmings on their laps into the collection buckets. They filed out quickly and quietly, not willing to make eye contact with Wyoming.

"You wanted to see me?" Wyoming asked.

Colorado got up, placing her scissors on the worktable and taking off her apron.

"We need to find that stone-fang."

"I know! That fucker Devon has it stashed somewhere. I know it! We're gonna have to give him another visit soon."

"He's spooked, hiding out in another location."

"How far can he go? He has no money and is cracked out of his mind half the time."

"He has family here too..."

"Yeah, the race-traitor cunt and her nigger boyfriend. I wouldn't mind having a go at them..."

Colorado rolled her eyes.

"We have to keep our heads low. Wash told me the Storm-Star is coming soon."

"Oh yeah? You really believe that?"

The compound was filled with people who believed the Storm-Star, some distant entity, would come about with Montana as its conduit. Wyoming remembered the years Montana spent researching esoteric Nazism, as well as records of other obscure texts from ancient China and so forth. He didn't pay too much attention. His eldest brother was obsessed. Montana hadn't been acting straight for the past couple of months. Anger, depression, and manic obsession were his three main moods.

"Little runt sleeping off his punch?" Wyoming asked Colorado. "He's lucky I didn't get to him first."

"Yeah. He's gonna be watched more closely, and he can't leave the compound anymore."

"Figures. Are we gonna do another run tonight?"

"Yeah."

"Montana wants to bring about the age of his glorious rule, eh?"

Colorado gave him a stern nod.

"Yes, he thinks it is time for the Storm-Star and the Fenris-kin to rise."

Wyoming growled with fury, pacing like the caged animal in the background.

"Special little shit, ain't he?" Wyoming spat, obviously jealous of the attention his younger brother was getting. "If Ma didn't get knocked up with another boy, that could'a been me."

"Enough! We have to remember the end goal." Colorado tried to calm him.

"Yes. After the Storm-Star rises, it will never set." he recited sarcastically. "Fuck it. I'm gonna smoke a bowl. You know where to find me."

Colorado, ignoring her brother, returned to trimming her pile of buds. The tedious and repetitive task relaxed her. After a few minutes, a hand landed on her shoulder.

"How's the trimming going?" Oregon asked.

"Fine." Colorado looked at her brother's left arm. It was scarred, angry red marks snaking up his forearm.

"Monty did that to ya?" She knew the answer. Oregon stared at his boots.

"I was hoping Idaho would cheer him up. I think the workings are getting to him."

"Do we need to do a supply run?" Oregon inquired. Colorado knew it would have to be done soon.

"I can start bagging some of the nugs. I'm almost finished."

"Remember, you have to take care of the problem. We can't let transgressions go unanswered." Oregon strolled out of the greenhouse.

She understood what she had to do, but she needed Wyoming with her. As runty as he was, Wyoming was the muscle and was eager to pick fights. He had a reputation as a "berserker" due to his violent nature and because of his inferiority complex, she was happy to let him have the title. Anything to keep the peace or keep the hothead from going rogue.

The cold night air chilled her as she walked from where the marijuana plants were kept to the main house, keen to check on Idaho. Where she dwelled with her family was unkempt and cluttered with various record tapes, some weapons and video tapes, along with standard household amenities. Upstairs in a sparse bedroom was Idaho, resting on his mattress. The sizable bruise formed where Washington hit him. Sitting by his feet, Colorado gently stroked his left leg. Moaning softly, her little brother came to.

"What the hell—What's goin' on, Collie?" Idaho garbled dazedly.

"Wash and Ori brought you back."

"Oh, fuck."

"Do you need an aspirin? Some water?"

"I'm fine. Just pissed. Next time I see Wash, I'm gonna fucking brain him."

"He said you were hesitant to come back-"

"Putting it fucking lightly." Idaho cursed, tenderly touching the bruise on his face. He winced and hissed in pain.

"I'll get you an icepack." Colorado offered, "Do you want to talk about it?" She was used to being an unlicensed therapist for her family members.

"No. Leave." Idaho turned over on his side, back to his sister. Colorado was more than happy to oblige. She closed the door behind her, leaving him alone in the dark.

Not satisfied with sleeping it off, Idaho decided some fresh air would clear his head. He opened the frail window, carefully making his way down the roof. He jumped, landing softly on his feet. It was nearing dusk, the land around him dark and shadows growing. Idaho avoided the barn on the left of the property, weary of running into his older brothers. He usually liked to go to the greenhouse near the woods, but thought better of it. Wyoming would be near the plants. The compound trailers were only a few feet away; their crowded placement giving him a chance to blend in.

The other residents of the compound milled about. Most of the men were out, busy patrolling the perimeter. Children played with each other as they waited for dinner to be made. Idaho lowered his head, avoiding the looks he received by the women. They knew who he was and likely heard about his escape.

"Hey, you." a voice carried above the den of child's play. On the wooden steps of one of the trailers sat Oregon's wife, Dahlia. She was beautiful, her grace hiding her true rugged nature. Oregon was the only sibling who was married. Montana and Washington were known for their affairs with some of the compound women, while Wyoming was perpetually unlucky with love.

"Don't worry. I won't tell." Dahlia reassured him, "Looking to sit a spell?" Idaho let his guard down upon the invitation and took a seat next to his sister-in-law.

"You can't be running away like this. What were you thinking?" she scolded him gently.

"Geeze, Dahl. I don't need a lecture."

"Sorry, Ida, but you know you have a purpose here. We need you."

"I've heard."

"Oregon tells me business has been doing good. Personally, I don't know why Monty chose this place, but I trust his instincts."

It wasn't unusual for his family to move, but why here?

"Who knows?" Idaho responded. Dahlia took the opportunity to wrap her arm around his slumped form.

"Whatever it may be, it's all gonna work out for the good. You'll see."

Idaho placed that statement under "famous last words".

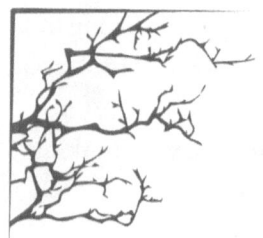

Chapter 13

Having completed his initial duties, Ash was enjoying The Grotto's Metal Monday's tradition. The patrons were either head-banging or moshing while various metal tracks roared in the background. Radimir and Daisy were serving drinks, while the kitchen was serving appetizers and finger food. Aside from the occasional spilt drink and appetizer, Ash did not have to clean up often that night.

"Ladies and gentlemen! How are you enjoying these head-banger hits tonight?" Attila's voice boomed on stage. An enthusiastic, guttural noise arose from the crowd.

"Fucking awesome!" Attila affirmed, "We have a special guest for you tonight! Please welcome *BludEngle-Necroheimr*! - A black metal band straight outta Indianapolis and has come here to share their dastardly dirges with you here in Rust Springs!"

The crowd went wild as the band came on stage, wearing dark clothing and corpse paint. Attila left the stage and the band immediately growled out their first song.

Ash covered his ears. The combined noise was intense. He needed to get some fresh air. Ash snuck out the back and into the alley. Snow flurries fell steadily on his hoodie and melted away in a flash. His mind went back to what happened here a couple of hours earlier. Idaho looked distraught and unwilling to return to his family. What the hell did they do to him? Why was he scared of his own family members? He knew not all families were cracked up to be nurturing. Foster kids were at times the result of broken homes. He wanted to trust and open up more to Jasper. A little voice would tell him to close off and protect himself. People were disappointing and, although hopeful, he didn't want to open himself to more hurt in his life.

A figure approached him and grabbed his shoulder when he stepped out on the sidewalk. He turned to the smiling face of Calvin Clarkson.

"Hello, young man. Seeking solace from the rampant heathenry inside?" the man asked. The smug and pious look on his face did not go unnoticed.

"Don't you have church services to attend to?"

Ash did not want to engage the man. Calvin chuckled.

"That's cute, but you seem upset. Something troubling you, son?"

"Like it's any of your business. I'll tell Attila-"

"Hey, hey. No need to involve your employer in this. I just want to talk. I understand you're new here."

Ash paused.

"How do you know that?"

"You'd be surprised how quickly word spreads through town. I heard Daisy's brother is involved in some bad things."

"So what?" Ash snapped defensively.

"What do you know?"

"Not much. I just moved here, man."

Frustrated with not getting the answers he wanted, Calvin sighed disappointedly.

"I'm sorry." he apologized, "I hate that this town is going to hell, literally, and the authorities won't do anything about it!"

Ash wasn't sure what to say. At first the guy came off as a stereotypical evangelist loon, but now he was apologizing. Aren't these guys always self-righteous?

"Please come to our congregation tomorrow and bring your friend Devon with you. We can help each other out."

"Uh, sure...I guess."

Ash was uncomfortable with how close Calvin's face was to his own.

"Great! See you later!" Calvin waved as he took off down the street and got into a silver Volvo. The car pulled away.

Ash looked at the business card. It was called *Golgotha Life Church*. Calvin Clarkson was the presiding pastor and the church was located a few blocks away. He wasn't sure why Calvin wanted to talk to him, but he didn't like the way he was asking questions. He shoved the card in his pocket.

"Hey, kid!"

Ash spun towards a wired-looking Devon jogging towards him. He looked panicked and wary, like someone was out to get him.

"What are you doing here?" Ash was surprised the tweaker was out and about.

"Kid – uh - what's your name."

"Ash."

"Yeah, yeah, Ash. I gotta talk to you guys. The fuckers are after me!"

"Who?"

"The Lodge. I-I remember what happened."

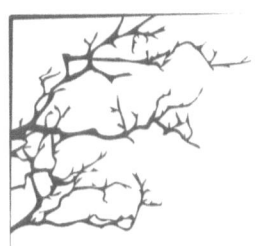

Chapter 14

"Take it from the top. You're not making much sense." Attila said, trying to make sense of Devon's manic and profanity laced ramblings. Attila, Devon, Daisy, and Ash huddled inside the back office. Coffee and cigarettes were passed around, bringing a sense of much-needed relaxation to the group. With patrons and performers gone, they listened to the tales of the meth cook.

"I told you. They are after me! I saw them outside my motel room!" Devon cried out fearfully.

"For the last time, who? The Loupcroix?" Attila asked, irritation marking his voice.

"No! The servants of the Storm-Star; I think that's what they're called. My God! They are fucking real!"

Ash was tempted to leave the room, as the cigarette smoke was getting to him, but was enthralled with Devon's tale.

"I'm not fucking with you cause I'm high but – God! I wish I was." Devon stopped to take a drag off his cig. His hands were visibly shaking as the cherry glowed brilliantly.

"So what happened?" Daisy chimed in.

"It was while ago, ya'know, before I left. I was going down to the barn after finishing my last cook. Montana wanted to talk to me about something so I was like "sure". When I got down there – "

...

Wyoming and Oregon carried a wooden crate over to the altar in the dusty barn-slash-temple that the Lodge used for fellowship and meetings. The two men got some crowbars to open the contents.

"Hey, uh, what's going on?" Devon stuttered. He could feel himself sweating.

"That's what we wanted to ask you." Montana said softly.

"Where's the two grand we've made from the bake sales?" Washington asked. "Bake sales" was their cute way of referring to the money they made from meth dealing.

"What?" Devon felt his face redden.

"You know what!" Washington marched towards him, his muscular frame bowing upon Devon.

"Where is it?"

"I don't know, man." Devon stepped back.

Oregon and Wyoming managed to open the crate pulling out a long blue stone. It was sharp and sparkled darkly in the amber lights of the barn. The shape reminded Devon of a fang.

"Oh, yes! They survived the journey!" Montana whispered excitedly, trying to keep his voice down. He grabbed the stone from Oregon, studying it.

"Devon! Don't lie!" Washington yelled again at Devon. "I saw you skimming last night. Where's the rest at?"

"I was using it to buy more supplies for the cooks, ya'know."

"Bullshit! Where are you hiding it! You're gonna steal from our people?"

"Your people? What the fuck about them? I'm the one staying up in that damn trailer cooking all day-!"

"Shut up!" Montana boomed.

The lights flickered slightly.

"Devon, where's the money? We've established you took it, and we want to know where you hid it."

Devon's pulse quickened.

"Yeah! Fine, I skimmed it, but I ain't telling you shit about where I put it! Fuck y'all!" Devon pulled out a gun from the waistband of his jeans.

The others drew their weapons angrily, sans Montana.

"It's okay, Devon. No one's gonna hurt you." He smiled.

"Nah, fuck this! I'm out!"

A metal surface ricocheted off the back of his skull. Someone kicked the gun out of his hand. It was Colorado, holding a shovel.

"You always have to make things so hard, Dev." Montana motioned for Colorado and Wyoming to pick him up. Devon was seeing double. Montana ripped his flannel shirt open.

"And because you have to make things so hard, I'm not going to show you any clemency."

Montana took the stone and stabbed downwards to Devon's chest, leaving a bloody gash. Devon screamed, bucking back.

"Get off! Stop, Monty!"

Montana cut him again; leaving another bloody gash. Devon wrestled out of Colorado's grip and grabbed the fanged stone in Montana's hand. The pain bit sharply into his hand and chest, but his survival instincts were kicking into overdrive.

"I'm gonna lay you out, bitch!" Wyoming growled, trying to grab Devon again. Devon kicked Wyoming in the crotch and elbowed Colorado in the face. He could see Oregon and Washington gunning for him. He twisted, sinking the fang deeper into his flesh and more importantly, snatching it from Montana.

"Get that bastard!" Montana yelled.

Devon headed toward the back door near the altar. He could get to his bike near the gravel path outside. Getting on his motorcycle and placing the slick and bloody stone in his saddlebag, he revved up the engine and speed off down the pathway. Curses and shouts rang in the air as the Loupcroix gave chase.

...

"That was the last time I saw their scary asses until the other day." Devon concluded taking another shaky drag. Devon lifted his ratty t-shirt. His abdomen was riddled with pink scars.

"What the fuck –?" Daisy gasped in horror.

"See! The fucker tried to make an example out of me. Kept cutting me with this jewel-fang-thing-I-don't-know! Point is I escaped and took the thing with me! That's why they're trying to get me!"

"So, all of this, over something you stole from them? Is that why those bastards were at your house? Is that why your friends were killed?" Attila put the pieces together.

"Dev, you could have come to me." Daisy said.

"Nah, I wanted to be on the down low 'till I figured out my next move. But know I can't wait anymore. They found out where I sleep – Shit's going south real bad."

Attila stayed quiet, crossing his arms and looking fed up with the ordeal.

"So what happened to the money? We know the stone's missing." he asked.

"I was never able to go back and get it. It was buried somewhere on the property."

Ash took in the tale so far. Montana was the ringleader of this drug gang or cult? What odd names for these siblings.

"Then after what happened tonight...man they're close, fucking close!" Devon croaked.

"What happened? Don't tell me they caught up with you again." Attila groaned.

"No, no, but I scored some shit on the street. It was some watered-down shit but it got the job done. I was taking a walk back down the alley to the motel and I heard some scraping noise - like fucking nails on a chalkboard – but I couldn't see where the hell it was coming from. I heard some growling or some shit so I hauled ass. I could hear something chasing me. Whatever it was, it was fast. It caught up to me and snarled right in my ear. I would have gotten bitten if I didn't move my head. I was so fucking scared; I screamed like a fuck'n bitch!"

Devon paused, licking the spittle off his lips and taking another long drag. Everyone was dead silent as they waited for Devon to finish. Not even Attila directed a derisive remark at the meth-head's direction.

"I started fucking gunning it. I'm pretty sure I ran over someone - a hobo or something - but I didn't stop until I locked and barricaded the door. Nothing happened for a while, but I heard that damn scraping and more growling again. It was louder than ever. My brain was going to burst. The door and windows rattled. It stopped and I heard a howl. There was a howl and for some fucking reason – couldn't stop my body – I peeked outside and saw...."

Devon stopped speaking abruptly. He looked up at the ceiling, spacing out in the rafters.

"What are you staring at?" Attila asked, "What happened next?"

"They were right...They're fucking real!" he gasped, "I thought the whole Storm-Star crap was some crazy shit they came up with but it's not! You should have seen it...I wish I didn't. It was fucked."

"See what?" Attila asked. Devon ignored him, chewing nervously on his dirty nails.

"We should get Dev back home. It's getting late." Daisy rose from her chair to lead her brother outside. Attila put out his cigarette and walked toward his back office, Ash following.

"You can get going if you want. It's late." Attila told him over his shoulder, "Sorry for the mess. Devon is the poster-child for the worst future brother-in-law a guy could have."

Ash bit his tongue, not wanting to tell him about Clarkson.

"Did you need to talk to me about anything?" Attila turned around to face his employee.

"Aah!" A sharp pain shot through Ash's shoulder.

"Are you okay?" Attila inquired, concerned about Ash's cry of pain. Ash ran towards the men's restroom, pain searing hotly on his back. He winced and groaned. Did he pop his stitches?

"Hey, dude, you alright?" Concern laced Attila's voice. Ash did not answer his employer who was on the other side. His back was on fire. Removing his shirt, he turned around to inspect the wound. White fur grew through the scars, strangled by the stitches. Mind racing, he plucked one of the hairs. It was soft and stained pink with blood.

"*Whatthefuck?Whatthefuck?Whatthefuck?*" he chanted internally. A loud knock silenced it.

"Ash, are you okay in there? It looked like you were hurting. Is it the stitches?"

"I'm fine!" he lied, "It's a little irritated is all. I'm gonna go home and take some medicine."

"Alright. Be safe." Attila sounded unconvinced.

Ash put his shirt back on when he heard Attila trotting off. He was sick with anxiety. What was going on with him? Ash's mind combed through what he knew from TV medical shows. Maybe he had some bizarre infection. Should he go to Jasper? What would he say? Hesitation settled in his guts until he mustered the courage to walk out of the bathroom. He made it to the parking lot, watching Devon and Daisy conversing. Devon still looked uneasy. His story sounded crazy, but Ash was starting to believe him to a small degree. After what happened in the woods the other day, it was evident *something* was going on. Did Devon see the same creature he encountered? Rust Springs was weird, no doubt, and things were only going to escalate.

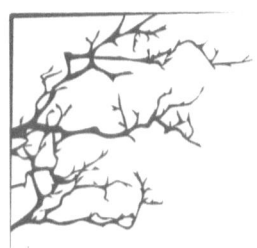

Chapter 15

Ash's skin itched; anxious to get inside. He found Jasper in the den, resting on the couch.

"Hey, kiddo. How was work?" he greeted.

"It was g-great!" Ash stuttered nervously, "I'm going to go bed now. I'm so wiped."

"I can see."

"It was kinda rough. This preacher guy, Calvin, was yelling at Attila about stuff and Devon came by and was talking about how he was being stalked by these Storm-Star cult dudes."

"Geeze. Calvin never shuts up. Such a sensationalist hack." Jasper put his herbal tea down and rubbed his temples.

"What's his deal, anyway?"

"Just another boogie-man for him to go after." Jasper rose from the sofa. "He's always advertising for his books and tapes, along with exorbitant donation requests to his ministry. Such a charlatan. I don't even know if he believes what comes out of his mouth." Jasper took another sip of his tea.

"Yeah, he feeds into the paranoia and hypes up the media he criticizes." Ash observed, "It's way weird."

"Smart." Jasper smiled, "You're catching on."

A scratch at the door alerted the two men. Jasper stood and walked towards the front door. Raini and Stormi rushed inside, wet, dirty, and covered in an orange substance.

"Crazy dogs. Had a good time in the springs, did you?" he asked as the dogs woofed excitedly.

"Do you usually let them roam around? What if they get hit or something?"

"Nah, they can handle themselves. Besides, Dalmatian-mixes are high-energy dogs and I can't dedicate that much time to caring for their exercise needs." Jasper explained. Ash could tell Jasper was sickly looking. His age did not help matters either.

"How's your stitches? Any better?"

Ash's blood froze in his veins.

"Yeah, yeah. They're fine." Ash said. At the mention of them, the wounds tingled uncomfortably.

"Do you need me to look at them?"

"No, I'm good. Like I said, I'm going to turn in for the night."

"Well, alright. Let me know if you need anything. I'm here if you need to talk."

Ash rushed upstairs. In his room, he quickly disrobed and touched the hair on his back. It grew out a little longer and was smooth and straight. The skin around it felt tender and sore to the touch. He plopped on the bed, lying on his side as he reflected on his body.

"What is wrong with me?"

Turning out the lights, his worries gave way to troubling dreams.

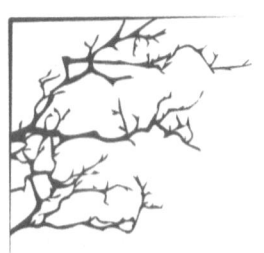

Mosaic

The space was a black abyss; aside from the sparkling sands and glittering mountains of various minerals. There was a brilliant light ahead of him. As if sitting on a large throne, a golden, candid skeleton with rainbow-jeweled fangs. It was massive; as tall as a mountain.

Out from the shifting sands rose other monoliths of its kind; raised to strike.

The bizarre encounter became terrifying as the creatures pushed towards him. As hard as Ash tried, he couldn't move his legs in the now quicksand ground. The bodies curved upward and parted like a morbid curtain to reveal a giant maw of a massive creature. He couldn't even scream when the rows of large fangs rushed to meet him.

...

There was another victim dead in the street. The optimistic morning sun did nothing to enlighten the grim scene.

"Got another one." Cooper sighed. Stockden, his partner, nodded. The body count was racking up. The disturbing thing to Stockden was this was in a residential, quiet neighborhood.

"Got quite a load on him." Cooper said as he rose from the body, "And some interesting tattoos, like the others."

Indeed, the dead man had tattoos indicative for the Aryan Brotherhood and baggies of meth in his possession.

"The meth's a bit different."

"Not really. Neo Nazi gangs often deal crystal." Stockden countered Cooper.

The Ripper's case frustrated Stockden, but there was a pattern of targeting suspected white supremacists. There were other casualties; mostly clientele of the extremists.

Neighbors were gathered at the crime scene tape, trying to get a view.

"I bet you a hundred dollars there is a big dog or something that killed these people. Maybe a vigilante?"

"Likely some twisted soul."

The two officers jotted down notes while forensics took pictures of the gruesome mauling.

Stockden saw Traynor reviewing the scene. The man looked irritated. He was curious of why he had not convicted the offenders with crimes.

"Wanna get something to eat after this?" Cooper's stomach growled audibly, "I haven't eaten anything yet."

"Sure." Stockden could always rely on Cooper's appetite, even after as nasty crime as this.

"You think Traynor's acting...weird?" He looked around to make sure no one else was following them.

"Yeah, apparently I'm not the only one."

"What do you think it is?"

"Stress, maybe?"

"Stress?"

"This Ripper thing has been a hard nut to crack for him."

"What about the skinheads he let go?"

"Technically, we couldn't hold them on anything."

So Cooper didn't "see" after all, which was okay in Stockden's opinion.

"Huh." It could be his skeptical nature, but Stockden knew something was up.

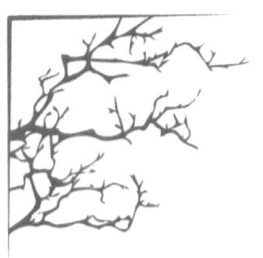

Chapter 16

"So where is this "Reich Rebel" person we're supposed to be meeting?" Vasquez fidgeted in his seat, eager to start the day.

"Somewhere downtown it seems." Mullen said in between sips of his coffee. They sat in the lobby of the hotel they were staying at. Vasquez got a notification from a friend in Cincinnati that an associate of Storm-Star Lodge members was in Columbus.

Vasquez combed through the file for an overview. "General" Custer Delaney was a former member of an infamous white supremacist gang named the *Rebels of the Reich*. Their goal was to train members and acquire funds to dismantle the American government. They would conduct training sessions in isolated areas across the country, and commit various crimes in order to obtain the money necessary to buy weaponry and rent safe houses.

"I remember these guys-!" he said excitedly to the chagrin of Mullen.

"Shhh! Keep it down! You don't need to alert everyone in the whole town." Mullen almost spilled his cup of complimentary coffee.

"Sorry." Vasquez lowered his voice, "I remembered these guys. They were a band of bank robbers; crimes stretching from Nevada to Pennsylvania."

"They got caught a couple of years ago. Most of the members went to jail and their terrorist activities were brought to light." Mullen pointed to one member's picture. "Except one."

"Yeah, Delaney snitched on them. As a result, he got a reduced sentence. What does he know about the Loupcroix?"

"From his account, Montana and Washington used to run with them before they left. He could give more insight and history into the Order."

"Looks like it." Vasquez rose from the lobby chair and walked with Mullen to the car.

It wasn't long until they made it to the Delaney residence. It was located in an old, but quaint working-class suburb in the city. Fall decorations of cornucopias and leaves covered the dwelling. As they approached the house, Mullen could hear children playing inside.

"Sounds like Delaney did well for himself after all." Vasquez observed. Mullen's own home was devoid of the sounds of his daughter. Vasquez knocked on the door and a woman answered. She looked tired in her jeans and yellow blouse, a portrait of motherhood.

"Yes. How can I help you?" she asked.

"Mrs. Delaney, we are Detectives Mullen and Vasquez." Mullen introduced, "We wish to speak to your husband. Is he home?"

The warm smell of sloppy joes filled his nostrils.

"Ah, yes. In the backyard." she said, trying to look composed but Mullen could see an uneasiness flash across her features. He and Vasquez followed her to the back door, passing though the living room and kitchen. At the table, a little girl and two boys were coloring and talking to each other about Power Rangers and princesses.

"Children, please go upstairs and play now." Mrs. Delaney commanded them. The offspring obeyed; collecting their art supplies and giving the two detectives curious looks as they passed by.

"Sweet kids." Vasquez commented. Mrs. Delaney did not acknowledge it.

"He's out by the shed." she told them plainly. Mullen walked over the threshold. The backyard was small and he could easily see a sturdy bald man moving to the shed and organizing various tools.

"Custer Delaney?" Mullen called out. The man walked out of the shed and looked at them confused.

"Yeah. That's me." he said.

"I'm detective Mullen. This is my partner, Vasquez. We are here to talk to you today concerning the Loupcroix brothers." Mullen said. Custer looked resigned, as if knowing why they would want to talk.

"Alright, detectives. What do you want to know?"

"We were wondering if you've heard anything about your old associates, Montana and Washington Loupcroix."

"Montana and Washington. Those are names I haven't heard in a good long while." Custer sighed.

Vasquez shifted uncomfortably in the lawn chairs Delaney provided them, finding one of the legs was shorter than the other one. The clear, crisp air chilled his lungs.

"What can you tell us about them? You were vague on details during the initial investigation." Mullen asked.

"Well, for one thing, they were pretty intimidating. I mean they looked wild, like they were raised off the range. But considering their lifestyle, it wasn't too far from the truth." Custer explained.

"Elaborate."

"I've met their father, Bennett. Rough son of a bitch. He's a vet but had a fall out with the government. He married and moved northwest, lived in wood cabins away from everyone. Totally off the grid. Became a regular at gun show circuits and meetings for people...like myself. Preached the same old hate, but rubbed other groups the wrong way."

"How?"

"Well, for one, he was critical of the Christian Identity movement. Ya'know, where Jews and minorities are Satan's spawn and whites are God's true chosen. Bennett was more of a trailblazer type with this pseudo-Norse religion he was pushin'. He espoused these "star beings" and his true religion for whites; renouncing Christianity as a Jew religion meant to cripple Aryans. He believed Christian Identity supporters were no better."

"How did that go over?"

"Terribly. Bennett could be volatile when pushed. He became a loner as a result, aside from those of a similar mind. Neo-Nazis in particular could relate to his reverence of the Norse Gods and Hitler's relation to the occult. He did have an odd interpretation, though."

"What do you mean?"

Custer leaned back, seemingly struggling how to explain Bennett's philosophy.

"Bennett believed some two star thingies will come down to earth to purge it of "mud people" and other undesirables at the end of times. An entity will come as a Messiah and usher the Aryan race into a new age. That's all I remember. Gives you a picture of how his kids were raised to think."

Mullen mentally reviewed his notes. Custer's account matched that of the cult, which now could be classified as doomsday in nature. The situation in Rust Springs just got more dangerous.

"Back to Montana and Washington." Vasquez said, "What were they like?"

"Well, they were the oldest of the siblings and thick as thieves from what I could tell. Montana was more of the leader. He's charismatic and likeable. Wash was more reserved and quiet. He followed his brother's lead. Took orders like a good soldier." Custer continued.

"What were their goals?"

"They were initially part of our group. We trained them and they did "jobs" with us. We kicked them out after the incident."

"What incident?" Vasquez leaned forward.

"They were with us for about a year. We had a safe house in South Dakota, outside of Rapid City. Montana, Washington and Jace Striker went out to rob a family. They did not tell us where the guns and gold coins came from. Later, we found out they killed them: a father, a mother, and their boy. We told them to leave and we moved out before suspicions could set in. A week later, they were pulled out of the river." Custer's voice was strangled by regret, eyes falling to the ground. Mullen whispered to Vasquez to look into Striker later.

"And that's it. We never saw them again. I don't know what else to tell you other than I'm grateful to be out from under that mess."

"Thank you for your time, Mr. Delaney." Mullen said, "Enjoy the rest of your evening with your family. You have a good thing going here."

Mullen's noticed Vasquez's surprised face in the corner of his eye. He would usually leave with a business card, not another word. He was happy Custer reformed and made a life for himself. The children were indeed precious, as any parent would know.

"Thanks. They're the best decision I've ever made. I mean, we don't have much; me being a mechanic and my wife works retail but we try to make it the best we can." Custer said.

"Yes, well, sometimes that's all that matters." Mullen walked back towards the house. Vasquez shook Delaney's hand, giving him a contact card if he had any more information.

They gave the Delany family a polite farewell; eager to discuss the new information.

"That was enlightening. Not only are the Loupcroix the head of a doomsday cult, but are murderers as well. Lucky for Delaney, he got out of that mentality." Vasquez said.

"So it would seem." Mullen replied.

"What do you make of Bennett Loupcroix? Sounds like a piece of work."

"We need to look him up. If he served in the military, there should be a record of him somewhere. If the Storm-Star Lodge are the edge of the fringe, things could get more dangerous. We need to proceed quickly and with caution." Mullen stared out to the Delaney residence with Vasquez wondering if they were on the same page. Kinship and bonds meant a lot to the Loupcroix. They stuck together under a shared vision for the future. Vasquez hoped they would be able to figure out the relationship between the Ripper case, which they were supposed to be focusing on, and the Storm-Star cult. The two detectives would make their way back to Rust Springs with new names and leads to follow.

Maw of Madness

"How long has he been doing this?" Oregon lay on the rough wooden floor, listening for any movements or utterances underneath.

"Past five days." Washington stood upon the tattered Oriental rug that hid the secret chamber underneath the barn structure. Idaho leaned his head against the pew. The barn was warmer than outside, but he hated attending these petty meetings. On each side of him was Wyoming and Colorado, who also looked a bit bored. The men of the militia and some of the women took the rest of the pews.

"You hear?" Washington spoke, "Folkvagnr is upon us! This is the time to prepare. You know the protocol: secure the compound and scale down operations."

The meeting was adjourned. People rose and formed their own discussion groups or exited. Wyoming mumbled something about some "owed debts", while Colorado shuffled towards her older brothers. Idaho took it as a cue to leave, but Wyoming blocked him.

"Where are you fucking going?" Wyoming snarled.

"Out. What's it to you?" Idaho looked over his brother's shoulder, desiring nothing more than to run out the barn doors.

"Yeah, right. I hear Wash has a job for you."

"Bullshit."

"Ida!" Washington yelled, "Come here."

"Told ya, fucker." Wyoming smugly smiled, walking off. Idaho reluctantly approached his brother, worried of what would be asked of him.

"You need to see Monty." Washington moved to the podium, leaning on it. "He needs to talk to you now."

"Why? I hadn't seen him in a month..."

Washington gave him a look; a look that promised consequences if he didn't listen. Idaho abruptly bit his tongue, his blood chilling in his veins. Washington grabbed the carpet, throwing it, and pried the trap door open. A startled sound left Idaho's lips. He could sense Montana's presence in the dark pit. It was a sensation he hated.

"You okay?-" Oregon asked.

"I'm not going down there." Idaho's stomach lurching.

"You can and you will." Washington said with a tense voice. Oregon gave him a nudge and Idaho descended the steel ladder. When he was about halfway down, the door was slammed shut. Total darkness encased him. The only sure foundation was of the cold steel in his hands.

It's everything, but nothing. Kind of how Montana described the Storm-Star. A walking contradiction, where its existence would render the world a void. Without it, however, no being or object would come to fruition. His brother described it as ascension to greater cosmic knowledge and communion to Aryan ancestors. Idaho descended into the grand chasm. He struggled to find a reason to continue. He could try his luck in convincing his siblings to pull him up.

"Ida?" Montana's voice echoed. He dare not answer. "Come closer."

Idaho still did not respond. His mind conjured experiences from past sessions with his brother. He loathed them; he truly did. The conjurings, if they could be called as such, invaded his mind. Indescribable visions of the Storm-Star in question. The closest it could be in his mind was a spiral. It could be a spiral, yes. It extends from a point and spreads its influence. Spirals are also synonymous with delirium, a senseless dance across the cosmos. It is fundamental by nature in its design. Spirals ensnare and entrap. A more appropriate comparison is a circle. An endless but complete loop destined to go on forever; infinity and immortality. They do say the definition of insanity is repeating the same action over and over with the expectation of a different response.

But it's whole. Comprehensive.

Spirals are out of control, while circles are ordered. Neat.

Order and disorder.

It's both.

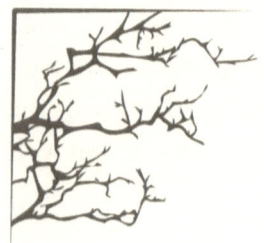

Chapter 17

"You look like shit, Ash."

The bright lighting in the club did not help in disguising the exhausted and haunted look on his face. Ash suffered an aching soreness that penetrated to his bones. He had a troubled sleep and was exhausted. Everything hurt on him. Ash could confirm Attila's comment; he did feel like shit.

"Rough sleep? You look tired." Attila pointed.

"Yeah, I was just trying with the whole goth look ya'know, try to fit in around here." Ash weakly attempted humor.

"It's not working for you. You're a better fit as a grunge type any way." Attila teased back. "Besides, janitors don't need goth wear. Hell, with all the shit you have to clean – "

Attila was interrupted by Devon throwing a fit outside. The two men walked to check on the commotion. Devon pushed Daisy away from him.

"Goddammit! I don't need rest. Not when they are after me and shit!"

"Listen to me! You need to calm down. You were up all night. Devon, we can take you somewhere else." Daisy tried to reason with him. The tweaker sobbed.

"It's not going to matter. They're going to find me either way. Probably plotting my fucking demise as we speak."

"That's the drugs talking – "

"Ha-ha-ha!" Devon laughed madly, "Meth is the only reason why I am alive. Do you know what fucked up shit they do on the farm? Sure, it looks like some skinheads goofing around but these

98

fuckers are serious! They will kill to get what they want! And Montana...boy...I don't know what state of mind he's in now but if he is anything like I remember, he's even more batshit. Fuck, this is like Kansas all over again. I can't stay. I gotta skip town." Devon mumbled frantically.

"Shit. Ash? Can you take Devon to the convenience store? Looks like he can use a cig." Attila said.

"Sure. Come on, Dev. Some nicotine will do you good." Devon was still frantic, but accepted Ash's offer.

"Okay but seriously, I gotta leave afterwards." Devon picked at his skin.

...

The cheerful chime of the gas station doors greeted Ash and Devon as they entered.

"I'll be over here, Dev." Ash said as he walked towards the drinks. "Will you be alright?"

"What am I? A fuckin' child?" Dev snapped, "I got it."

"Okay." Ash whispered to himself as Devon went to the counter. He reviewed the beverage choices in front of him. He decided to grab a cola, clutching and pulling the cool door of the display refrigerator.

"Ash! Funny meeting you here!" Calvin Clarkson, local televised pastor and Rust Springs' first line of defense against Satan and the occult had arrived, making his presence known with his shrill voice. Ash stared dumbly; as he was not expecting to see Calvin at that moment. He almost forgot about the invitation he got last night.

"I was on my way back to the church. How are you doing?"

"Uh- Fine. Just getting a drink."

Devon came from behind.

"Who's this? Mister Roger's molester brother?" Devon hissed, opening the pack of cigarettes.

"Devon..." Ash warned.

"Oh! Is this Devon? Daisy's brother? Nice to meet you." Calvin extended his arm out to Devon.

"Don't fucking touch me, asshole!" Devon growled like a wild animal, slinking away in search of a nicotine fix. Calvin was unsettled by the response, but shook it off and continued conversing with Ash.

"What's his issue?" Calvin asked politely as possible, "Is he on something?"

"Maybe? He's having a rough day."

"Well, there's nothing the love and grace of Christ can't fix! So, are you going to take me up on the offer and consider bringing Devon to the church?"

Ash paused. The bar would not be opened for a couple of hours, but at the same time he did not want to be sucked into Calvin's hijinks; even if he was curious and entertained by his outrageous character. He'd never been to church either.

"C'mon. I know you have to work, but it will only be for a little while. I won't keep you too long." Calvin pleaded. In the background, Devon had managed to light a cigarette inside the store to the vexation of the owner.

"No smoking inside, sir." the cashier said.

"Fuck off!" Devon hollered the man, flipping him off.

"Er, sure." Ash hoped this wasn't a bad idea.

"Cool beans. I'll show you the way." Calvin was pleased by the answer.

"C'mon Dev. Let's go before we get kicked out." Ash called.

"Where are we going?" Devon mumbled as he gripped the cigarette between his lips.

"Some place to chill. It'll be safe." Ash reassured the twitchy addict.

"Ok. As long as there isn't other fags like him." Devon pointed at Calvin.

Golgotha was a fairly modest building for a tele-evangelist on the way to mega-church stardom. The pastel-green colored structure was once a storefront back in in the 1960's, as evidenced by its mid-century aesthetic. A neon white cross was plastered above the glass front doors.

"Welcome to the house of God!" Calvin chuckled warmly, "It's not much but we are planning to move to a bigger facility in the next year or so now that the ministry is growing."

People milled around between the wooden pews, observing the newcomers. They looked like they were cut from the white-bread Americana cloth inspired by a Norman Rockwell painting.

"Gang! I want you to meet Ash and Devon." Calvin introduced them to a small circle of colleagues who worked at the church. Ash waved shyly while Devon smoked, not caring to give attention to anyone else in the room. Calvin didn't seem particularly happy with Devon smoking inside but if it calmed him, it was the lesser of two evils given Devon's erratic mood.

"Follow me to the back, Devon. I got a room set up for us here."

The interview was to be conducted in a conference room where three chairs were arranged. Two cameras on stands were facing the seats.

"What's with the cameras?"

"Don't worry, it's for documentation purposes only. I plan to share this with the proper authorities." Calvin told him. "Help get some attention outside of Rust Springs."

"That's good and all, but I hope you obscure our identities or something."

"Scout's honor."

Ash could only hope Calvin would keep his word about the situation.

"Okay, everyone. We're going to get started here in a bit." Calvin organized some folding chairs in a circle. A middle-aged homely woman approached Ash and Devon.

"Hello, gentlemen. My name is Kathy. Would you be interested in some coffee?"

"We're fine, ma'am, thank you." Ash said. Devon was checking out the golden candleholders near the altar, as if assessing the value.

"Take your seats, boys!" Calvin waved to Ash and Devon.

"Pretty bossy, huh?" Devon wasn't questioning why he was here, considering what Ash had mentioned to Calvin. When everyone was seated, quick introductions were given. Devon didn't seem to care.

"Now that we are acquainted, why don't you tell us about yourself, Devon?"

"You don't need to know anything, asshole-" Devon ground his teeth through his cigarette.

"Okay, okay. No problem. Why don't you tell us about the Storm-Star then?" Calvin snorted, unsatisfied with how conversation was going.

Devon stared at Ash, cracking his knuckles on his right hand. He messed up big time.

"It's nothing you would want to know...bad shit happens there."

"Like what exactly?"

Devon chuckled, sitting up straighter.

"You don't know what you're messing with."

"Oh, I believe I do. The powers of darkness themselves."

"This shit ain't like anything you learned in Sunday School, Mr. Molesto. Ash, I wanna leave."

"Don't toy with me, Devon. I see Satan's work in this town-"

"Motherfucker! You don't fucking get it! None of you do!"

The room fell silent, aside from the congregation whispering amongst themselves. Devon and Calvin had their eyes locked on each other.

"Let's calm down, everyone." Kathy placed her hands outward, urging for calm.

"You're right, Kathy. Thank you." Calvin sighed, "Heh. I tend to get a little passionate when it comes to breaking the devil's stronghold, but we should keep calm. There are important matters to discuss."

Devon chuckled darkly again. This time sounding unhinged.

"So you want to know what the Storm-Star is?" Devon asked.

"Yes. Please." Calvin answered. Devon paused flicking ashes from the cigarette on the floor of the church.

The church buzzed, eager for salacious details on the mysterious cult in Rust Springs. Ash could see the wheels turning in Calvin's mind. He nervously considered about the consequences of Devon's confession. It could make him more of a target than he was already. Depending on how Calvin spins it, Ash could be in danger himself.

"Well, it's a cult that wants to resurrect some star-god-dog-thing. They don't like the government or anyone who doesn't look like them...uh...they do rituals some times in the barn."

"Are you saying they are located in the rural areas?" Calvin interrupted.

"Y-yes..." Devon said, saying too much already.

"Wow, Devon, thank you for your bravery in coming forward with this information." Calvin pulled out a note pad. "Now, we are armed with more knowledge to fight these devil-worshipers. Is there any more you could share with us? What about their end goal?"

Devon's face instantly turned grim. The cigarette hung limply in his mouth, the cherry light giving his face a haunting glow. He did not speak but only stared off into space, turning his face upwards towards the church rafters. An uneasy silence settled over the group.

"You want to know about their objective?" Devon put out his cig on the floor.

"Y-yes." Calvin said shakily. Devon laughed. It was not the normal joking laughter one would associate with telling a joke or a funny anecdote. It was bitter and condescending.

"You morons. You know what they want: to bring about the Folkvangr age."

"Uh, true but how?"

Devon laughed again. His demeanor changed. His eyes were wide and unblinking, staring down Calvin, who shrank back in his seat.

"The Storm-Star will come. In this form we know him as Nidhoggr, the great dragon who chews on the world. He will consume the inferior, purging the world for the Aryans. The Fenris-kin will serve beside him, his dire howls signaling a new reality: Folkvagnr." he hissed.

Ash remembered accounts of people possessed by demons. The normally twitchy and paranoid Devon was gone, replaced by a wild-eyed unknown. The rest of the group shrank back in fear of what Devon would do. Ash followed Devon, who raced past the isle of pews to the entrance.

"Gotta leave…" Ash heard him mumble in front of him. A cold wind blew in his face as Devon opened the wooden double doors of the church.

"Wait! Where are you going?" Calvin cried out.

"Sorry, I have to watch him!" Ash looked back at Calvin and the rest of the Golgotha congregation members.

"Please come back. We have more to talk about!"

"Yeah, sure."

Ash would not make the mistake of hard commitments with Calvin again. In the threshold, he could see Devon trying to break into a car parked on the street.

"What the hell are you doing?" He approached slowly.

"What does it fucking look like I'm fucking doing?"

Ash was hesitant to ask more stupid questions or stop Devon from his task after eyeing his pocketknife, which he was currently using on the door. The glass shattered on the driver's side window and Devon unlocked the door, proceeding to hot-wire the car.

"Dev, please, we should be getting back to the club. Your sister is waiting for you –" Ash pleaded.

"Fuck her. She can live out her post-porn existence with her nigger boyfriend. If she left me once, I can leave her again."

The engine roared to life. Ash jumped back to avoid being run over by Devon. How was he going to explain this to Attila and Daisy? The smell of burnt rubber filled his nose as Devon fled the reach of the Lodge.

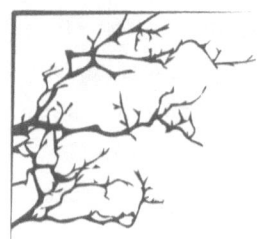

Chapter 18

Having your wits about you on the mean streets of Rust Springs West was a must. As a woman of the streets, they were her home. She couldn't remember how long she'd lived out here. Time lost all meaning to her now. It was day-by-day, night-by-night.

Find shelter and survive. The cold weather became worse as she got older. Fall and winter were the worst to her. The heat of summer was at least tolerable but the cold permeated her bones, making them painful and achy. The alcove of an empty church seemed like an ideal place to rest. She parked her shopping cart of goods and sentimental junk; digging for a trusty, ratty blanket.

She wrapped the soft fabric around her. She placed her body against the stone wall in an upright position, facing toward the street. She got accustomed to sleeping with one eye open. There were many dangers for homeless folk. The shadows of the night bothered her as well. She had to make sure they didn't grab her.

The sleep came shortly after setting up for the night; stiff yet peaceful. There was a commotion near the street corner. It sounded like a bear growling.

Fear passed through her. Was it the shadows? She opened her weary eyes, trembling. She peered around the corner of the smooth alcove. It was the shadows, consuming something red, bloody, and with blonde hair. One of the shadows reared its head, sniffing. She ducked back, not knowing what to do. She prayed to God that no harm will come to her. She closed her eyes and waited for the noises to stop.

After a few minutes of silence, she slowly re-opened her eyes; terrified of what she might see. She looked at the street corner and saw a mangled, bloody corpse. She wanted to vomit and promptly did so; evacuating what little food she ate today. She found a pay phone nearby, rustling around for some change she had stuffed in her pocket from panhandling earlier. She fed the dime and picked up the phone, dialing 911.

"Hello, 911. What's your emergency?"

"I need to report a killing on Malone Street."

"What? A murder, ma'am?"

"Yes. The bodies were taken by the sh-shadows."

"Excuse me?"

She hung up. They probably thought she was crazy. She had to leave before the shadows found her too.

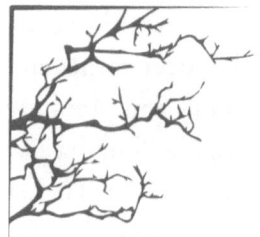

Chapter 19

"**D**id you hear? They found two more bodies." Vasquez said over his desk to Mullen. His partner did not pay attention to him; apparently busy talking with someone over the phone and reviewing paperwork. The surface of Vasquez's desk was fairly bare except for a single file.

The file tab was labeled "Striker, Jace"; the Rapid City murder accomplice who Custer Delaney named during his interview. Inside, the file was filled with various documentation concerning Striker's criminal history. Physical assaults, assaults with deadly weapons, drug possession, burglary, and fraud were just a fraction of his extensive career. Based on the young age at which Striker embarked on his life of crime, Vasquez could only guess the background he came from. Along with the Reichstag Renegades, Striker was also associated with a skinhead group out of Texas. Similar to Delaney and the Loupcroix, their crimes took place over many different states.

Vasquez noticed the most recent criminal charge was for possession of marijuana in Kentucky. After that, Striker seemed to disappear off the face of the Earth. He used the computer database to retrieve more information on family and friends. He came up blank. What could have happened?

The possibilities were endless: overdose, name change, death. He scrolled down, only to find a report of Striker found dead from a self-inflicted gunshot wound in El Paso. Vasquez groaned internally. Another dead-end; the same as what he found with Bennett Loupcroix. The patriarch has military records and some former residences from that time period but after that, nothing. Bennett didn't want to be found and used aliases and fake identification for his clandestine lifestyle.

"I finished talking to the boys over in Ridgeland, West Virginia." Mullen interrupted Vasquez's thoughts.

"Wow, West Virginia. What did you find there?" Vasquez inspected the notes placed on his desk.

"A relative of the Loupcroix. Apparently, Bennett had a brother named Vermond. They both served in Vietnam but they lost touch with each other a couple of years later, being off the grid and such. It would seem that a Columbia Loupcroix lives outside of Ridgeland in the hollers."

"Cool. I wonder if she knows what her family has been up to? Then again..."

"The Loupcroix are extremely secretive and elusive people. I don't think we will be well-received."

"Should we leave tomorrow?"

"Sounds good."

Hands slamming on a hardwood startled them both.

"You boys still dicking around with that cult stuff? I thought I told you to lay off." Traynor growled, "You're supposed to be working the Ripper case."

"No, we're checking another angle, sir." Mullen eyed Vasquez, signaling to clear the desk. Traynor got close to Mullen, reaching over to his ear.

"I suggest you boys drop it. We're short on resources as it is. I don't need my detectives chasing their tails over a non-factor in this case."

"How do you know?" Mullen asked. Traynor laid a hand on Mullen's right shoulder.

"I know you haven't been the same since the divorce, Mullen. I see you slipping, but I know you're better than this. For the sake of your career, I hope you take this as a second chance."

How dare he say something like that! Vasquez balled his fists, waiting for Mullen's response.

"I appreciate your concern, sir. Vasquez and I will follow up on Ripper leads." Mullen's tone was even. How could he be calm after such a grossly disrespectful comment? Traynor looked them over once more and left; stiff in his walk.

"Man, what an asshole." Vasquez was still angered by Traynor's disrespect.

"Don't worry about it." Mullen slumped in his chair. "Whatever gets us more time and him off our backs. You're gonna have to go to West Virginia without me."

"What about Traynor?"

"We'll think of something."

Vasquez stretched, relaxing tense muscles. "It would be nice if he could drop off the face of the earth – "

Boom! A large explosion shook the police department. The shockwaves shifted the papers around on Vasquez's desk and rattled the pencils inside a coffee mug.

"What the hell was that?" Vasquez exclaimed amongst the rest of their co-workers scrambling to determine the cause. A couple of people rushed towards the direction of the explosion fire to investigate. Mullen and Vasquez followed through the corridors into the back-parking lot. Squad cars and various models of unmarked cars filled the concrete space. Near the center, several vehicles were set ablaze. A figure dressed in uniform blue was seen fleeing the flames. While someone went back inside to call the fire department, Vasquez broke away from the on lookers to approach the man, who he recognized as Officer Deane. Deane looked shell-shocked from the explosion.

"What the fuck happened, man?" Vasquez asked.

"I-it's Traynor!" Deane panted. "He got in and started the car and it exploded!"

Although Vasquez could not see Traynor inside the car, he could smell the familiar scent of burning flesh. After working a particularly malicious arson case in Cincinnati, he could never forget the sickening odor.

Looks like they got their wish.

The fire was put out, leaving behind the shell of the squad car. The charred bones and ashes of Traynor were found as well. The scene was taped off while investigators did their work. After some observation, Mullen and Vasquez discussed their theories.

"We know Traynor was fishy. Is this some form of retaliation?" Vasquez asked.

"I believe so. After all, it was his vehicle. We should interview Deane." Mullen said.

Deane was shaken but willing to give a recount of what happened.

"I was out in the yard with Traynor. I heard him cursing something about being "cut out" and wanting to pay a visit to someone. The he got in the car and..." Deane sniffed.

"It's okay, buddy." Vasquez reassured. He knew Deane was a good guy. Whatever Traynor's schemes were, he was not likely involved. He didn't suspect anyone in the department was either. They disliked Traynor's leadership just as much as he did. If the Loupcroix were instrument to this, it was all the more urgent he and Mullen find Columbia and talk to her.

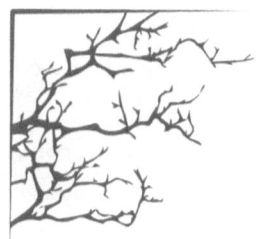

Chapter 20

The cool water soothed Colorado's throat. She had finished her shift tending to the plants, sipping water from a mason jar. She touched one of the marijuana trees, its vibrant green leaves tickling her fingertips. While they provided a means for her family to accumulate the funds and resources for the Lodge, the plants would lose their usefulness as the prophecy came closer to fruition. She sat the jar on a workbench in the greenhouse, making her way to the barn. She was happy with the fact that she didn't have to deal with Devon; her older brothers decided to take on the task. Colorado was trained but didn't care to fight. Those days when her father would demonstrate weapon use and self-defense techniques for the family and whoever took up their cause, she preferred to help out around the compound instead. Common chores were less stressful than fighting or evading authorities. The consistency of the tasks and what they provided for the community gave Colorado a sense of stability in a shaky world.

Once inside, she looked past the pews, which seated so many of their members. Continuing towards the podium, she found the tattered Oriental rug on the floor. Her big brother slept below. It reminded her of the story of Christ's crucifixion. Occasionally, he would rise from the dead and they would be called to provide sustenance and water. However, for two weeks, he fasted silently - ensnared by a trance that few would comprehend.

The carpet shifted as the secret hatch door opened. Colorado stiffened, alarmed and elated by the movement. Montana rose weakly from the chamber, squinting in the grey light coming from the door.

"Monty?" she asked.

"Collie...you wouldn't believe the things I've seen. The glory of Folkvagnr is near."

Colorado rushed to his side, helping him up to his feet.

"Was it as pretty as you said it was?"

"Even greater." Montana laughed, looking around. "Where is everyone?"

"Wash, Ori, and Wylie are out after Grayhart. Ida is in the house."

Montana groaned at the mention of Devon's surname.

"Goddamn idiot. I'll have to catch up with him when he returns to discuss a few things..."

Colorado didn't say anything, knowing Devon was a dead man if they caught him.

"Let's go to the house. I want to see Ida." Montana told her. She obliged, staying close to his unsteady form. She could tell he lost some muscle mass but he was still formidable as ever. He looked elated; manic even. Vitality coursed through him. How could he be so energetic? He must be ecstatic from his visions. It gave her joy as well. It was turning out to be a good day for her. She didn't have to hunt a traitor, and Montana is back to lead them once more.

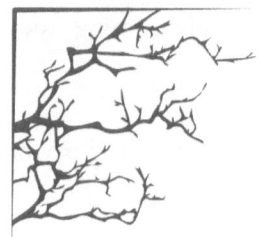

Chapter 21

"Did you see where he went?" Daisy asked about her absent brother.

"Up the street but he disappeared from view after a while." Ash said.

"We should go after him."

"No." Attila said sternly, "Devon's made his choice. He doesn't want to be here. Just let him clear his head."

"Clear his head? He wanted to leave the damn state!" Daisy argued, "He has no money and he's driving a stolen car! We have to get to him before the Loupcroix get him or worse."

"Can we just call the cops and call it the end of the day?"

"Hell no! You know the cops won't do shit, even more so for an addict like Devon." Daisy snapped.

"You heard Ash." Attila rose from the bar stool he was sitting on. "He obviously doesn't give a good damn about us. You need to stop coddling him. He will seek help when he wants it and we can't keep bailing him out. I still have to pay for the damages to the motel room he trashed!"

Daisy walked away, trying to hide the tears starting to stream down her face. Attila hung his head.

"What did he tell you?"

"Uh, something about porn. What's that about anyway?" Ash asked when Daisy was out of earshot.

"It's something we don't like to bring up but hell, Devon told you anyway..." Attila muttered.

"Did Daisy...?"

"Uh, yes, but that's all I'll say about it. If you're curious, you should talk to her about it."

"She would be okay with that?"

"Depends on how you approach it. She's had to deal with people recognizing her before. Sometimes it's not a problem but others...it got ugly."

A beat of silence passed between them.

"For another time. You need to get to cleaning before we open."

Gathering his supplies, Ash debated internally if he should ask Daisy about her adult performer past. She was beautiful, but it was surreal to him to encounter someone from the industry. Ash did not have too much experience with porn outside of some Hustler mags, and he only had one girlfriend a while back before he moved to Rust Springs. Must've been some upbringing Devon and Daisy had to take them to where they were at now. Daisy cared for Devon, yet, he was unsure of the latter's feelings. Uncharacteristic for the flavor of the club, soft instrumentals were played on the sound system as he completed his tasks silently.

A couple of hours into opening, a particularly vicious bar brawl broke out. Ash was not close enough to see how the fight started, but it seemed like a spat between two jealous lovers. While the bouncers escorted the offending parties out the door, he wiped vomit off the floor.

He decided to wash up in the bathroom before he was stopped by Daisy.

"Uh, shouldn't you be at the bar?" Ash asked her.

"Shouldn't you be cleaning?"

"I finished doing that..."

"Never mind. We need to talk."

Ash followed Daisy's lead to the office and locked the door behind him. She had a worried expression on her face. Ash wasn't sure of how to proceed.

"I know what you're thinking." She said flatly. A nervous blush crossed Ash's face as if she read his thoughts.

"You're wondering about the porn, aren't you?"

"Honestly, we don't have to go there if you – " Ash was getting even more red.

"Relax. I'd be better to tell you before you start hearing any rumors. Have a seat." Daisy said reassuringly.

"Honest, you don't have to. Not judging – "

"Ash, shut it and listen. It will help put everything between Devon and I into perspective."

Ash twiddled his thumbs, not sure of what to expect.

Wichita, Kansas 1980s

Daisy clutched her books and grabbed her bag as she exited the noisy school bus. The tree-lined streets of her suburban neighborhood portrayed the serene idealism of the American Dream.

Just one more month and she will be able to leave this dump. Indeed, graduation was around the corner. Along with her studies, she wanted to focus on her drama club play: A Western version of *A Midsummer Night's Dream*. Although not a fan of the theme, she enjoyed the chance to be someone else through acting. Anything to escape from her family.

"Daisy!" her mother's shrieked through the screen door in front of a generic, beige single story home. Daisy dreaded to find what had angered her mother, Diana, this time. The house was dark with open windows providing the only light inside the home. Her mother was in the kitchen, wearing her "power suit" and tapping her polished nails on the counter in an irritated manner.

"Do you know where your brother is? The truant officer called and said he wasn't at school when he left this morning."

Daisy could only guess he was in the park somewhere smoking pot or at the arcade wasting quarters on cabinets and pinball machines. Devon was a year younger than her and behind his grade due to his lack of devotion to his schoolwork. This only incensed their strict and overachieving mother.

"No." she said simply, not wanting to add more to the conversation. If only she could be excused to go to her room.

"Okay, go upstairs and get to work. You have only a couple of weeks left 'til graduation. We need to keep this ship running tight. Did you pick out a dress for the prom? What about college applications?"

Daisy had found a dress more her style or was at least unique enough to stand out from the pastel-colored crowd. A classmate of hers even asked her out.

"You're not going with a boy are you?" her mother asked.

"What's the point of going to prom without a date?" Daisy replied incredulously.

"You shouldn't. After all, it's important for women to be independent and at your age, boys shouldn't be the focus."

As Diana droned out her feminist ideals, Daisy tuned her out. She had mailed out two applications to some schools with notable theatre programs. While her mother wouldn't approve of her creative ambitions, Daisy wanted to become a professional actress. She was not sure she would be able to get accepted though.

"Look at my relationship with your father..." the Grayhart matriarch continued. Daisy rolled her eyes. Their hen-pecked and emotionally unavailable father would be home soon, only to not spend time with them. He would just disappear into the office. Grayhart wasn't even his last name; he took his wife's name upon marriage.

Daisy walked to her room, where she found her dress. It was black and lacy, but looked better than the cookie-cutter crap the other girls in the school wore.

She heard a tap on her window. Opening the blinds, she saw Devon.

"Dev, you better leave." Daisy opened her window. "Mom's gonna be pissed if she sees you."

Devon brushed her off.

"Yeah, whatever. Don't you wanna come with me and Ronnie? We're gonna have a great time at the park." he invited.

"Sorry, Dev, but I don't like your friends. Ronnie's racist and dumb as hell."

"Maybe you're just a stuck up bitch! Still gonna do that acting gig? You know mom won't vouch for ya. Dad's too busy being scarce to care anyway." Devon searched his pockets for a cigarette.

Daisy knew Devon was hurt by the lack of relationship between him and father. Devon hated their mother as she did not care much for having a boy, initially. She got pregnant again in order to have a girl.

"What are you going to do with yourself, Dev?" Daisy asked her brother. Devon took a long drag as he considered the question.

"Ronnie and his circle have connections. I'm gonna help produce and run product for them. Besides, have you tried speed? Shit's the best. Way better than grass. You can turn a quick buck off of it too, nowadays. You're looking at the future Meth King of Kansas!"

"Sure." Daisy rolled her eyes, "Nice to see you have great aspirations for yourself."

"That's right!" Devon missed the sarcasm. *A knock at the door.*

"It's Mom!" Daisy whispered, "Get out of here!" Devon ran towards the sidewalk in front of the house. Mother opened the door.

"What are you doing?"

"I thought it would be nice to open the window and let some air in." Daisy pretended to do homework, picking up a calculus book and a pencil.

"Have you been smoking? I smell smoke."

"No. Must have been the neighbors."

Diana gave Daisy a scrutinizing look.

"Okay, but get cracking on your homework. Graduation is soon. I still have to send out those invites..." her mother trailed off, moving to get tasks done. Daisy flopped on her bed, reciting the lines of Shakespeare, hoping for acceptance to a university of her choice.

Later that night, Diane Grayhart watched with disgust as her son stumbled through the front door, no doubt drunk.

"You're late." she grumbled angrily. Daisy was determinedly fixated on the dishes she was washing. She hated when her mother and brother fought, sensing the tension between the two.

"So w-what? I was with muh friends." Devon slurred.

"So what? You smell like skunk and booze - and it's 10 pm on a school night!"

Ernest Grayhart, the timid patriarch, was nowhere to be found. No doubt he was hiding in his study. Typical.

"I know you were hanging out with that Ronnie kid all night! Do you know he's a no-good punk? He is preventing you from graduating high school!"

"Why do you fucking care? You never gave a shit about me!"

"I give "a shit" about your future and our reputation! Your father and I have a status in this town to maintain. Why can't you be like your sister? She's graduating this year and going to business school."

"There you go again. Comparing me to her. You know what? Fuck you!"

Diane slapped her son across the face. Devon roughly shoved her, pushing his mother onto a plush recliner. He escaped out the front door, running into the warm spring night.

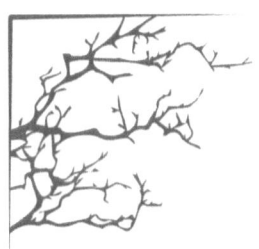

Chapter 22

"That was the last time I saw Dev, until he showed up in Rust Springs." Daisy finished her recounting of painful memories.

"Did you ever get accepted?" Ash asked. Daisy shook her head.

"No, so I moved there from Wichita to California. I worked at various small-part gigs, attending community college, and working night shifts."

"Sounds exhausting."

"Yeah. It sucked."

"How did you get into skin flicks, though?"

"It's hard finding legit gigs. That's when I met my first agent and boyfriend, Xavier. He was a smooth talker and full of shit. He introduced me to the world of adult entertainment and some scummy producers. Not long after, I had my debut as "Bellatrix Velour". I broke it off with him after I caught him sleeping with one of my co-stars."

Ash considered the content of her story. Even normal families have their set of issues, and relatives may not always get along with each other. He gained insight into their bond as brother and sister. Daisy and Devon only had each other when they were growing up. After Daisy left to go to California, Devon felt betrayed and left to fend for himself. There was one part of the story missing.

"How did you meet Attila?" he asked. Daisy chuckled.

"It was at a film shoot. He was part of the production crew when he met me. I don't know. We talked and one thing led to another. After I retired, we decided to move to Ohio to get away from the

L.A. mentality of stardom and fame-mongering. We wanted something real."

Ash nodded. Love can be found in strange places. Daisy's interest in the gothic subculture and fashion sense seemed to mesh well with Attila's former religious affiliations and interest in the occult.

"Don't be sorry for me and my brother, Ash. We made our own decisions and we have to own them. I don't deny my past. I'm not necessarily proud of it, but I don't regret it either. Sure, I've met my fair share of industry scum-bags, but I also have met friends. Without porn, I would have never met Attila. I don't know how Dev feels, but he chose the cult and drugs and he needs to own it."

"What are you going to do with Devon?"

"I guess Attila's right. I can't help him. I don't know where he went but where ever he is, I hope he's safe."

"He did mention some crazy stuff about the cult to Calvin – "

"What? You two went to go see him?" Daisy gasped. He winced.

"I know, but Calvin said he had information on the cult."

"Ash, Calvin likes to exploit people and situations for his own gain. Who is to say he didn't do the same to you or Dev?"

"Well, if what Devon told us is true...we could be in more danger than we thought. Look what they did to him!" Daisy rose and ran out the door. Ash got up.

"Where are you going?"

"I'm going to go find my brother."

The road was dark and covered with freshly-fallen snow. Attila and Ash searched the roads and highways snaking out of Rust Springs, hoping to find Devon alive. Despite her foul-mouthed objections, Daisy was convinced to stay behind. Attila did not want to take chances with her life. There was no telling what they would find on the road.

"Are you sure you remember what the car looked like?"

"I could pick it out of a line-up if I needed to." Ash confirmed.

Their last chance was to check Interstate 70, which provided a straight shot to Indiana. The headlights on Attila's car fell upon a single vehicle on the side of the road.

"Hey! That's the one!" Ash hailed while Attila pulled over behind the abandoned car. Ash stepped out into the snow and approached the car cautiously, flashlight shining ahead of him. It was dead and the driver's door was open. The snow collected in the seat turned pink, highlighting the blood pooled in the seat.

"There's blood here." Ash grimly observed the damage. This was bad. Attila trotted behind him, rifle in hand.

"From the looks of it, Dev was hit with a bullet from the passenger side. See the window?" Ash turned his head, noticing the spider-web pattern around the telltale hole. Drag-marks accented with blood made a trail into the woods. Following the trail, it was not long until they found a severed finger lying on the ground. Bad was an understatement.

"The hell? Is that-?" Attila's disgusted and horrified tone of voice made Ash's gut clench. There was a bit of blood on the ground, but not enough to denote a life-threatening injury.

"We need to go back to the truck stop." Attila urged Ash towards the car.

"Why?"

"I gotta call those two detectives we talked to a couple of days ago. I got their business cards in my wallet."

"Daisy said the cops wouldn't do anything for anyone like Devon. Besides, you said the police chief was corrupt."

"But those two are different. They aren't intimidated by Traynor." Attila told him as they got back in their vehicle. Ash remembered his ill uncle at home.

"Well, let me tell Jasper about what happened. I don't want him to worry like last time."

"Good idea."

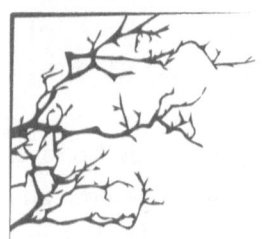

Chapter 23

Ash sat at Links Diner located in the busy truck stop, while Attila contacted Mullen and Vasquez near the restrooms. Ash had spoken to Jasper, who told him in a short conversation, he would be waiting for him and wished him well. Jasper sounded fatigued and disoriented. Ash chalked it up to whatever was ailing his uncle. The waitress brought him coffee and a cup of ice, unaware her customer was carrying a severed pinkie finger in his pocket.

Attila was squeamish about handling Devon's finger so he gave the duty to Ash, who was used to handling dead things. Attila managed to find an old ashtray in his car to store it in. His boss told him to put the finger in ice in order to keep it cool for later reattachment. Ash made sure to cover the tray as to not draw attention to what the contents were. It was also beneficial to Ash, who was starting to be nauseated by the scent of bloody flesh emanating from the appendage. He saw a rough-looking trucker walk inside with a lot lizard and take up the booth across from him.

Ash assumed they had intercourse an hour ago from the stench covering their bodies: that of sweat, tobacco, latex, and assorted bodily fluids. The prostitute in particular smelled foul, like sickness. Ash deduced the trucker was smart in wearing a condom after all.

The pain came back. He wished he was outside in the cold to numb it. Sipping his coffee, he promptly spit it back out when the warm liquid when it burned his mouth.

"Ow!" he yelped.

His teeth felt like they were going to fall out of his mouth. With his tongue, he wiggled a loose incisor. With a slick pop, it came out.

Spiting it out in his hand, the white tooth was clean aside from the bloody root.

"What the fuck?"

His shoulder was flaring up as well. His mind was panicking and going in different directions. What should he do?

"Well, Vasquez and Mullen should be here soon." Attila said, startling an unaware Ash.

"Damn, you're jumpy." Attila noted, "What's that on your lip? Blood?"

"Yeah. I think I bit my tongue." Ash lied.

"That's a lot of blood for a bit tongue. What's in your hand?"

"Nothing, okay?" Ash said, storming off. Attila looked confused, but did not question further. Ash got out of the booth and went to the restroom to check himself out. He was thankful the restroom was empty, except a man in one of the stalls. Indeed, when he lifted his upper lip, one of his canines fell out. Ash was pretty dutiful with his dental habits. He was alarmed, not sure what to make of his tooth or the increased senses he was experiencing. Pocketing the tooth, he quickly walked out and rejoined Attila. The man had ordered two cups of drip coffee and some cream.

"Everything okay?"

"Yeah."

"Jasper is doing well?"

"I dunno. He's been kinda quiet. I asked him about his condition though."

"What is it?"

"He didn't elaborate."

"You need to learn how to be persistent."

"He got all defensive about it. It seems to bring him sadness...and anger."

"That's weird. All the year's I've known Jasper, he never mentioned anything about that. Well, he has gotten worse over the years."

"What?"

"You see how skinny he looks now. He wasn't like that before. How is he at home?"

"Decent, but like he's distracted or something."

Ash and Attila fell quiet. What malaise befell their friend and relative? Ash remembered the locked basement. Jasper said it was his personal space, aside from his bedroom, for him to use. What was down there?

High beams lit the window, blinding Ash. When the car shut off, he saw two familiar people exiting the cruiser. The detectives had arrived.

Attila and Ash gave an account of the events of the past couple of days regarding Devon, the Loupcroix, and what they found off the road. Mullen and Vasquez discussed what they found on the cult, and what took place this morning at the police station.

"It's all I found of him." Attila told Mullen and Vasquez. The detectives observed the greasy and long-nailed finger, wrapped in a paper towel with ice.

"And you said there was nothing else?" Mullen asked.

"Besides the tire tracks and the abandoned car, no." Attila confirmed.

"Hmmm." Mullen uttered after a brief pause, "My best guess is he was taken by his captors -"

"And we need to figure where exactly "where" is." Vasquez said.

"It had to be the Lodge. They've threatened him before, and Dev's screwed with them in the past." Ash said.

"We can't know for sure." Mullen told the group, "Didn't you tell us that Grayhart has ties to a biker gang? What are the chances it isn't one of his friends?"

No one said a word.

"We'll look into it. We need to take the...appendage in as evidence." Vasquez said.

"No shit? Traynor's dead?" whispered an astonished Attila.

"Yeah, the press is all over us and we are gonna have the Feds involved at this point." Mullen said.

"What comes next?" Ash asked.

"Understandably, we've had to change our plans. Vasquez is going to head to West Virginia early tomorrow to check on a lead. I'm going to stay here and keep an eye on the Fellowship and determine who killed Traynor. It's not ideal, but we might have no choice but to send for federal help. Shit's about to get real dicey. The cult seems to be ratcheting up their antics with Grayhart's disappearance." Mullen said.

"Ugh, Daze is gonna freak out. For better or worse, Devon is the only family she's got." Attila sighed.

"We know about Mr. Grayhart's past. It's sordid and unfortunate how people can be sucked into this mess." Mullen said, referring to Devon's falling in with the cult.

"And about the murders?" Ash asked.

"We honestly don't know. We've sent samples to OSU and other forensic labs, but they are as lost as we are. Saliva is a mixture of human, animal, and something else. From what we could tell from surveillance, the cult does not have any large canines on their premises that could do such extensive damage. Therefore, we believe a separate party is involved." Mullen informed him.

Ash was uncomfortable at the mention of the forensic results. If it wasn't human or fully animal, what could it possibly be? He recalled the park and the weird changes happening to his body.

"That thing from the park when those homeless people were killed. I think it's the Ripper." he told them.

"I remember you mentioning it in the report. You said the perpetrator looked half-human." said Vasquez.

"I guess it wanted what Devon stole, but why?" Ash asked.

Mullen looked into Ash's eyes.

"You know, it could be the trauma speaking from the experience. I'm sure Grayhart, a known drug user and cult member, didn't help with his account of the odd goings-on."

"We've found the Lodge is involved in drugs. And, like Mullen said, Devon could have been hallucinating. A man does not turn into an animal. It's impossible." Vasquez said.

Attila shook his head.

"After the shit we've been through the past couple of days, I'm not sure if anything is out of the realm of possibility." he said as he took out a cigarette from his pocket.

"Hey! If you wanna smoke, do it outside!" a waitress yelled at him as he lit the cig.

"Ok! I hear ya!" Attila barked back, waving his hand. He grunted as he got out of the booth and walked out the glass doors of the diner.

"You find the severed finger of your girlfriend's estranged brother and you have to smoke in the cold..." he griped as he stomped off. Attila was stressed; Ash could tell.

"I need to make a phone call. Tony, join me." Mullen said. The two detectives rose from the chair, taking the finger and wrapping up their visit. Before they left, the detectives informed the two to stay safe.

"Yeah, I'm not gonna sleep much tonight." Attila snuffed out the rest of his cig. "Knowing there's crazy out there."

Ash was beat. He couldn't wait to sleep. In fact, he slept on the ride back to his car, dreaming he was in a warm bed away from the cold world.

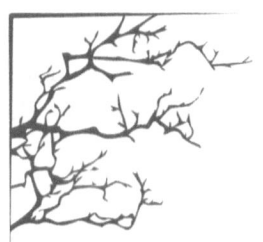

Chapter 24

Devon groaned as he came to, slowly orienting himself to his new surroundings. Strange etchings and runic markings marred the walls inside the dark room, illuminated by the low light of a lantern. Dread washed over his body like a bucket of ice water. He was in Montana's private ritual chamber. Only a select few came in here; as the other members made use of the barn for their separate services. The bindings around his body kept him stiff and still, while the cloth bandana between his teeth warned him that calling out for help was not an option. No one around here would help anyway. He was made aware of the pain emanating from his shoulder and right hand, reigniting memories from hours earlier.

...

He clutched the wheel. The desperate tension of leaving Ohio drove him forward on his solitary journey. Devon had none of his possessions and hardly any money, but it didn't bother him. He had gotten by with less before. His current high spurred him forward. He could always hustle some cash though meth making, and could use the funds to acquire new material goods. If push came to shove, theft was not beneath him. In his world, you grab what you can get and exploit any situation or weaknesses of others.

The sunset painted the sky orange as purple clouds obscured the rest of the atmosphere. It was a nice change from a grey overcast. The road was desolate so far. Devon was alarmed by the appearance of another vehicle. He sped up more, paranoia setting in. He could not make out who it was. It wasn't a cop, but the make and model of it seemed terribly familiar.

Looking into his rearview mirror, he saw a figure rise from the truck bed. He slammed on the gas pedal. He had to get away now! His brain started to hurt as his vision inexplicably became blurry. He could hardly see what was in front of him. He pushed the gas pedal on the car, RPMs redlining, and briefly closed his eyes.

Opening them, Devon saw the familiar, ominous blue truck was gaining on him. It roared beside him. Heart pounding, he swerved out of the way.

Bam!

The impact had Devon seeing stars.

Boom! Crack!

He lost his right-side mirror to a gun blast!

"Fuck!"

If one of those things connected with his body, he was done for. His brain was an angry hornet's nest, buzzing with panic and manic energy.

"Ack!"

A bullet scraped his shoulder.

"Shit! Fuck!"

He swerved off the highway and almost crashed into the embankment, his face nearly colliding with the steering wheel. He was too startled to react properly. The sound of shattering glass and the pain in his shoulder told him he was hit. He veered off the road into a shallow ravine. The car was totaled with a jarring crash. Devon worked to get the seat belt off, his flight-or-fight instincts summoning an urgent call to action. Fingernails scraped the metal clip fastening the belt to him as his head was buried into the wheel.

The burn of the airbag on his face pushed him up. It didn't stop him from trying to escape the wreck. He knew he had to get out of the car, but his body revolted. The lights of the truck were on his back. He tried to make it to the prairie grass but to no avail, his body still refused to move. He closed his eyes again. Opening them, he saw

STORM-STAR 131

the stopped truck in his peripheral vision. Turning his head to the left, the truck and its occupants stood out clear as day. Oregon was driving, having parked the truck parallel to Devon's car. Wyoming howled his head off in the truck bed, ecstatic over the prospect of violence. Washington, in the passenger's side, aimed his rifle straight at Devon.

Oregon pulled a little ways in front of where he was. Wyoming leapt out of the truck, while Washington stalked over slowly. The trio looked frightening as

Devon's vision was becoming clearer. Fear sped up his heart as the door was wrenched open. Devon was dragged out by his shirt. Wyoming, after throwing Devon on the ground, proceeded to wail on him.

"Back off, Wyoming." Washington ordered his brother.

"Why? This fucker is going to die anyway. I can't beat his stupid ass a little bit first?" Wyoming stood over Devon, who lay on the ground, too paralyzed with fear and pain to do anything. He quivered slightly with adrenaline, knowing he was going to die here.

"You're shaking, Devon." Washington said, a hint of taunting in his voice as he got closer. He pressed the barrel of the gun near Devon's face, the black hole greeting him like the evil star they heralded. "You're the lucky one today. Compared to what I'm going to do to your coal-burning sister, this is nothing."

Despite the vague threat and the face of his impending demise, Devon raised his middle finger defiantly to Washington. Wyoming slowly pulled out a large machete from a side holster.

"Fuck you and your shit-heap family." he grunted painfully.

Shnk!

Severed bone and flesh on his hand, Devon's' finger rolled out on the ice in front of him. He let out a horrible scream. Washington's left foot connected with his injured shoulder. He screamed louder while Wyoming gloated in the background.

"See! I told you he needed a beatin'!" Wyoming flicked the blood off his blade.

"Shut up!" Washington bent down and scowled at Devon.

"Let's take him back. He needs to face judgment for his betrayal. With the setback you caused us, I'm sure Montana would like to deal with you personally."

...

"You should have ran when you had the chance."

Devon's eyes tried to adjust to the darkness, but he knew that voice. His heart skipped a beat.

"Nice meeting you back here, Devon." Montana Loupcroix greeted. "Sorry about your hand, but you know how my brothers are."

The pain shot up his arm from his finger stub as if on cue. Devon bit his lip, not wanting to cry out. This was the reason he left in the first place. Montana scared the shit out of him. He couldn't see much of the man in question.

"I'm sure you know what's coming." Montana said, uttering a weird, gasping rasp at the end of his sentence.

Devon couldn't move or beg for his life. He was unsure if it was the drugs wearing off or the sensation of the same presence the night he left. The room spun around in his head, while an eerie glow illuminated the walls. Diagrams, foreign symbols, and crazed illustrations littered the walls of the bunker. Devon heard an odd and repulsive chewing sound emanating from Montana's direction. He looked only to see the man was not there. Instead, a black galaxy filled the dismal void of the room. An odd swirling presence made itself known.

"It eats it way through...the wyrm that gnaws at the world." Montana's voice was not his own. Devon couldn't comprehend and thoughts, not his own, compelled him to do the unthinkable. His mind cooled as something deep flowed out of him. The body stilled and he was no more.

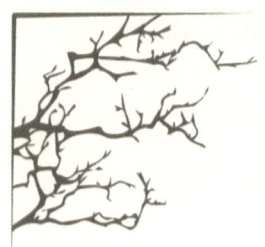

Chapter 25

The maw opened again. It had a sucking energy, which made a vortex around him. It threatened to swallow the earth whole.

Idaho curled up in his bed, too paralyzed to move. A bright orange light flickered through his open window, accompanied by the familiar scent of burning wood.

Bonfires weren't uncommon but, from the intensity, it was bigger than any he'd seen before. Curiosity got the better of him as his fear subsided and he swung his legs off the edge of the bed, stepping out on the cold floor. Unobstructed by the dirty glass, the window gave an all-inclusive view of the scene below.

Idaho could see Wyoming and Oregon sulking around the bonfire. They were waiting for something. There were other compound dwellers about; watching the scene before them. What was the occasion?

Washington and Colorado appeared, carrying something wrapped in a ragged tarp. Unceremoniously, they dumped it on the fire. The scent changed as the tarp and its contents were burned. Soon, a familiar stench invaded his nostrils. It was like that time Wyoming roasted a live raccoon over an open pit. He was filled with a sickening terror. Idaho gripped his forehead as his brain jolted. Images came through his mind. Devon lying there, dead in the bunker. Montana's ominous presence made itself known in his mind, magnifying the malignant dark star. As soon as he thought his brain would burst, the pain subsided. The floor greeted him, concluding he fell down. Idaho reached for the soft blanket crumpled on the floor. He knew what was cast upon the fire.

A knock at the door.

"Aren't you gonna join us?" Oregon asked.

"No!" Idaho was disturbed they would do such a thing so publicly.

"Well too bad. Plus, Montana wants to talk to ya for a bit."

Idaho pulled on his pants to follow Oregon outside; his only choices were coming quietly or being dragged out. The fire was bright and the people were drinking and reveling. Montana was in the shady porch of the house.

"Hey there, little bro." he greeted, "Have a seat."

Idaho sat on the lawn chair. A beat of awkward silence followed.

"We're gonna change things. You'll see."

Idaho didn't say anything. He was scared of the changes Montana was talking about.

"It'll be beautiful. All of the pain and strife of this work will be over."

Montana rose and walked inside the house.

"Why don't you join them?" he asked, "Ori, make sure Ida is taken care of."

Oregon led his brother to the fire.

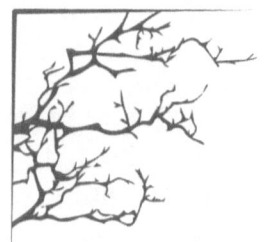

Chapter 26

Ash sat on the front porch of the vacant house, the adjacent light pole illuminating the snow with a stark, orange color. Jasper and the dogs were nowhere to be found, yet his car was parked in the driveway. Usually, Jasper would be at home, sleeping upstairs in his bedroom. Jasper was probably out for a walk with Raini and Stormi. He was hesitant to call the cops just yet, but Ash assumed the worst.

All the murders.

All the cult activity.

All the crazy questions he had regarding his heritage and what was going on with his body. He had to talk to Jasper. There was no other option. He needed to know what was going on with him. A deep pain shot through his core.

"Damn it." Ash cursed to himself as he shifted uncomfortably on the step. He went inside to find some pain medication. Ash turned on the lights and stumbled over to the kitchen. Inside the cabinets, he found some opiates. The pain was becoming a persistent throb now, increasing as he extracted one of the white pills out of the bottle. He still needed something to take it with. Staggering over to the fridge, he found a milk carton inside.

"Ah!" Ash gasped as his heart beat faster. It was going to burst out of his chest. He put the pill in his mouth and desperately swallowed it. Clutching the carton, he brought the container to his lips and drank its contents. The thick liquid's taste and smell caused him to gag due to the nausea swelling within him. He dropped the carton; spilling milk all over the floor as he proceeded to vomit. The bile soaked pill lay uselessly on the floor.

Ash's vision was becoming blurry and tunneled and he struggled to keep his balance. Ash slipped on the spilled milk as he tried to make his way to the bathroom. He ended up seizing face-down in the hallway, muscles tightening and relaxing erratically. The pain was all consuming at this point. His consciousness faded as his senses sharpened. He could only stare blankly at the floorboards as his body twitched and pulsed with new life.

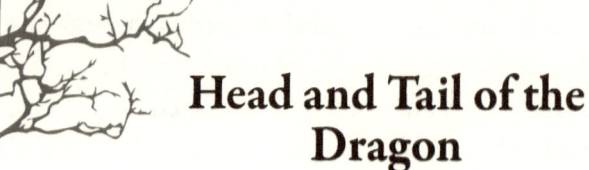

Head and Tail of the Dragon

He cursed the blood that ran through his veins as readily as he did his enemies.
They were easy to kill, striking terror into them.
But an enemy on the ropes can be dangerous when cornered.
No matter.
He got what he needed from them.
Pain struck through his abdomen, forcing up blood and stomach fluid.
He didn't have long for this world.
He would make every second count.
His scars and scoreboards of hatred against his mottled skin.
He left the borders of the enemy encampment, eager for home and rest.

...

The emerald fields were joyous and lively with Folkvagnr's chosen.
The forest and great halls housed those faithful and strong.
Waterfalls and winding rivers nourished the souls of those who suffered and languished under the black sun.
The Storm-Star rises over Folkvagnr; the fifth Aion reigning forever more.

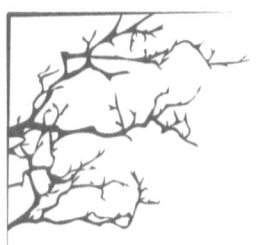

Chapter 27

"Don't talk to me. I gotta unwind." Daisy entered their townhome in a new residential development of Rust Springs. Attila was silently agreeable. After the night he had, he was ready to eat and watch some TV to relax. Daisy climbed upstairs and Attila microwaved some Chinese leftovers, desiring to doze in front of the television. The greasy noodles were comforting and hit the spot. Attila sat in his recliner, flipping through TV channels with no particular interest in mind. Local news was buzzing about the murders, along with Traynor's death. Various commentators, including Calvin Clarkson, gave their theories about what was going on.

"It was the Storm-Star cult, that dangerous group infiltrating Rust Springs!" Calvin exclaimed with confidence. "Inside sources have confirmed my claims of sacrifices and abuse taking place at the compound."

The noise from the TV hit a crescendo as Attila flipped to another TV station. Calvin Clarkson was giving a fiery speech to a congregation in a large church. His tweed jacket blended in with the cheap carpeting on the stage.

"My friends, we are living in the darkest of times." he addressed the crowd, "The media preaches debauchery and violence, while these satanic religions are being propped up as spiritual alternatives. You've heard of the Church of Satan and the Wiccan faith, but recently I have had the displeasure of discovering another insidious group in our mist and they have recruited locals into their secretive drug cult. My team and I are currently looking into this matter for the sake of our community here in Rust Springs."

The screen shifted to a shot of people convulsing on the floor set to dramatic music and effects.

"Have you ever wondered why our world seems to be declining into darkness at a fast rate? Bombings, terrorism, cults and occult groups gaining popularity; the new Millennium on the horizon. I have a solution to protect you and your family from harm."

The camera showed several books and video tapes on a table. It quickly devolved into a sales pitch.

"For 100 dollars, you can receive this complete collection of resources for the new era - "

The video jumped and the audio was cut off, switching to Clarkson in front of a desk topped with office supplies, books, and little cross.

"Hello, my name is Calvin Clarkson and I have some important and disturbing news to share."

"Goddamn." Attila whispered, his fist tightening around the remote.

"There have been rumors of disturbing activities happening around Rust Springs and there needs to be some light shed on this topic."

A montage followed, showing various people in the community, most from the church, giving their account of what they witnessed.

"I heard they were devil-worshippers."

"My neighbor's cat and dog were killed by them."

"I've heard some bizarre sounds from the compound."

The camera cut back to Clarkson.

"It sounds scary but that's just the tip of the iceberg. Wait 'til you hear from an actual ex-member of this dangerous group. Thankfully, he escaped and here is his harrowing story."

Sure enough there was Devon, uncensored bearing witness about the Storm-Star Lodge. Every detail was laid bare; a private conversation allegedly treated with the upmost confidentiality was thrown out there for the world to see, including the murderous Loupcroix family.

"I can't believe this." Attila told himself. How did this come out? Devon wasn't the one to share this type of information. Ash was with him the last time they saw him. Maybe he had something to do with this. Scenarios of how the cult would react raced through his mind. What if they were going to be targeted next? How could Calvin do something like this? He knew full well Daisy and Devon could be in danger. The fact that he would throw their names out there. With the piling of dead bodies nearly every night, it could cause a panic with innocents being hurt in the process.

Attila flipped the channel in anger. Damn Clarkson could not keep his mouth shut! Late-night sitcom reruns flashed on screen, obnoxious laugh tracks droning along after cheesy jokes were made. Attila escaped inside the inane plots and dialogue of one such show. Should he check on Daisy? Her reaction to Devon's disappearance and possible murder was distant. She was hurting due to the last words she said to her brother. He sighed, feeling useless.

...

Daisy lay in bed, hoping to get some sleep after a long day. Her body was restless. Something was tearing at her on the inside. Anxiety about Devon threatened to keep her awake. Foolish hopes that her brother would survive whatever happened to him popped in her mind. Daisy remembered the stories he would tell her about drug deals going south, clandestine criminals and wild locales that he traveled to during his career. While they were close, the two never saw eye to eye on certain things. Devon acquired racist leanings in high school in part to gain acceptance from a father figure he never had.

Speaking of their parents, she doubted her mother would care about what happened to her or Devon. Diana always hated her son and disowned her own daughter after learning about how she made her living for the past couple of years. Dad was intangible as always, hiding behind his paperwork inside his stuffy office. *Fuck it.* She was better off figuring this out on her own without having to deal with their drama. Something was going to give concerning the cult if they were responsible for her missing brother. She would find a way to take matters into her own hands by then. Attila had his collection of guns. If justice could not be served by conventional means, it would be time to do something drastic.

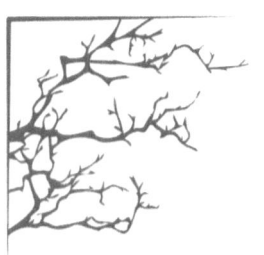

Chapter 28

The compound buzzed with activity around the large bonfire. People drinking and smoking with children playing around them.

Idaho slumped on a busted lawn chair. He couldn't say he was exactly celebratory considering what had transpired. He didn't want to be here. Wyoming, partaking of a freshly-rolled joint, spun a tale to drunken men nearby about catching Devon. His brother making light of terrorizing another human being enraged him, especially one who had the guts to leave. He couldn't say he knew Devon particularly well, but he did know no one deserved that type of treatment. In the end, Grayhart had no chance. Montana was the law and death was an acceptable sentence for traitors in their circles. His family was more than willing to murder on behalf of the Lodge. The heated wood made his hair and clothing smoky.

"Hey, lil' fucker." Wyoming jeered in a jovial manner. "Why the long face?"

"Go away." Idaho responded, not in the mood. Wyoming laughed, coughing from the smoke as he did so.

"You-you wanna hear how I got Devon? You know what? Imma do the same to his mudshark sister and her nigger fuck-buddy – "

Wyoming was caught by a swift boot to his balls. He dropped to the ground, dry heaving and loosing his grip on his blunt. Idaho stomped off. He hated everything.

"Ida! Ida, wait!" Dahlia called. Idaho ignored her. He needed to leave. Dahlia trotted behind him.

"Just talk to me, Ida." Dahlia insisted. He turned around, ready to let her have it.

"What?" he asked heatedly.

"Don't let Wyoming ruin your night – "

"It was ruined from the start! How could you be celebrating at a time like this?"

"What do you mean? Montana is back to guide us – "

"No! How can you be so happy when a man just died?"

Dahlia's face went cold.

"Well, he deserved it."

Idaho let out a derisive sneer.

"You well know Dev wasn't a saint, and he stole from us on top of it. It's up to leadership to decide."

"Yeah, that's what I thought." Idaho huffed, leaving Dahlia.

"Why do you care?" she called after him, "All of our suffering will be over when Folkvagnr arrives. We will be free."

Idaho kept walking. She was like everyone else in this fucking place: believing in the deranged mythology of his father.

Idaho hated being different. Why couldn't his family be normal and sane?

"Goddamn it." He kicked over a small pile of fire wood. The pain he incurred from the action made him even more enraged. He grabbed the ax lying nearby.

He had to end it.

He walked to the door of the farmhouse. Opening it slowly, Idaho tried not to awake the slumbering Montana on the couch. The leader was in a deep sleep. The axe was slippery in his hands. He hadn't killed anyone before, let alone a family member. Would Montana struggle to close the wound, pulsing blood out of his neck? Or would it be a clean and quick decapitation? Idaho gulped, focusing of the various times he's killed animals during hunting trips with his father.

He inched closer, placing himself right over his brother. The axe raised above his head. His muscles were tense and his stomach quivered from nerves. Idaho swung downwards.

Something stopped the path of the blade. Not realizing what was happening, Idaho bore down harder. Montana opened his eyes, revealing a bright blackness. Idaho retreated in horror. The axe was suspended in mid-air, frozen. Montana rose stiffly, turning his head towards Idaho's direction.

"Traitor!" he roared.

The resonance of the voice was awesome; it vibrated the windows. Idaho was hoisted into the air by an unseen force. He screamed in fright. The windows to the house shattered. The lights flickered rapidly and died. He was flung on the floor, cracking his head against the hard wood.

He was barely cognizant of the voices around him.

"What the fucking hell-!"

"Is that an axe?"

"What's going on?"

"Haul him up!"

Colorado grabbed Idaho by his arm. He rose unsteadily, using her for support. Through his parted eyelids, he saw Montana's upper body hanging off the couch. Washington and Oregon were trying to wake him up, adjusting his position.

"Monty, say something!" Oregon urged. Montana seized, gripping the couch tightly as he coughed.

"He's alright." Washington muttered. Idaho looked for the axe on the ground. It had disappeared. Damn, his head was killing him. Looking left, he saw the axe imbedded into the wall above the television.

"What happened?" Washington glared at Idaho.

"I don't – know- " Idaho fumbled his words, not grasping what transpired.

"Idaho." Montana sighed, "I can't believe you would – "

"Would what?" Oregon asked, trying to make sense of what happened.

Montana pointed to the axe.

"He tried to –?" Washington questioned. The others gathered were outraged as well.

"You bastard! Lock him up!" He heard Wyoming in the back. Idaho fought with two men attempting to subdue him. He wasn't going to be tied up somewhere like Devon. As others piled on, his struggles ceased. There was too many of them to fight.

"Where should we put him?"

"There's an abandoned trailer somewhere in the back." Washington told them, "Keep him under lock and key until the time comes."

They dragged him from what seemed like miles, passing curious on lookers. It was a walk of shame; silence marked the disbelief and disappointment. Idaho couldn't look at their faces. An old silver Airstream was where he was placed, shutting him in the dark. There were no lights, windows reinforced by wood or steel plates.

"Let me out!"

He yelled himself hoarse for thirty minutes, succumbing to the fact no one would save him. It was as before: the black light drowning him; shadows washing over.

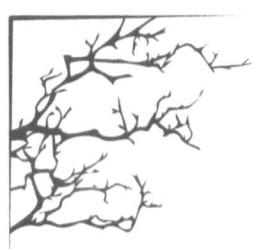

Chapter 29

Ash shivered, lying on his bed. The first thing he noticed was he was naked under the covers. He did not know why or how he got that way. Honestly, it freaked him out.

"What happened last night?" he thought, recalling the pain. Currently, he was refreshed and settled. His fingers caressed his back. There were healed scars, no stitches. What? He touched again to make sure he wasn't dreaming. No white hair either. How could that happen? He looked at his hands. His nails were hardened and thick, stained a dark ebony color. He flicked his tongue over his teeth.

The tooth.

After finding a pair of boxers and a shirt, he rushed to the bathroom to check his mouth. Opening his mouth and pulling back his lips, he found the location of the missing tooth only to find it replaced by a fresh white incisor. Indeed, the pink healthy gums cradled the new sharp canine. His relaxed mood upon awaking gave way to anxiety. Looking in the mirror again, he swore his brilliant green eyes had become encircled with a faint golden color. Turning around, he saw the scars on his shoulder were completely healed as if no injury occurred to them.

Ash clutched the sink basin, trying to get a grip on his tumultuous emotions through the porcelain. He needed to talk to Jasper about what happened last night.

Ash climbed downstairs to find his uncle. There was no sign of the ill man, save Raini and Stormi, who he found dozing by the television set.

"Maybe he is still sleeping. But he is usually up early." Ash remembered. Indeed, the wall clock said 10:00 am. Back upstairs; he knocked on Jasper's bedroom door. Not getting an answer after the first knock, he tried again.

"Jasper?" Ash called.

"Ash?" a raspy voice asked on the other side.

"Yeah, it's me. I was wondering what happened last night. All I remembered was I wasn't feeling well. Maybe we can talk?"

A pause.

"What's on your mind?" Jasper finally said.

"Do you know what I was doing last night?"

"Working?"

"No. I came home because I wasn't well. The last thing I remember was passing out on the floor."

"Well, you looked fine to me last night. You were in your bed when I checked on you."

"Well, I don't remember getting into bed..."

"I have no idea. Maybe you were more tired than I thought." Jasper coughed. "Sorry, Ash, I got sick and I didn't want to over-exert myself. I had to run some errands late, and I decided to take the dogs with me."

"That late at night?"

"Well, I had to go to the supermarket. Seemed a good time as any since I wanted to get it out of the way and rest."

Ash sighed, frustrated he couldn't remember. Maybe Jasper was right. He was tired. He swore he didn't make it up.

"It's okay, Ash." Jasper reassured, "Are you going to call in sick today."

"Nah. I'm doing great, thanks. I'm gonna get ready." Ash replied.

"Good. Well, I'm going back to sleep. I'll see you later."

"Ok. I won't keep you."

Ash turned away from the door to find Raini and Stormi staring at him. He did not even hear them come up the stairs. Raini trembled nervously, while Stormi gave a low growl; both agitated by something. Ash scooted between them, making sure to not make any sudden movements around Stormi. In his room, he quickly got dressed and collected his wallet. Ash refreshed himself with mouthwash as fast as he could, not wanting to irritate his sensitive teeth. Since he wasn't hungry, Ash went to the kitchen instead to call Attila. After a few rings, he answered.

"Hey, man what's up?"

Attila sounded tired and distant.

"Jasper's not well...and some more crazy shit happened last night."

"Yeah. I know." Attila said harshly. "I thought the shit with Devon was bad enough." A brief pause. "Hold on, we will talk about this later. See you in a few."

Attila ended the call, leaving Ash to his own devices.

Ash found the daily newspaper on the porch, wrapped in protective plastic. The front page screamed about two more murders that occurred overnight. This time, the attack focused on brutal dismemberment, with a removed head and pelvis between the two victims. Another article referenced a curious aurora seen across the sky. Turning inside the page, Calvin Clarkson's face appeared alongside caption: "*I know who's behind the murders! –A Cult!*".

Ash frowned. Clarkson had given him his word not to say anything about the interview to the public. The article spilled every dirty detail he could recall from the conversation. Ash was surprised by the revelation that Clarkson decided to share with his audience. At least, neither Devon nor himself were explicitly mentioned. On the other hand, he was concerned of the potential backlash. Devon was a wanted man, and Ash was sure the Loupcroix were watching and listening. Guilt stemmed from bringing Devon to that meeting; getting him involved in this mess.

What should he do? An apology was in order. Ash leaned back in the chair. No, he would explain it to them face-to-face tomorrow.

Ash hoped they would forgive him.

Ash threw away the nasty news; collecting the crossword puzzle and funny comics sections for a distraction. Working on the puzzle, Ash sensed the prickling of a static energy in the air. The hairs on his arms stood on end, and a distant droning sound numbed his ears. The air in Rust Springs was different this morning.

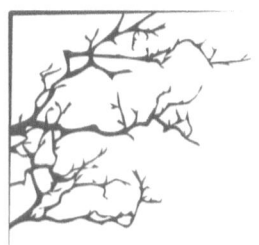

Chapter 30

The Appalachians were bare and snowy against the blue sky. Old homes and trailers clung to their edges, vaguely resembling the cliff dwellings of native tribes in the American west. Driving into the downtown valley of Ridgeland, West Virginia, Vasquez found the Sherriff's office. The department was smaller than Rust Springs, but it was a little coal mining community. Vasquez opened the front door to be greeted by a cheery, blonde office clerk.

"Good morning, sir! What is your business this morning? May I direct you to someone?" Vasquez flashed his identification.

"Yes, I am Detective Antonio Vasquez of Rust Springs. I'm here to speak with Sherriff Jeb McRoy."

"Oh, yes. We have been expecting you, Detective Vasquez. You can meet Sherriff McRoy in his office. It's the first door on the right."

Vasquez thanked her as he made his way to the office. Sure enough on the right, was a door labeled with McRoy's name. He knocked.

"Come in!" answered a gruff voice. Vasquez opened the door. An older, slightly pudgy gentleman was collecting and organizing files. He looked up at Vasquez when he entered.

"Ah, you must be Detective Vasquez." The man extended out his hand. "Jeb McRoy. Welcome to Ridgeland."

Vasquez shook his hand and sat in the chair before the desk.

"Getting to the business at hand, Columbia Loupcroix has isolated herself in a holler she owns. Had it passed down from her late father, Vermond. The other family members had moved on to parts unknown a few years ago. No known criminal records, but they

151

aren't the friendliest folk. They are known to be armed and therefore, possibly dangerous."

"So what's our plan?"

"Well, if she won't cooperate, we will have to do it by force. But she's not that much of a problem for as long as I've known her. A recluse as well, so I don't expect company."

Vasquez felt more at ease by McRoy's testimony, but the Loupcroix were an unpredictable and dangerous gang. He had no idea what may lay in wait for them at the holler.

...

"Dammit, Traynor! Where did you put your stash?" Mullen grumbled to himself as he searched Traynor's apartment. Mullen had combed through Traynor's office, hoping to find clues as to whom or what killed him. When nothing of importance was found, Traynor's home was the next best bet. He always had an inkling that something was up with his superior after the Storm-Star group came to Rust Springs. Even with all the complaints, Traynor would refuse to investigate, stating there was no ground for concern or proof of criminal activity. In his eyes, the cult was a minor nuisance. If the higher-ups could not find any proof of graver offenses, why bother pursuing the issue? The whole thing smelled fishy. Why would Traynor cover for these people?

Mullen upended file cabinets and drawers inside Traynor's dwelling. Traynor had gotten divorced years ago and developed an opulent taste. Expensive gold jewelry, luxury furnishings, and a high-end entertainment system were proof.

The bedroom was simple and modern with silk sheets on the king-sized bed. Mullen looked through the nightstand and dresser drawer. Just underwear and undershirts. In the closet, various casual outfits and suits hung neatly on the rack. Mullen couldn't see anything on the shelf except an empty duffel bag. The floor of the closet was much more cluttered with various boxes and luggage.

Uncovering the lid of a banker box, Mullen looked through the paperwork inside. Random notes referring to different locations and names along with monetary figures. Shifting the items, Mullen uncovered a safe. It was fairly small and fireproof. He kneeled to investigate the dial lock. Without a combination, the department would have to crack the safe. Maybe Traynor wrote the combination somewhere. As anal as Traynor was, there was little chance he would be so careless as to leave the combination for someone to find.

"Deane! Get in here!" Mullen called. He heard rushed footsteps coming to the bedroom. Officer Deane popped through the door.

"Yes, Detective Mullen?"

"Help me remove this safe. We gotta get it back to downtown. Make sure we get this place roped off and monitored. If Traynor was working with someone, they might come back here to hide the evidence."

Mullen and Deane managed to move the safe out of the apartment, unaware they were being watched.

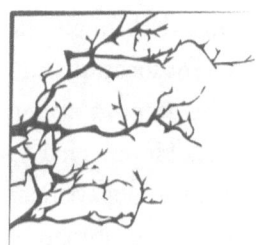

Chapter 31

Idaho didn't know what time it was. From his jittering body, he knew he stayed awake through the night. He never felt so hopeless and low sitting in the solitude. His family could only see him as an asset; something to control and use. He would never have any control over his life as long as he was with them. It was up to him to make a change.

Idaho walked around the cramped cabin, hands feeling around for any weak points from which to escape. He had to get out and warn Devon's family. The wooden plywood over one of the windows was his best bet. No instruments to break it, looks like he had to make due with his fists. He formed a fist and hit the board as hard as he could. The plywood splintered and his fist was aching, the splinters settling in the wounds. He used his other fist. This time the board had a decent sized hole in it. He looked at his hand; blood flowing from tiny cuts and stinging from the impact. One more and he was free. The final punch was thrown, destroying the board. Idaho was able to remove the rest of the wood from the window. He grabbed the ledge, easing himself through the small window. It was a tight fit but he was able to get out. He dropped to the ground on his knees, the dry grass rustling against his jeans. It was late in the afternoon. Patrols were more lax this time of day, but he had to be cautious still. The woods should be clear, but one could never be sure. Alert and adrenaline pumping, Idaho's breaths were shallow as he navigated to the forest at the edge of the property. There was a back gate he could escape out of. He weaved through the shadows casted by the residential trailers.

"You guys are over-reacting. Ida is still a kid, no matter how big he is now." Dahlia said. He paused, listening from the side of the structure.

"Dahl, we can't keep babying him. He has to fulfill his part of the bargain." Oregon said.

"I know but you don't have to mistreat him like that."

"We can't take any chances. He has to be there or the Folkvagnr won't work."

Dahlia fell silent and the creaky door to the trailer opened and slammed shut. Idaho's mind was swimming with questions. It was never clear why he had to be there on that day. He knew he had some power Montana could use in ritual working, but they acted like he served an equal and independent purpose.

"Beta, what's your position?" Oregon asked. A click and static came over the radio.

"Working towards the south perimeter." a voice chirped on the other side.

Shit. He had little time. Idaho moved faster, not stopping until he reached the south gate. The exit was chained and padlocked. The only way was up. Clutching the chilled chain link, Idaho climbed. The fence made so much noise, but he didn't care. The only thing that mattered was freedom. In the corners of his eyes, the guards' flashlights were coming closer. He was at the top of the 12-foot fence; the only obstacle was barbed wire. The cruel sharp barbs gave him pause. They would surely cut into any flesh that touched them. The sound of the guard's voices was enough to urge Idaho over.

Gripping the top of the chain link, he tentatively put his hands on the stiff cords. He leaned forward, going over the edge. The barbs were piercing his hands, making him bleed. This was it.

With a lunge, he flipped over the fence. On the way down, the back of his jacket caught on the barbed wire. It stalled his decent as he wiggled to get free. The material gave and he fell. He landed on his side, his fall cushioned by dead leaves. It still hurt, but at least he wasn't severely injured. He took off into the night woods, the naked trees greeting him with their skinny branches.

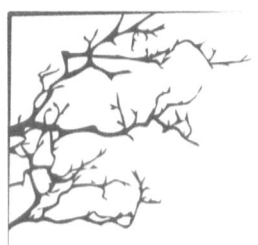

Chapter 32

Ash mopped around the bar area, while Radimir stocked the bar with various liquor bottles. Guilt nagged at him, but the show must go on. The concert with *Eldritch Enema* was tonight, and everything needed to be ready and in tip-top shape.

"Ash, do you know what is wrong?" the Eastern European asked.

"What do you mean?" Ash focused more on his work than the astounding fact that the normally reserved bartender was speaking to him.

"Daisy seems unwell today. Attila looks depressed too."

"Ah, well...it's family issues." Ash dunked and rung the mop to slap it back on the floor. Attila told him earlier to keep the issue of Devon's disappearance between them.

"Reminds me of my cousin, Kazimir. I don't know where he is now - Honolulu or something - but he's an idiot. Always running off and what not." Radimir scoffed. Ash continued to mop, sloshing soapy water around in circular motions. He had not seen Attila since he first arrived, when Ash had showed him his tooth and healed wounds. He wouldn't be surprised if he was still upset by the news report.

The man was in disbelief that something like this was possible. He asked questions of when Ash first noticed the signs and of Jasper. It was a moot conversation, as Ash didn't have much information about either, and Attila became busy with starting up operations for the day.

He would go to a doctor with Jasper, and ask about their family history concerning illnesses or other conditions. He was nervous about what he would find. The doors to the club burst open. There stood a familiar face, panting heavily and sopping wet from the rain.

"What are you doing here?" Radimir asked Idaho. "We are not open."

"Please, I need help!" Idaho panted, "They killed Devon!"

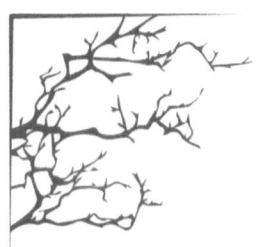

Chapter 33

Vasquez approached the isolated property in the center of the holler. McRoy was behind him in his truck, not wanting the out-of-town detective to wander around his jurisdiction alone.

The house was ramshackled and dilapidated. The wood was old and water damaged, while the roof was missing shingles. Various rusted machinery and antiques were piled outside. Tall grass and weeds grew unimpeded on the property.

Vasquez exited his car, hearing McRoy slamming the door of his truck.

"Since Columbia is a bit of recluse, I don't expect her to be too welcoming." McRoy warned, "Other than that, she's no bother."

As they walked among the weeds, a figure approached the rickety screen door. A haggard looking woman stood there, her posture defensive. She was pudgy with long graying hair tied in a ponytail. Her face was hard, and her eyes suspicious of their presence.

"What do you want, Sheriff?" she rasped harshly.

"Columbia Loupcroix, we have a few questions regarding the activity of your kin-folk." McRoy responded.

"Bah! You don't wanna know. None of y'alls' business anyway..."

"Ma'am, we have reason to believe your family has been related to the recent murders going on in Rust Springs, Ohio." Vasquez said.

Columbia looked at them funny.

"Don't be tryn'a pin things on me! I haven't had any contact with them in years! Besides, they're crazy, but they haven't done anything illegal. But like I said, I wouldn't know."

"Columbia, don't be difficult – ." McRoy interjected.

"I'm telling you the truth, McRoy." Columbia sounded wounded by his accusations. "I want nothing to do with that...madness. I've seen what an obsession like that can do to people, and I want no part of it."

The woman sauntered over to a rocking chair on the porch, taking a seat. She gave a deep sigh.

"What family members?"

"Wyoming and Colorado Loupcroix." Vasquez answered her.

"Oh, yes, Monty and them. Last I heard, they were still in South Dakota or something."

"Do you know if they were involved in any criminal activity?"

"No, aside from that white power mess, I..." Columbia trailed off, gears switching in her mind. "I remember them talking about moving westward for a bit. I heard from Yuki- or Yukon- who I don't talk to anymore by the way. He was talking about Montana getting a movement together and -"

She laughed.

"You'll just think I'm crazy-"

"No. Tell us." Vasquez told her, "Any information can help."

"They were talking about the Storm-Star, that stupid propaganda we were fed as kids. Most of my siblings and cousins believe to some extent. Others have taken it farther."

"How far?"

"They think the Storm-Star is some great being that will "save" the white race. *Stupid crap.*"

"Isn't that what you told me when you came in town?" McRoy said, "It's on their website?"

Vasquez nodded.

"Website? What?"

"Were not sure ma'am but it seems your uncle's side of the family were involved in some murders in South Dakota."

"I wouldn't know, but I-I shudder to think they've been making a movement of it...it's unhealthy."

She rose from the rocking chair, retreating back inside the house. "Columbia – "

"Leave my property. I have nothing more to give you, detective." Columbia slammed the door in their face.

Vasquez and McRoy retired to where their vehicles were parked. Despite their best efforts, they couldn't get Columbia to share more about her family.

"Well, I best be getting back home. I have some info to relay to Mullen." Vasquez said, "It's not much, but it does warrant cause for concern."

"Well, good luck to y'all." McRoy said, scratching his head. "If there's anything I can do to help, let me know."

Vasquez was ready to go home. What was Claudia doing in their shared apartment? Thanksgiving wasn't too far now. He was considering inviting Mullen whether the man wanted to or not. He couldn't shake how disturbed Columbia was when he told her about her family's activities. It gave him goose bumps. If she was unnerved, the Loupcroix must be plotting something truly evil for Rust Springs.

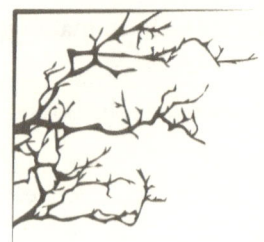

Chapter 34

"So, you saw him die?" Daisy asked. Idaho nodded.

"Yeah. I'm so sorry." he muttered, not looking her in the face. Radimir, Lucy, and Ash surrounded Daisy inside the booth, trying to give her some sense of comfort. Judging by her shaking frame and the tears in her eyes, they were failing in their efforts.

"What did they do to him?" Daisy asked, her breath hitching as she struggled to keep her composure.

"They found him trying to escape town. The caught him and brought him to the compound for his...punishment." Idaho tapped his fingers on the clean, smooth table.

"For what? What did Devon do?" Lucy asked in place of a clearly distraught Daisy.

"He stole one of the fangs and betrayed the Lodge."

"What is that?" Radimir asked.

"They are sacred to my family. They're supposed to act like a cosmic tuning fork. My brother uses it to make contact with the *other side*."

The group didn't know how to take Idaho's answer. It was a bizarre thing to Ash, but what could they expect from a cult?

"So that's what Wyoming was talking about when he attacked Devon." Daisy whimpered, "How did they -?"

"By fire." Idaho stated, not wanting her to complete her question. Ash could tell he was deeply troubled by what he saw. Idaho, though Loupcroix blood coursed through his veins, was different than his siblings.

"He didn't suffer. Montana must've killed him in the chamber before they put him on the pyre - "

"And that's supposed to make me feel better! My brother is dead because of your fucking family! Why didn't you call the cops?" Daisy's pain and rage surfaced.

"I'm sorry! I didn't know until I had to participate. Plus, the cops won't do anything, not with Traynor calling the shots. Believe me, I hate my family as much as you do. They've done nothing but spread misery and hate. I'm done with their bullshit!"

"You want to leave?" Radimir asked.

"Damn right I do!" Idaho spat. "That's why I'm here."

"You said Traynor was involved." Lucy asked.

"My family grows pot and they sell and distribute it in the area. Traynor accepted part of the profits in order for him to turn the other way and not interfere with my family."

"Well, that makes sense. But, you know Traynor is dead." Lucy told Idaho. Surprise crossed his face.

"He is? Maybe that's what Washington and Oregon were talking about; tying up loose ends."

Daisy stood and pushed Ash and Lucy out of her way as she exited the booth.

"Where are you going, love?" Lucy asked her.

"In the office; I got some calls to make. Be ready to get this show on the road by five." Daisy disappeared in the back of the club.

Radimir sighed.

"What are you going to do now, Idaho? Go to the police?"

"No." Idaho shook his head. "I can't go there. I know Traynor was involved in my brother's shit, but I don't know who else might be involved."

"Mullen and Vasquez are good men. They have been working with me and Attila. We're the ones who found Devon's finger." Ash bit his lip at the last sentence. Idaho tapped his fingers nervously.

Vasquez was out of town on a lead, and Mullen was busy figuring out what happened to Traynor. He had to convince Idaho to talk to Mullen.

"Why don't you stay here, Ida?" Lucy offered. "We can get you help after things have settled down."

Idaho smiled.

"That sounds good. Thank you ma'am."

"Great. Are you hungry? Let's get you some food."

Lucy and Idaho left, leaving Radimir and Ash by themselves.

"We should get back to work." Radimir told him.

"Yeah, uh, I gotta make a call first."

"Use the phone at the bar." Radimir slid out of the booth.

Ash found the old corded phone on the counter. He quickly dialed Mullen's number. After several rings, he was awarded with a voicemail recording.

"Hello. John Mullen is not available. Please leave your message after the tone." a computerized feminine voice told him.

" Detective Mullen, this is Ash. I got Idaho Loupcroix with me at the bar and he needs to talk to you about the cult. Call me back at The Grotto. Thanks."

Ash hung up, biting his thumbnail. He needed to clean still. Maybe he could meet Mullen after the concert. Hopefully, Idaho would be put in protective custody beforehand. He put his hands in his pockets as he made his way to the janitor supply closet. He was surprised to see Daisy walk out of the office.

"Ash, if you see Attila, tell him I'm going back to the house. I'll return in a bit." she told him.

Ash didn't bother to question her motives. He could hear her at the bar talking to Radimir about having a shotgun tonight just in case. What did they have in mind? Considering the viciousness of the Loupcroix family, there was little doubt they would need to worry about their safety. Especially, if they figured out where their missing brother was.

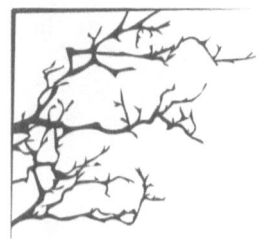

Chapter 35

"What do you mean he escaped?" Washington yelled at Oregon and Dahlia. "He was locked in the trailer!"

"I didn't think he could escape." Oregon whined.

"This would have never happened if you just talked to him!" Dahlia interrupted. "He was upset about what happened to Devon-"

Washington slapped her across the face. She fell on the floor. Washington gave a scowling and stern look.

"Colorado, take Wyoming and go find him. Oregon and I have to plan our next steps." Washington ordered her.

Dahlia sat up and rubbed her stinging cheek. She looked briefly at her husband, hurt he didn't defend her.

"Go now!" Washington yelled at her again. Dahlia ran outside the barn.

"Montana told me of his visions. The Storm-Star is on its way. We need to gather together and enact our final strike -" Washington told her brother as she scanned the grounds for Wyoming, knowing her brother's preference for hanging around the marijuana growing. Sure enough, he was smoking outside the greenhouse.

"What you want, Collie?"

"We gotta find Idaho. Come with me."

"That little shit ran away again? Well, where should we start?"

Colorado considered the options. Before, Idaho would just go into Rust Springs and explore. This time, he might have gone to get help. He would not go directly to the cops, but maybe a person or group he thought would listen to him, a contact from the outside.

"I might have an idea. Let me think."

"We're done thinking. We gotta act!" Wyoming griped, itching for some action.

They scoped out all over Rust Springs where Idaho would usually hang out. They had no luck, however. Their little brother was smart enough not to visit his old haunts. Colorado wracked her brain trying to figure out where he could have gone. The other three volunteers were in the back of the pickup, patiently waiting as they drove around. An idea popped into Colorado's brain. She could be wrong, but she had a good guess.

"You gotta hunch of where he might be?" Wyoming asked her impatiently.

"Oh yeah."

"Where?"

"To the only people who could relate to what's going on."

Wyoming stopped.

"You don't mean..."

"One in the same. The Grotto." Colorado finally said.

"That faggot bar?" Wyoming asked, "Are you sure?"

"Don't ask how I know. Trust me."

"Ok, girl." Wyoming said, "Can't hurt."

The pickup roared down the street, heading to the nightclub.

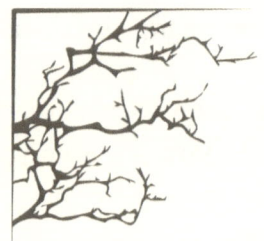

Chapter 36

Mullen rubbed his temples, reviewing Traynor's records and notes found in the deceased police chief's apartment. Names of dealers, dealing locations, routes, numbers; it was all here. Even the name Loupcroix was written several times.

Traynor was *dirty* after all. Mullen was not surprised by what he had found. He was enraged that Traynor would engage in misconduct and corruption, but relieved he had the evidence needed in order to nail the Loupcroix group. Surprisingly, Traynor didn't hide the evidence better or get rid of it after it served its purpose. Still, there was nothing about a combination to a safe.

Mullen walked into the evidence room as his fellow officers cut into the steel door of the safe. The grating sound of the saw was followed by a metallic snap. Removing the door revealed bundles of cash in large bills.

"All that money..." Deane said.

Indeed, the former police chief had a lucrative side business in the Loupcroix dealings and likely others they did not know about.

"Mullen!" Lieutenant Carter called to him. "I just got off the phone with Vasquez. He said the Columbia Loupcroix thing was a bust. The only thing she mentioned was that Montana Loupcroix was going to lead the white race."

"Damn." Mullen cursed under his breath.

They were no closer to understanding the cult, other than this Montana fellow being a messiah figure in this mess. He walked over to his desk. There was a missed call on his voicemail. Mullen tapped the button on to listen to the message.

"Detective Mullen, this is Ash." Mullen's heart pounded as he listened.

"I got Idaho Loupcroix with me at the bar and he needs to talk to you about the cult. Call me back at Attila's Grotto. Thanks."

Mullen stopped the machine. This was the break they desperately needed. Idaho would know more about the cult than anyone else. Why would the kid leave though? The Loupcroix didn't sound like the nicest people. Maybe it was due to abuse or some other disagreement. Either way, they would be looking for him.

Mullen quickly punched the number of Attila's nightclub into his phone.

"Can I help you?"

"Yes, please get me on the line with Ash Jagerhund." Mullen told the stranger. After a few seconds, he heard breathing on the other end.

"Hello?" Ash asked.

"Ash, it's me, Detective Mullen."

"Oh, so you got my message?"

"Yes. Where is Idaho Loupcroix?"

"He's here with us. He said he ran away from the cult after he saw Devon get killed."

"Devon? Devon Grayhart?"

"Yeah."

Mullen knew he would need Idaho to come to the station. Traynor's vault was cracked and soon they would know about the extent of possible corruption.

"I'll be there as soon as I can. Make sure Idaho is ready to go. Keep a low profile." Mullen told Ash.

"Will do. Though, Idaho is concerned due to Traynor's dealings with this family." Ash replied.

It all adds up.

"Okay, stay put."

Mullen quickly made his way out of the building, putting on his overcoat. He was one step closer to finding out the truth to this mystery.

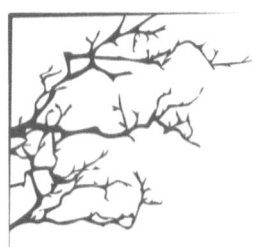

Chapter 37

The door chimed as he passed though the threshold into Don's Liquor Mart: "Rust Spring's Premiere Booze and Spirits!"

Attila was the only one in the store, sans the clerk.

"Prima donna band mates; fuck me!"

He was not looking forward to trying to find half the stuff on the list, a lot of it foreign sounding to him.

"You alright?" The pug-looking clerk peeked above his newspaper.

"Fine, man. I just gotta find some things."

"Let me know if ya need help."

Attila figured the guy wanted to keep an eye on him. He peered up at his reflection in a nearby security mirror. Combined with the CCTV, there wasn't much trouble he could cause without incriminating evidence attached, if he was that type. Fortunately, Attila was an upstanding, tax-paying citizen.

There was a case of beer that drew his attention by the freezers. He checked the list again. Perfect! One of the fancy German beers on the list found by chance.

Only twelve to go...

The next item: Sake? Who the hell drinks that? Attila found himself going deeper and deeper into the shelves of intoxicating substances contained in clear, colorful bottles. He almost forgot missing out on the show.

Another cheerful chime. Attila, in a far corner of the store, looked up at the security mirror. A skinhead type stumbled in, clearly injured from his bloodied arm and leg.

"Holy -!" the clerk shouted.

"Please, it's still out there..." the stranger passed out.

Attila's ears caught another chime. A dark figure wearing a hooded jacket approached.

"Quick! We need to get help – "

The power cut out, turning the store dark. Only the streetlights illuminated the store within. A flash of movement in the mirror. The clerk slumped over, felled by an unknown force.

Attila kept crouched looking at the mirror in fear.

"What...what the fuck are you?" the skinhead cried, shivering on the floor.

The assailant attacked the skinhead in an inhumane manner. A wet crunch near the bodies resonated in Attila's core. Was the attacker eating them?

The convex reflection distorted the killer who cautiously moved where Attila was hiding. Attila held his breath, looking for a means of escape.

He could hear the shadowy figure take deep whiffs, approaching halfway up the aisle and suddenly turning tail. Another chime, signaling the killer had left. The lights flickered back on a few seconds later. Attila peered around the corner, finding nothing but rivers of blood on tile. He took brave steps towards the two dead bodies.

"Fuck..." Attila shuddered.

The stench of blood was overwhelming. The bodies were mutilated beyond recognition. Attila stared into the glassy eyes of the clerk. It was like that time at the park. Attila was assaulted by the memories of that night. He needed a phone. He ran to the back office, dialing 911 on the desk phone.

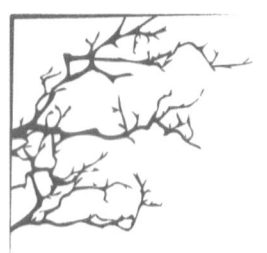

Chapter 38

A sh watched as the crowds lined up outside. It was the largest crowd he's ever seen at the club, a hundred or more people clamoring to see the famous metal-industrial group: *Eldritch Enema*. Ash was excited too, anticipation warming him in the chilly air. The sun was setting and darkness would consume it once more. A dirty Buick pulled up, revealing Daisy with a cigarette in her mouth and carrying a heavy duffel bag.

"Hey, Ash. Help me with these will ya?" Ash walked over to her and picked up one end of the bag.

"What did you put in here?" he asked, arms straining from the weight.

"Some supplies for tonight. Is our detective friend coming over?"

"Yeah. Mullen said they unlocked the safe contents and had to review them first. He should be coming over to get Idaho soon."

"Good. As much as I feel bad for the kid, I don't want him hanging around here. Everything good to go?"

"The band's here although they are wondering where Attila is since they told him to go get some booze. Radimir and I had set up the stage but the band needs to do a sound check."

"Why the hell is he not here already?"

"He had to get a few things for the band." Ash shrugged.

As serious as Attila was about this event, it was odd for him not to be on time. The two were startled by a loud noise. It was the bassist of *Eldritch Enema*, Leilani Kurz, the only female member and capable in her own right. Ash knew she could kick his ass.

"Where have you been? Dave is pissed that the sound isn't set!" she yelled at them. "And where's the hooch?"

"I'll be there in a bit, Leilani. Sorry about this." Daisy answered her. The other woman walked away with a huff of frustration.

"C'mon." Daisy said as he gripped the bag. "This has turned out to be a pretty shit day already. I'm not going to have some divas fuck it up."

Daisy walked through the backdoor, Ash close behind. Once at the stage, the rest of the Eldritch Enema members confronted them.

"Where the hell were you?" David Makala dug into them, "We got a concert in 20 minutes and your – "

"Sorry, I'll get you guys going in a bit here-"

Ash noticed Daisy's flustered expression, tired and stressed. Attila where are you?

Daisy motioned Ash to join her as they got the stage ready. Ash went backstage to talk to the band. They were busy putting on their outfits: black and riddled with spikes, studs, and leather.

"Yo, you got an ETA on the drinks?" David asked again. David Makala was the front-man, lead guitarist, and singer of the band. He was known for his tempestuous personality compared to his brother's cooler demeanor.

"Yeah, we gotta get on stage soon. Need to loosen up a bit, yeah?" Solomon Makala, the guitarist and back-up vocalist for Eldritch Enema, said.

"We apologize. There was a situation at the liquor store according to my manager, but I'm gonna take care of you tonight. Are you ready to go in ten?" Ash explained.

He didn't skip a beat. He was impressed that he was able to say that in one go. He was a little star-struck by being in the presence of *Eldritch Enema,* but didn't want to take up their time. Besides, he was too shy to tell them he was a huge fan.

"Fine." David huffed, not happy without his pre-performance drink. "But you better deliver after the show."

Mullen stepped on the damp asphalt in The Grotto parking lot. He was anxious to apprehend Idaho and spirit him away to the police station before his murderous family had an idea of his location.

Blam!

A whack to the back of his head had Mullen seeing stars.

"Eat it, pig!" a loud, angry male voice yelled.

"Shh! We have to be quiet." a soft female voice said.

"Like the fuckers inside can hear us any damn way!" the man retorted. Indeed, the metal music inside could be heard out in the parking lot.

Mullen clutched the back of his aching head, hoping he could get out his pistol with the other. A booted foot kicked him in the stomach.

"I can't be having you stopping us from getting our little brother." the man's voice said, smug and mocking.

"We need to move, now!" the woman urged, "Wash wants us in and out."

"I fucking know, Collie! I can handle it! Fuck, you sound just like – "

Mullen took advantage of the lax pressure on his back and moved. Wrenching someone's leg, he heard a cry of pain. He reached for the gun but a sharp, metallic clack made him pause. The angry man glared at him, holding a sawed-off shotgun to his face. Within a heartbeat, Mullen was brutally executed.

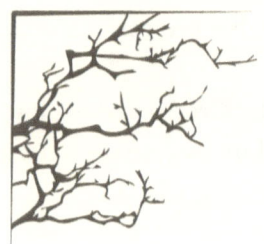

Chapter 39

Inside the band played their boisterous music. The harsh lyrics telling tales of abominations from beyond the mortal realm, and the untold desecration they will release on the world...if they are awakened. The song made Ash feel rowdy and excited. While the energy from the crowd was intoxicating, Ash kept his distance. The crowd was going wild, moshing and dancing to the music. Radimir, Daisy, and Lucy were busy serving patrons. Attila was doing sound and watching the show from backstage.

Ash perked up. He heard a bang outside. It sounded like a car back-firing or a gunshot. He was surprised he could hear anything over the music. Ash was reluctant to miss *Eldritch Enema,* but he should do his due diligence and check the commotion outside. He left the crowded floor and strode to the alleyway exit.

"And this is why we disarm people first, fuck-face."

Ash's insides turned to ice. He recognized the ornery tone of Wyoming Loupcroix. He looked over the doorframe and saw Wyoming and another man standing there.

"God, it hurts like a son of a bitch!" the unknown man complained.

"Walk it off, pussy. We got a job to do."

Ash's heart leaped when he saw them walking towards him. He ducked back inside and shut the door, mind racing. What should he do?

He decided to lock the door to provide a better barrier between the patrons, himself and the armed gunmen. The door in question was old and not as sturdy, but in his mind it was better than nothing.

Ash ran out of the kitchen to find one of his co-workers. He had to warn everyone. He ran into someone as he turned the corner, taken aback by the sudden impact.

"Ah – sorry, Ash!" Daisy yelled over the music, "Hey, what's wrong?"

"We need to get out! I saw Wyoming outside! They have guns!"

"What?! Guns?!" Daisy yelled back, trying to confirm what she had heard.

A gunshot and scream interrupted them. The music abruptly stopped; patrons fleeing for their lives. Ash spotted Colorado and another woman at the entryway with their firearms raised. Another shot hit a spotlight, blacking out part of the stage. *Eldritch Enema* was lost in the crowd of the terrified audience.

"Everyone get out!" Daisy roared over the din.

The patrons needed little encouragement as they sought a means of escape or a place to hide.

"Get down!" Daisy reached for a pistol underneath the bar shelf and took aim at the two women. A short scream told her she had hit the mark.

Colorado pushed her friend behind her, firing back at Daisy from the cover of some lounge chairs. Ash, on his hands and knees, crawled back towards the kitchen. Daisy didn't notice the departure; occupied with the firefight. Ash saw Wyoming and Radimir in a struggle of their own. The scent of blood filled his nostrils. He could see the other gunman dead on the ground near the back door. Radimir was seriously injured as he grappled Wyoming.

"You're a tough bastard, I'll give you that." Wyoming pulled out a knife from his pocket. He quickly plunged the blade into Radimir's arm.

The bartender cried out in agony. Ash lunged, succeeding in knocking Wyoming back. A dark fog settled in his mind, crazed by the violence.

Wyoming was enraged, kicking and punching. Ash held tight, finding purchase on the angry man. As if second nature, he bit down on Wyoming's fist. Surprisingly, his teeth did not shatter. Instead, they succeeded in taking a chunk of flesh off the knucklebones.

"Get off, fucker! Shit!" Wyoming snarled.

Ash was knocked away. He tasted the blood in his mouth, licking his lips.

"You're dead!" Wyoming roared, rearing to attack.

Ash grasped Wyoming's hand with unhuman speed. He growled from the depth of his being, flashing his blooded teeth. A gory mist sprayed Ash's face. The fog abruptly lifted. Ash's vision dizzied him, and the metallic tang of blood in his mouth made him ill. Wyoming lay dead before him.

"Is-is he-?" Daisy trailed off, her gun lowering.

The back of Wyoming's head had a hole that was seeping blood onto the tile floor.

"Y-yeah." Ash responded shakily.

They didn't even respond to the footsteps behind them.

"What happened? Y'all alright?" Attila asked, "Jesus."

He rushed to Daisy's side, taking the gun from her. They held each other as Daisy cried. Ash looked at his boss as he held his fiancé. The man acknowledged his presence by facing him with a haunted expression on his face.

"What happened?" he asked softly.

"It was the Ripper."

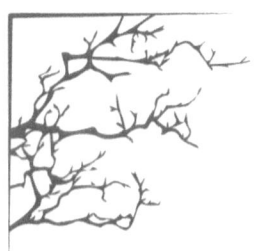

Chapter 40

Vasquez was enjoying a late dinner at his apartment he shared with Claudia. The leftover spaghetti from the night before was delicious; the spices having settled in the meat sauce overnight. Claudia was not home however. Vasquez got the note she left on the refrigerator door this afternoon. A family emergency; she had to leave suddenly for New York in order to help her mother care for her ailing father.

It didn't concern him much. He looked forward to being in her arms tonight after an unfruitful time in West Virginia. However, silence was fine too. It was calming after dealing with insanity all day.

Ring!...Ring!

A phone call? At this hour?

Probably Mullen wondering if he got back into town yet Vasquez picked up the receiver.

"Hello?"

"Detective Vasquez? This is Officer Deane speaking."

"Oh, yes, Deane. Tell me, what's going on?"

"Mullen's dead. We found his body in the parking lot of The Grotto."

Vasquez was dumbstruck.

"Vasquez? Hello?" Deane beckoned, trying to reach him, but he was far away in his mind.

He never had a partner die on him.

Never.

Was this real?

"Sorry." he finally said. "So he's gone?"

"Yes, I'm so sorry. I know this is hard to process. He was going to take Idaho Loupcroix into custody. He had run away from the Storm-Star compound."

"I assume he is in custody now?"

"Yes. There was a disturbance at The Grotto nightclub. Wyoming Loupcroix is dead."

"Did he kill Mullen?"

Vasquez hoped the man died shortly after killing his partner, preferably in an excruciating, agonizing manner.

"We are not sure. Mullen was not in the best shape when he found him. He – "

"It's okay, Deane." Vasquez didn't want to have the mental image haunting his nightmares. "Fill me in when I get to the station."

"Will do. See you in a little bit."

Vasquez slumped back down in his chair, burying his head in his hands.

"Damn, Mullen." he whispered to himself.

How was he going to approach Sarah and Lydia with this? Mullen had a family who survived him. Vasquez sighed deeply. It was an occupational hazard, but you never expect it would be you or someone you know, let alone your partner. It hit too close to home, too close for comfort. He expected to be emotional and weepy, but it never overtook him. Instead, he was numb, a sense of purpose made him push forward. He had to take action. Vasquez rose and quickly freshened up; changing clothes and washing his face. He grabbed his keys out of the bowl and walked out the door, marching down the stairs of the apartment building.

"I'm going to finish this case we started, John. Even if it means joining you in the afterlife." Vasquez promised internally.

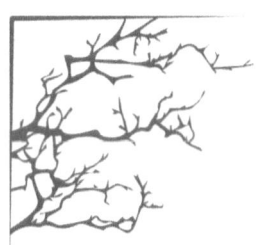

Chapter 41

A sh was relieved to come home after giving statements to the police about what happened at the bar. Unfortunately, Colorado and her other accomplices escaped when the turn of the battle was not in their favor. At least Wyoming was dead. A pang of regret shot through Ash.

"Why did I even come here?"

With all of the crazy things that have happened in Rust Springs, he questioned his sanity as to why he would continue to live and work here as if everything was normal. The drive home was uneventful as usual for Ash, passing through the empty back roads with shot nerves and exhaustion. He was paranoid on his trek back to the house. The dimly lit road was surrounded by dark foliage with no telling of what lied in the darkness. Soon, Ash saw the familiar post light. He was eager to get inside and not leave the house for a good while. Looking around the property, he saw the lights were on inside and Jasper's car was parked out front.

"At least he's home. Weird shit happens when he's not."

He hissed audibly as irritation returned from earlier. With every step, his nerves flared up like an open flame. His stomach quivered with uneasy anticipation, as if he was about to do something that was forbidden.

A steady blue light caught his attention. It was coming from the right side of the house. Ash's head was throbbing, but he investigated anyway. Azure-colored light beamed out of a basement window. The window was painted black, obscuring others from looking in.

What is Jasper doing down there? The fantastic light work shone through in some places where the paint was scratched. Crouched in the wet grass, his eyes strained to see though the light. He could hear a lot of awful growling and low chanting. The droning incantation swelled into a booming pitch that rattled Ash's teeth. With a final roar, the chanting stopped and the light seared his eyes.

Ash yelped in pain, tumbling away from the window. His body spasmed painfully. Ash whimpered as he fell helpless to the jerky movements of his body. His breaths became rapid and shallow, the November air freezing his lungs. He panicked. His vision tunneled, threatening to blind him. It was as if death had returned again.

"*Let go...Just let it go...*" something whispered deep within him.

"Ah!" he gasped.

The pain he experienced last night was back. This time at full force. Ash fell to the slushy ground, curling in pain and crying. Too hot and tight in his clothing, Ash writhed on the ground. He was dying. The biting wind blew, and Ash was relieved the stifling heat was gone. The pain still remained. He convulsed again, his limbs twisting and transforming.

Ash wished for someone to fix him. To stop this agony. To make him normal. His teeth lengthened, tasting blood from his ruptured gums. Warm tears rolled down his dirty cheeks, giving a final, desperate breath.

...

He ran through the dark wood, sinews burning with new strength. It was all so new yet right in his bestial heart. The pack stopped. The mottled alpha led them in a new direction, catching something in the wind.

Their prey...

"Fuck this man. I don't like this at all." Daren said; breaking the silence in the small car he shared with Thomas.

"Easy." the other man growled, "We got our protection right here." He patted a sawed-off shotgun in his lap.

Daren and Thomas waited thirty minutes for their client to arrive by the tracks near the center of town. They were both on the edge after what had been happening to some of their other Lodge members getting killed by someone or thing that was obviously targeting them.

"It's the Ripper. People are scared of him." Daren commented again.

"Shut it!" Thomas snapped, his nerves grating. "They're late that's all."

He did not like the look of things either. He reconsidered.

"Alright, if the bastard doesn't wanna show. I guess that's that." Thomas got ready to turn the ignition back on. A scrapping sound got their attention.

"It's him..."

"Shh – "

Thomas left to check the back of the car. His screams and gunshots told Darren the Ripper had gotten to him. Handle on the door, the last thing he saw was spotted fur and jaws breaking through the glass.

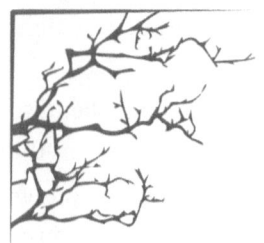

Chapter 42

"That's a lot of damage." Daisy flipped through the photos of their nightclub, uttering a mirthless chuckle. She wanted to cut the head off of every Loupcroix she could find. They killed her brother and attacked The Grotto, nearly destroying the business her and Attila built together. She needed a smoke now, but could not bring herself to find her missing pack of cigs.

"Here." Attila murmured, offering a fresh one with a lighter.

"Thanks, baby."

The flood of nicotine calmed her, but the action tonight wore her out.

"Damn. We gotta close the bar until we can fix the damage and replace the furniture. Not to mention the hooch spill and the blood..."

"Please shut up." Daisy groaned. "I don't wanna hear about it. Let's go to sleep."

Attila turned over on the bed. She briefly hoped Ash and her coworkers were faring better.

"We gotta go see Radimir tomorrow morning." Attila said.

"Yeah. He...took a rough beating."

Daisy was reminded of how bloody and torn Radimir looked behind the bar. Attila made a guttural groan.

"Seriously, babe. I can't explain it - it's unreal! That...thing I saw..."

"What did you see?" Daisy asked, concerned by his outburst.

Attila paused.

"It had to be the Ripper. He killed that man and the clerk."

Daisy could tell from his demeanor that Attila was having trouble processing the event. She thought about Devon and the message she left her parents about his death. It replayed in her mind:

"Hey, it's me. I know this is out of the blue, considering our history, but I just want you to know that Devon is dead. He was killed on the highway leaving Rust Springs. I don't know of any funeral details considering how he died and the situation I'm in now, but I thought I'd tell you. I don't care if you call back or visit...I wanted to tell you the fate of your son...my brother. Bye."

Blinking back tears, Daisy put out her cigarette.

"We need to keep a clear head. There is something clearly not right with this damn place." Attila said.

"Should we leave?" Daisy asked, already knowing the answer.

"Hell no! We got friends here and a business to look after. The cult and this other crazy shit aren't going to change that. We need to cooperate with the cops and figure out what is going on."

Daisy considered his words as she got under the covers. Made sense to her. She did want to leave either. Inside the darkest corner of her mind, she wanted to get revenge for what happened to Devon.

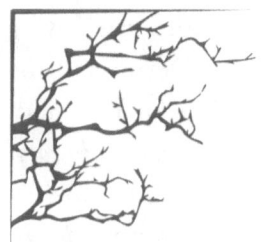

Chapter 43

T he morning light shone through the blinds, warmly waking Ash from his slumber. Stretching out, he recalled the violent vivid dream he had last night.

"I don't even remember getting in the bed. Maybe I was too tired..."

Ash noticed his skin was unusually clean, like he had been washed. At least he was wearing a t-shirt and boxers unlike last night. He did not remember getting in bed, taking a shower beforehand or passing out in front of the house. The television could be heard from downstairs.

"Jasper? You down there?"

No one answered. Ash descended the staircase. The dogs were moving around, observed by the jingling sound of their tags. There were no lights on, save for the TV. Jasper was on the couch with Raini and Stormi nearby on the floor, viewing a game show. Their tails wagged slightly when Ash appeared.

"Hey, Ash. Did you have a good sleep?" Jasper turned his attention to his nephew. He was taken aback by the greeting. His uncle sounded better today than he did yesterday but more haggardly than usual, his face pale and bloodless.

"Uh, did Attila tell you what happened?"

"Yeah, he called me this morning. It's insane."

"I came home last night and there was a strange light."

"Oh, I had to get some foodstuffs before you got home. What do you mean by "light?""

It was weird how Jasper was nonchalant about the whole thing. He was more concerned and protective when he was in the hospital.

"I saw a bright blue light downstairs in the basement. I peeked through the window outside." Ash continued.

"Huh, that's funny. Why would there be anything like that going on in there? Nothing but old junk." Jasper replied. "No, no. You came home really tired and you went to bed."

"To bed?"

How did he remember all of that? It was so vivid.

"Yes. In fact, I checked on you and there you were. Out like a light."

Ash grunted a little bit, frustrated. That wasn't a dream last night. It was too real, too natural. It was disturbingly liberating. Those men...whatever happened to them?

"Breaking news!" a newscaster announced, "Two men found dead by the Rust Springs depot -."

Ash sucked in a breath. Footage of the police at the scene; blood on the tracks. His heart pounded in his ears as his limbs fell limp. Ash needed to get away. He needed some space. A walk would be ideal. He threw on a thick jacket and went outside.

The sunny weather and the fresh air invited him outdoors. Raini and Stormi frolicked in the woods behind the house. There was the soft sound of men's voices in the distance. Ash followed it. There was a man and woman digging around for something. Were they the poachers he saw earlier? He wasn't sure. The woman snatched something bloody and ragged up from the earth, a plaid shirt that had seen better days.

The sight of it triggered something within Ash. The dogs galloped past him towards the couple. The pair ran off, dropping the shirt.

"Hey! Come back!" Ash called after them.

The couple kept running to a dirt pathway behind the property. They jumped in their car and sped off. The dogs seemed to lose interest, focusing on the flannel cloth. With Raini and Stormi carrying one end of the shirt, they brought it back to Ash. He was disappointed he couldn't figure out why the couple was there, except for the shirt. Coaxing the cloth out of Stormi's mouth, he inspected it.

It was indeed familiar. He rubbed it between his fingers, dried blood peeling off. He would have to ask Jasper about this. Why was it on his property?

There was a time where he would ignore things and sweep them under the rug. This was not the time. Ash walked back inside the house.

Jasper glanced at the cloth, no expression on his face. Raini and Stormi were alert as well, sensing the tension.

"Where did you get that?"

"It was out in the woods. The dogs were playing with it." Ash neglected to mention the couple in the woods.

"Looks like some rubbish they found."

"I saw it in my dream last night. It was what one of the victims was wearing the night they died."

"It's not evidence, Ash. A *dream*? Besides, there's a lot of people who could be wearing this type of shirt."

"No, it's too uncanny." Ash knew what he saw.

"Ash, you're shaking." Jasper commented.

"Jasper, does our family have a history of illness?" Ash asked, hands clenching into fists. Jasper gazed down to his lap, contemplating his next words.

"Sit, Ash."

Ash was not enthused with Jasper's tone, but followed his order and sat on the cushioned chair.

"My illness is hereditary, yes. My father, your grandfather, was affected by it. Your grandmother did not have it, but she had other complications that shortened her life, sadly." Jasper explained, "I do not know what it exactly is. All the doctors I have been to do not know either, other than it's terminal."

"What are the symptoms?"

"They manifest in different ways. Mainly mental illness, physical deformities and general degradation of health over the years." Jasper gave a wet cough. "Which is what I'm currently experiencing at a fairly young age."

The weight of Jasper's clarification hung heavily on his soul. The only relative he knew was going to die.

"The illness manifested earlier in my life rather than later, which is the norm." Jasper continued. "I have no clue about your mother. She seemed perfectly healthy the last time I saw her. Who knows? As long as you don't have the symptoms, you might be perfectly fine."

"I've been blacking out lately." Ash admitted.

"Hmmm..."

"That's why I was asking if there's a history of illness in our family."

"Let me see your back."

Ash lifted his shirt over his head. Jasper looked him over.

"Nope, you look perfectly normal. The scars have healed well." Ash frowned. The scars shouldn't have healed so fast.

"What about you? I don't see you having any deformities."

Jasper sighed.

"No, I don't have any and neither did your mother. I wouldn't worry about it. I've had plenty of time to resign myself to my fate. Death comes to us all eventually. Some sooner than others. Don't sweat it, kid. Focus on enjoying the life you've got."

Still, Ash was not satisfied with the discussion. So his characteristics are hereditary, but what about the train tracks in his dream? The pain? It was too vivid. He looked at the dogs, searching their faces for an answer. They stared back dumbly, as if not having a care in the world. What did he expect from a pair of dogs anyway?

"Do you have anything planned for today? Ya'know with the bar being closed and all?" Jasper asked.

"I'm gonna check in with Attila and go see Radimir."

"He's the bartender, right?"

"Yeah. He got roughed-up bad."

"Fine with me. Send Attila and his crew my condolences. I'm going to go back to sleep." Jasper pulled the plush throw over his body.

The dogs followed Ash into the kitchen where the telephone was. He dialed Attila's home phone, but did not get an answer. Ash remembered his boss was still at the hospital. It was time to go over there and meet them.

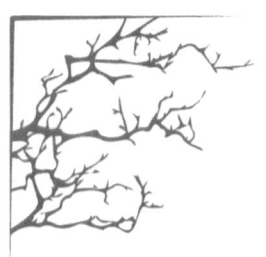

Chapter 44

Montana reclined on the bed, attended to by Colorado. A cup of water sat on the bedside while broth was given to him by the spoonful. The siblings, Dahlia and a few of the "inner-circle" surrounded him.

"Wyoming? Damn them." Montana whispered.

Colorado kept her head down, ashamed for not being able to protect her brother or at least, bring his body home. The rest of the Loupcroix siblings seemed shaken with the exception of Washington, who was always stoic.

"We shall honor him for his contribution to our cause. It is a great tragedy to lose a true brother."

The group held a brief moment of silence for their fallen. Colorado vowed to give the same dedication to the final hours.

"I need to rest." Montana interrupted. "I have to prepare for Folkvagnr's arrival."

"We should figure out how to get Idaho back." Washington added.

"Do you know where they are keeping him?" Montana asked.

"I have an idea. Likely in custody by the RSPD."

"Get him back." Colorado hung her head, ashamed for the botched operation. She was happy Montana wasn't angry. There was more of an emphasis on finding their little brother and the glory to come.

"I'll start getting the others prepped for Zero Day." Oregon said. "I'll go with Wash for back-up."

Colorado perked up, eager to help. She still feared Montana's power, but had peace. Soon, all that they were working towards would come to fruition.

"Good. Like I said, the Storm-Star will rise." Montana smiled approvingly.

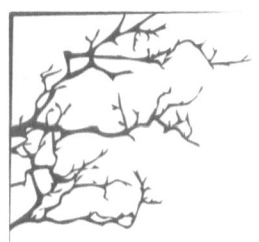

Chapter 45

The bombastic bagpipes echoed over the cemetery. Police in their clean pressed uniforms bore shiny badges with a black line across them. Solemn pallbearers carried the casket to its final resting place. Before it was lowered in the grave, attendees spoke their eulogies and laid their flowers on the polished wood of the casket. Vasquez was the last one to approach. He brought no flowers; only a letter. Vasquez had given his speech earlier to the public at the chapel, for the sake of his fellow officers and Mullen's family. He nearly choked when he saw Sara there in her little black dress, quiet and innocent.

This letter was something for Mullen, something that could not be expressed openly with others listening. This was between him and his partner. Vasquez placed the envelope atop the flowers and stepped aside as the casket was lowered. Watching the first shovel-full of dirt cover the letter gave him some satisfaction. With the ceremony completed, the crowds broke off to find comfort in conversation. Vasquez walked alone to the cemetery office, finding three familiar faces.

"We wanted to give this to you." Daisy placed a flower bouquet and a small wrapped gift in his hands.

"We're sorry for your loss, detective." Attila said. "It hasn't been easy for us either."

Ash gave a sad smile.

"Thanks, Mr. Gadsden and Ms. Grayhart." Vasquez said. "I'll be sure to give the flowers to Angie and Sara."

"Good. That's nice to hear." Daisy said warmly. For a while, no one spoke. They had the same question on their minds, but did not know how to articulate it.

"What now?" Ash asked bluntly.

"After reviewing the evidence, Idaho Loupcroix's statements and considering what happened to Mullen, the city wants to get the FBI involved." Vasquez informed them.

"That sound's good."

"I'm unsure. The FBI has been getting skittish over the years concerning these types of situations, you know. Just stay away from the compound and cult members. These people are highly organized and dangerous."

"Don't worry about us. We can handle ourselves." Attila reassured. Vasquez wasn't convinced.

"And the Ripper is still on the loose. Didn't you say you ran into him, Attila?"

"People think I'm outta my mind but, shit, they don't know the half of it."

Vasquez saw the look in the man's eyes. He was rightfully scared.

"I don't think you're crazy." the detective replied. "There is something...odd going on in this town. The cult and the Ripper...I'm going to get to the bottom of this."

Vasquez left the trio behind, descending the hill. Mullen's widow and daughter were returning to their vehicle.

"Sandra!" he called to her.

She turned, smiling.

"Antonio. It's good to see you." she gave him a hug. "How are you?"

"Doing good. I'm engaged actually."

"Oh, and who's the lucky lady?"

"Claudia."

"Best wishes to you both."

Little Sara waved at Vasquez.

"Hey there!" Vasquez bent down to the girl's level. "How are you doing, sweetie?"

Sara hid behind her mother.

"Sorry, she's a bit shy."

"That's ok." Vasquez stood, "I was like her at that age. Hard to believe, huh?"

Sandra laughed at the remark.

"Please, let me know if there is anything I can do for you." he told her.

"Of course. Thank you."

The mother and daughter waved goodbye. Vasquez wasn't up to joining the others at the bar. The wounds were still fresh. He'd drink alone at home. Driving away from the beautiful cemetery, he craved the taste of warm whiskey. He would not drown his sorrows; instead, he would focus to take down those who killed Mullen.

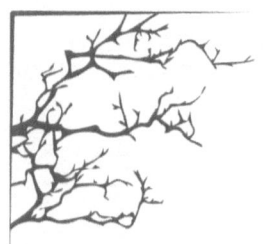

Chapter 46

Ash did not care much for hospitals. In fact, he downright hated them. The smell of sterilized surfaces and sickness was overpowering. Not to mention the equipment that would poke and prod him at check-ups. It was all very unpleasant. Fortunately, he was not there for himself. Attila led him and Daisy to the room where Radimir was recuperating. The room was similar to the one he stayed at when he was attacked in the woods. Radimir slept upright on the bed, covered in gauze and IVs strapped to him.

"Poor, Rad." Daisy lightly placed her hand on the bed rail.

Cold settled in Ash's gut. Radimir's pale skin and bloody wounds highlighted the utter viciousness of the attack last night. Ash could still hear the gunfire and smell the blood. The fight with Wyoming in the kitchen; he'd tapped into something wild and primal. As much as it filled him with fear, he harbored a strange attraction to it. It was suffocating him; something was tearing to get out.

"I, uh, need to go to the restroom." Ash muttered.

"Ash?" Attila followed as he took off down the hallway.

He ducked into the nearest male-designated bathroom and lurched over a toilet. Waves of nausea ebbed and swelled with in him. His skin tingled as if lighting danced along it; his head was swimming. Ash growled at the discomfort. An urge to walk overtook him. His body was battling possession, wanting to bend over and relieve itself of this unnatural posture of man. Slightly hunched over, Ash exited the stall.

"Ash, are you okay?" Attila knocked from other side of the door. Ash turned the faucet on the sink and ran his hands under the cool water.

"Yeah, I'm fine!"

Attila came in and looked at Ash's reflection in the mirror.

"You look a little green, kid."

Ash doused his face in the water.

"Jasper told me about my family and his illness."

"Attila leaned on the sink counter.

"What's up? He never would go into specifics with me. I always thought it was something embarrassing."

Ash looked at himself. Water dripped off his chin and damp brown hair. The golden rings around his pupils seemed brighter as his emerald irises surrounded them.

"He wasn't specific with me either, only that it was hereditary and my grandfather had it too."

"Do you have it?"

"Jasper said it was unlikely." Ash paused, earlier recollections coming to his mind. "Some weird shit happened last night. Not sure if it was a dream or not..."

"Weird shit, huh?" Attila said sarcastically. "You're going to have to be a little more specific. A lot of fucked up shit has happened as of late."

Ash told him about what happened when he came home after the attack and the strange dream he had, along with the news report of the two men found by the tracks.

"Sounds like a messed-up dream to me, especially if you woke up in your bed in the morning." Attila said.

"But it was so vivid! Like I was there!" Ash raised his voice in frustration. Attila put his large hands on his shoulders.

"Okay, okay, calm down. I would be freaked out too. Hell, I still am! And stressed too! Business insurance isn't an easy thing and the Ripper - "

Attila paused.

Silence followed, both men unsure of what to say. *What was there to say?* Everything was crashing around them, the security of normalcy snatched away. The squeak of the restroom door opening startled them.

"There you are!" Daisy said. "I was wondering what happened to you guys."

"Jesus!" Attila jumped at the sudden intrusion. "This is the men's bathroom!"

"Oh, hush! There's no one else in here but us. Like I give a shit anyway. I've seen hundreds of different men's junk – "

"Daize, don't remind me." Attila gave her a disgusted look.

"What are you guys going to do today?" Ash asked before the couple got into an argument.

"Well, we got the funeral out of the way. We're visiting Radimir, now." Attila ticked off the different engagements.

"Why don't we see Lucy?" Daisy asked. "She'd probably want to see us. Plus, we could tell her how Radimir is doing."

Attila shook his head.

"No can do. I've gotta talk to the insurance people today. Maybe tomorrow. Ain't like the old girl is going anywhere. Call her up and tell her about Rad."

Attila and Daisy regarded Ash, waiting for his answer concerning his daily plans.

"I was going to hang around downtown." he admitted. "Jasper is not expecting me until later anyways. I have to get out of the house."

"We understand. Just be careful. If you need anything, you have my number." Attila reminded.

"Yep."

After saying their goodbyes, Attila and Daisy parted their ways with Ash in the middle of downtown. The young man looked around him. Despite the terrible happenings, the residents of Rust Springs were carrying on business like usual. Ash checked his wallet, finding he had some cash leftover. A delicious smell wafted to his nose. It was lunchtime at the pan-Asian restaurant, Golden Mountain. Ash decided he would check it out.

The inside of the restaurant was decorated with various items and images from Asian cultures. The most prominent among the décor: a huge wheel depicting the Chinese zodiac cycle. It loomed over a smaller circular table where a lone figure sat.

"Ash, my friend!" Calvin greeted. "Come over and sit a spell!"

Ash didn't expect to see Clarkson here. They always seemed to run into each other in the oddest places. It was if Clarkson haunted the streets and locales of Rust Springs like a restless spirit. He obliged the televangelist and sat across from him.

"I ordered some tea. Would you like something else to drink?" Clarkson asked him.

"No, tea is good. I like tea." Ash said absentmindedly. Clarkson nodded in approval.

"What brings you to downtown today, Ash?"

The cheery nature in which the question was posed rubbed Ash the wrong way. Was Clarkson living under a blissful rock?

"Well, let's see." Ash began in a scathingly sarcastic tone, "I attended a funeral, and visited a severely injured co-worker who is in the hospital. Oh, and I am currently unemployed due to the fire at the bar last night..."

Ash slumped his head.

"I am slowly losing my mind here."

Clarkson stared at Ash with a shocked look with a limp smile plastered on his face.

"I am so sorry. My prayers go out to you and your friends." Clarkson's expression saddened. Ash rolled his eyes. A waitress appeared with a tray of tea, a plate of lemon wedges, and sugar.

"Are you gentlemen ready to order?"

"Yes. Get me an order of pineapple-fried rice and Siamese chicken." Clarkson said. "Is that enough to share between two people?"

"Yes, sir."

"Calvin, you don't have to." Ash protested, fingers rubbing his temples.

"It's on me, Ash. It's the least I can do. Besides, you look like you could use a good meal."

The waitress went away with the order. Clarkson passed a small cup of green tea to his lunch guest. Ash accepted the drink, uttering a small thanks. Taking a sip, he found that he did not like the taste of green tea by itself.

"Try it with some sugar and lemon." Calvin suggested, "It improves the taste in my opinion, even though it's not a traditional way of drinking it."

Ash poured the sugar and added a lemon, mixing them with chopsticks. He took a sip. Calvin was right; it was a better flavor.

"Honestly, Ash, I am saddened by what has happened. Forgive me for my obliviousness. I have seen the news. I should have known better."

"Just forget it." Ash wanted to eat and forget his troubles, if only for a little while. Calvin seemed to not catch this sentiment.

"Detective Mullen was a brave man. I have been following the cult since their arrival and let me tell you, it takes courage to face these people."

"And yet, it was not enough to save him. Not Radimir. Not us. No one is safe from these people." Ash hoped Jasper was okay by himself. He looked fatigued this morning.

"It's important to focus on faith in these times. The enemy will try us, but we must persevere." Calvin chimed. Ash put his head in his hands.

"Well, you're optimistic. I'll give you that much."

Calvin sipped his tea.

"I know where my fate lies. When I die, I'll be raptured to the heavens with the other faithful. This fact alone gives me peace."

"You're sure about that?"

"Yes, I am. Are you?"

The waitress came by with the food. Ash's stomach grumbled. The chicken and rice smelled delicious. Calvin thanked the woman and bowed his head in prayer. Ash was chomping at the bit to eat but waited out of respect.

"Dear God. Thank you for this food we are about to partake in. May it nourish our bodies. Amen." Calvin prayed.

Ash and Calvin scooped the food onto their plates. Ash ate ravenously, while Calvin neatly ate with his fork. The rice was good, even if Clarkson's talk was grating.

"Did I ever tell you of my dealings with a New Mexican death cult?" Calvin asked.

"No." Ash said between mouthfuls.

"Oh! It's a kicker! A couple of years ago, I was called to assist a woman whose daughter was mixed up in this atrocious group who worshiped this "death-god" of sorts. It was a nasty affair. All of those sacrifices they made to this false god in hopes of some supernatural power. Their priest was some crazy brujo who would make these animal sacrifices and offerings of corpse flesh to this entity."

"What happened?" Ash was slightly curious.

"The daughter testified to police about the drug trafficking, prostitution, and corpse theft and the priest was arrested. She became a Christian after repenting, too."

"The point of that story was-?"

"The flawed nature of these cults and how quickly they fall apart. The Storm-Star Lodge is no different. Now that law enforcement is involved, it's only matter of time."

The rest of the meal was continued in silence. The ambiance of Chinese flutes and the water trickling into a nearby koi pond did little to calm Ash's nerves. He was growing irritated by the man's presence. His gums were itchy. How could this man view himself as morally superior after lying to him? Ash grabbed one of his unused chopsticks, twirling it in this hand. He wasn't a god, only a mere man. And like mankind, a flawed species subject to petty tribalistic quarrels and the acceptance of falsehoods. Could people like Calvin comprehend the bullshit they spewed, or did he wholeheartedly swallow it? Ash ground his teeth as he thought of crawling across the table and attacking the reverend. Not willing to submit to his dark urges, he snapped one of his chopsticks in half instead.

"Are you okay, Ash? You seem a little on edge."

Ash placed the splintered utensil down.

"Peachy."

"I've read through the website of the Storm-Star Lodge." he mentioned. "Never read so much racist filth before."

Ash stirred his tea. He didn't have time to read that tripe. All he knew was that the group was a bunch of murderous assholes worthy of his contempt.

"I should thank you. For letting me interview Devon. I saw the true evil of these types of works."

"No you only made everything worse with that media stunt you pulled."

"I don't know what you mean."

"By putting the cult's information out there, you put Devon and everyone in more danger." Ash snapped his chopstick in his hand. "And here, I was the damn idiot, who helped build a case against them for the cops."

"It all worked out." Clarkson said, "I am not responsible for Devon's death. He was marked when he defected."

"Yeah, yeah. Blame someone else like you always do for your faults. Did you learn that in seminary?"

Calvin placed his utensils on his plate, looking indignant.

"Look, Ash – "

"Spare me the lecture."

"If you need solace, you can always come to one of our evening services. I'm sure Kathy and I can help you. I can even offer some books from my library - "

"No, thanks." Ash said, abruptly standing. His agitation rose again, stifled by the environment. He had to go. Ash took money from his wallet.

"For the meal. Stuff that in your donation box."

He threw some bills on the table. Calvin protested, but he turned for the front entrance of the restaurant. On the street again, the young man headed away from downtown to the urban neighborhoods that surrounded Rust Springs. Brick buildings gave way to once-charming dilapidated Victorian homes on either side of Ash. Residents eyed him with suspicion as he walked past.

Ash approached a junk car lot. This part of downtown was shady; he kept alert. There were some men hanging out on the corner. They looked rugged and mean, dressed in tattoos and leather. Ash tried going around the men. They whispered among themselves, pointing at him. He didn't like the looks they were giving him. He was prepared to run or fight.

"Hey, get over here!"

Ash ran to the other side of the street. The largest of the three men cornered him, as Ash was flanked by the other two on either side. He tried to fight them, swinging but missing the larger man. His effort was rewarded with a punch that left him seeing stars. They were merciless in their desire to subdue him, taking advantage of

Ash's disorientation to bind his hands behind him. He thrashed in their grip, trying in vain to get away.

What did these men want with him?

"Is this the guy you saw?" one of them spoke.

"Sure is." another confirmed. "Devon left him there on the street. Wherever he went, he was in a big fuckin' hurry."

Devon? These guys new him?

"Let's go in the lot." a voice whispered in his ear, "We have some questions for ya."

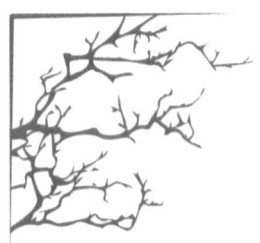

Chapter 47

Attila and Daisy walked out of the insurance office, drained by the whole process of documenting their losses and filing a claim.

"Can't wait to go home." Daisy muttered. "I need some coffee."

Attila groaned, seconding her motion. Their phone mailbox was filled with supporting words from their faithful patrons while their voicemail also contained requests for interviews from various news stations. Attila and Daisy ignored the reporters, as they wished to keep their privacy and sanity. The garish 70's interior of the rest area of the business complex transported them to a different era of time. The single person sitting on one of the absurd floral tables waved them down.

"Attila Gadsden? I'm Dan Harp from the Rust Springs Sentinel." the man introduced himself, "Can I interview you about –?"

"No." Attila grabbed Daisy and moved away.

"Please sir!" Harp persisted, "I need a moment of your time!" Attila tapped the button on the elevator, wishing for the doors to open soon.

"What are your thoughts on the cult?" Harp questioned, "In your opinion, is law enforcement doing enough to protect the city? What about the death of Detective John Mullen and Devon Grayhart's disappearance?"

"What about it?" Daisy snapped over her shoulder. Attila gritted his teeth and squeezed her hand firmly, not happy with her outburst at the nosy news hound.

"We're not taking any questions, Harp." Attila said calmly, "Please leave."

"Ms. Grayhart, your brother was a member of the cult. Do you feel his affiliation is to blame for the destruction of your bar?"

The violent blow landed on Harp's chin and knocked him down. Daisy stood over him, anger burning across her features.

"Look, asshole, my brother was many things, but he did not burn down our club. Those cult kooks did, and mark my words, they will pay!" Daisy yelled at him. She was snatched by her coat as a loud ding sounded behind her.

"Come on. We gotta go!" Attila said.

Daisy left the reporter on the floor, and stumbled into the elevator. The doors abruptly closed on them as it descended.

"What the hell was that?" Attila snapped. "You went berserk back there!"

"Damn it, Attila! He brought up Devon!"

"I don't care. We have to be smart about this. No more talking to the press, okay?"

"Daze! You can't just go over and do that!"

"That asshole was talking about my dead brother!"

"It doesn't matter. He's gone and we have bigger things –"

"How can you fucking say that? He was my brother. Regardless of who he was, I loved him!"

"Daze - "

"No! You never cared for him, Attila! And you know – whatever. Like you said, it doesn't matter." she began to cry. "You never liked my brother then, and you never will." She turned away from him.

"Daze, where you going? C'mon!"

"'Tila, I just need time to myself. I'll take a taxi home."

Attila was too tired and frustrated to argue.

"Fine." he huffed. Daisy turned her back to him once more. She fumed silently the rest of the way home.

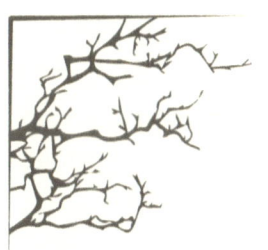

Chapter 48

"**S**teady there, kid." the grizzled older man told Ash.

The man had a gun aimed straight at him. Ash ceased his resistance, not eager to get shot. Fear and uncertainty ran through him. Wasn't Devon an ex-biker? What would they want with him? The herded him to the junkyard. Past the rusted car parts and abandoned vehicles was an old El Camino.

"Sit down on the bed there." the old man told him, "I'm gonna ask you a few questions."

Ash was silent, not knowing what to say or do. Looking at their 1% patch, Ash assumed they were outlaw bikers.

"What are you doing here?"

"Minding my own business. I wish you would do the same..."

"Hey! Get up asshole!"

They roughly grabbed him off the ground, pulling him up to the old man's level. Ash kicked out at one of them, getting someone in the shin.

"Aw, look, boys." one of the men said in a mockingly sweet voice. "We got a little fighter here!"

Ash's backside hit the cracked ground.

"What are you doing out here?" the man who pulled him up asked. He was grizzled and gray-haired. Ash assumed he was the leader.

"I'm sorry." Ash apologized, wanting to avoid a beatdown. "I don't want any trouble."

"Then what the hell are you doing here?" the man growled.

Ash did not know what to say; other than what would make them think he was crazy and kick his ass.

"Say, son, you look mighty familiar..." the man said, leaning down to get a better look at Ash. A realization crossed his rough features. "Are you a pal of Devon Grayhart's by any chance?"

"Uh, not really – "

"You sure? I've seen you around with him the other day. I was surprised he would show up around these parts."

Ash looked at the three men with confused looks. Who were these guys?

"Yeah, you look confused." the older man noted. "Well, let's say we're old business associates of ol' Dev. Name's Tobias. The others are Jess and Big Tim."

Ash looked at the attire of the men; jeans with tattered shirts and black leather vests. Ash was right in his assumption that Tobias and his crew were outlaw bikers.

"You see, he screwed us over in a major way. And I told his sorry ass never to set foot in Devil's Thunder territory ever again." Tobias recanted, "I guess he didn't listen." He looked at Ash briefly.

Hold him, boys!" Tobias commanded.

Jess and Big Tim roughly grabbed Ash and held him upright.

"Wait! No – what did I do? Let me go!" Ash struggled against his captors. Tobias raised his fist and aimed it at Ash's stomach. Ash wheezed painfully as the fist met its target: his solar plexus.

"Not until you tell us where Devon is." Tobias growled. The other bikers laughed as they held the limp form of Ash.

"Get up on your feet, fucker, and tell us where Dev is." Big Tim told Ash in a low voice. Ash struggled albeit feebly; trying to get free. Another punch laid Ash out on the ground. He rolled on his side and puked bile.

"Damn, Toby, you'll kill him." Jess said, voice wavering.

"Kid will wish he's dead when I'm through." Tobias snarled. "Get the crowbar. That'll loosen his lips."

Ash could hardly hear the biker's exchange, as his nerves ignited with pain and his heartbeat pounded in his ears. Was he dying? His mind blanked out as agony consumed him; the voices of his assailants muted in the background. He could hardly make out their yelling and screams.

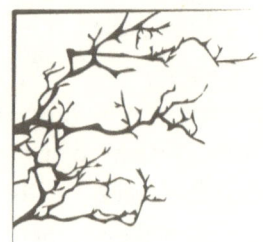

Chapter 49

Daisy left the bedside and her sleeping fiancé. She could not sleep. She was too pissed to close her eyes. She rose and walked downstairs. She pulled her robe tighter to her body as the chill night air hit her. She sat on the back porch, lighting a cigarette. The words of the day weighed on her mind.

She hated what the Loupcroix took from her, and the fact Attila did not come to her side.

"I shouldn't have lashed out."

She couldn't blame him for not getting along with Devon. Devon, in short, was an asshole. She loved her brother and sometimes that blinded her to his dark side. Daisy may have shared a bond of blood and hardship with him, but he was ultimately responsible for what happened in his life; paying the ultimate price for his choices.

But he didn't have to die like that. Nobody deserved to die like that. No one except for the Loupcroix. She took another drag and swiftly snuffed the cigarette. She knew what she had to do.

Daisy strode back inside. She wanted to see the Loupcroix bleed. She got dressed and went to the gun cabinet, taking her pistol and a shotgun Attila owned. The man was none the wiser, sleeping deeply on their bed. Daisy felt a pang of regret looking at him. She may not see him again. What if she got hurt or worse? She shook her head.

No.

She would be fine, but she had to do something. Daisy wanted the Lodge to know that her family and business were not to be messed with. She left the bedroom; Devon consuming her thoughts.

Before she knew it, she was on the road with nothing but weapons and a taste for revenge. Daisy looked for the turn Devon mentioned to her. The compound had to be close.

"Anchorage Farms." she read off the blue and white faded sign. This was it. Daisy turned left, proceeding with caution. There was a muddy dirt road lined with trees. She could not see anyone, so Daisy took it as a good sign.

Gat! Gat! Gat!

Sparks flew out from the hood of the car. Daisy ducked as she slowed to a crawl. The gunfire ceased. Daisy laid on the front seats and grabbed her pistol.

"Get out of the car!" a rough voice demanded. The door opened on the passenger's side. A pair of hands gripped her tightly and pulled her roughly out of the car.

"No! No! Fuck you!" Daisy kicked. She was thrown to the ground, the impact jarring her bones.

"Stay down, bitch, or I will blow your damn head off!" her assailant demanded.

"Is that? – " another person asked.

"Holy shit! It's Devon's sister!" another man said.

"Tell me? What brings you here?"

"My brother." She got on her knees. "You killed him!"

"How did-?"

"Idaho, told me."

"He did, did he?" yet another man huffed, squatting to her level. "Ah, Wash and I will get him soon enough."

"Oregon, they want to know what's going on." someone told him.

The man, holding a gun to her face, was one of the Loupcroix family members.

"We'll show them."

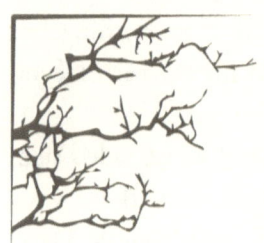

Chapter 50

Vasquez pulled into the police department parking lot. There were many unmarked sedans at the building this morning. The FBI had arrived into town from the looks of it. Vasquez exited his car, carrying a box of donuts and a cup of coffee. It was all he could stomach today and hoped to carry them in without anyone noticing. He didn't get much sleep last night after gathering the notes he and Mullen collected over the past months. He wanted a few minutes to himself before he got back to work. A little smile played on his lips, thinking about how Mullen would get annoyed about all the junk he ate.

"Hi, Antonio!" a happy female voice called out to him across the lot. Vasquez saw a portly, older woman walking briskly towards him, beaming from ear to ear. He recognized her as Deputy Mayor Janet Whately. Vasquez groaned internally as he put on a false smile. Janet Whately was an A-type personality, who never seemed to have any emotion besides total elation. Her sunny disposition offset the dour demeanor of Rust Springs' presiding mayor, Kathleen Meyer.

"What a nice morning for once! Even the sun is peeking out of the clouds!" Whately cheered.

Vasquez looked up at the sky. Squinting his eyes, he could see a faint ray of sunlight fighting to burst through the clouds. There's a silver lining to everything, according to Janet, that is.

"I should thank you for all the hard work you and your partner – God rest his soul – have put into this case. Without it, we would've never made it this far." Whately took Vasquez's hand in her own.

Vasquez was uncomfortable with the close contact. It was not out of the ordinary for Whately to be physical and casual towards her constituents. She saw it as a way to better relate to them, but it more often than not, resulted in awkwardness.

"Thank you, Deputy Mayor." Vasquez rushed, not wanting to linger on the subject. "Where is Mayor Meyer?"

"She will be here shortly – wait, there she is! Over there!" Whately exclaimed as a silver Toyota pulled up beside Vasquez's parking spot. Meyer stepped out, greeting them with a hand wave. Whately left him behind to greet the tall, lean, dark-haired woman. Vasquez took this as a signal to proceed to his office. The main foyer was buzzing with activity, as local police and federal agents, worked together. Vasquez climbed upstairs to his cubicle. He was happy not to have been noticed as he sat at his desk. As he was about to take a bite out of a chocolate donut, an announcement was made.

"Everyone to the conference room. We are going to review details related to the Storm-Star case and plot our next course of action." a suited man said.

So much for a quiet breakfast. He knew he shouldn't complain. He had to finish this thing for Mullen, and for the sake of Rust Springs. The force crowded inside a room where a projector screen and a dry-erase board were filled with various photographs of the Loupcroix suspects and crime scenes. They triggered vivid memories of the terror and death that plagued the city. Vasquez paused at the picture of Mullen's broken body lying on the dry pavement. He diverted his gaze away from the sight, the pain of losing his partner still fresh. People were taking their seats. Meyer and Whately were upfront next to an older gentleman wearing a navy-blue suit and tie. Vasquez took a seat up at the very front. The room was filled with droning talk of many tongues. The static tones were hushed when the suited man rose, and took his place at the podium.

"Good morning everyone. I'm FBI Special Agent in charge, George Carbine." the man introduced himself. "My division is working with the Rust Springs Police Department to bring Montana Loupcroix and his Storm-Star Lodge to justice. Through the combined investigations of U.S. Marshalls, FBI, ATF, Rust Springs Detective Vasquez and the late Detective Mullen, we have a clearer picture of the danger the Storm-Star Lodge presents to the community. Today, we will plan our next steps."

"Now, it seems we are caught in a turf war of some sort between local drug dealers, but that's not the case." Carbine continued with the details.

Vasquez tapped his pen on his clipboard. He was restless sitting in the small chair. Wouldn't the Loupcroix still try to get Idaho back? They had no qualms about killing an officer of the law and attacking a nightclub full of patrons. A warm hand lay on his shoulder.

"Hey, it's okay." an agent told him.

"Anything you want to share, Vasquez?" Carbine asked. Vasquez rose, coming to the front of the crowd.

' "Yes, there was an investigation into the exact nature of the activity we were monitoring. The Storm-Star Lodge are a white supremacist sect that came here about a year ago. They've come to Ohio to anticipate the coming of some entity they revere. Until then, it seems they've supplemented their income with drug and stolen firearms dealings."

Someone raised her hand.

"Is it true one of the key members is dead? Wouldn't the others want their brother out of custody?"

"Yes, Wyoming Loupcroix was killed in a firefight at Attila's Grotto. And I fear the Loupcroix might make an attempt to get their brother back. He is important to their group."

"How?" Carbine asked.

"They are basically a doomsday cult. They have nothing to look forward to in this world, aside from resurrecting this Storm-Star being and the Fenris-kin. We are still unsure about the particular details."

"Does this have anything to do with the passing of the Hale-Bopp Comet? Seems like they are obsessed with astronomy by the terms." another person questioned.

"No. I don't see a connection with their materials. It seems to be a title to describe the nature of the two entities. We need to approach with caution. Like with what we saw in Waco, these types of cults can turn deadly upon confrontation."

Vasquez could see the mayor and deputy mayor looking on as he gave the presentation.

"Noted." Carbine interrupted, "We need to send some tactical teams around the property - "

"Sir!" another agent came bursting in the room. "I have word that two RSPD officers were found shot and killed off of Union Road."

"Union Road is near the location of the compound."

"Yes, Anchorage Farms!" the agent replied, panting.

"Get ready to roll out. Things have escalated." Carbine announced to the room.

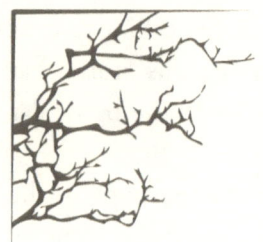

Chapter 51

Idaho rested in his holding cell. He had been in there since the attack on The Grotto. It was lonely. He played odd games to amuse himself. He paced, counted cracks on the walls and conjured abstract images from patterns on the tile floor. Interactions with others were brief, only when it was time to be fed. Was this how solitary confinement was in some supermax prison somewhere? He remembered father talking about those hell-holes they put men in.

"Remember, humans are social creatures by nature. No matter how much of a loner one might be, we crave to interact with our own kind. The American prison system goes against that instinct. You take a normal man, leave him locked up and alone for years and tell me if he comes out the same. It's plain unnatural." the Loupcroix patriarch would say.

Idaho remembered the quote inspiring such dread when he was younger. It made him not want to ever go to jail. Yet, the actions of his family will most likely lead to this route. Montana's transgressions were bad enough to warrant a life sentence at least. Idaho lay on the cot, trying to focus on fond memories. Traveling extensively cross-country and experiencing different environments were fun and exciting when he was younger. He made new friends only to lose them again, finding enchanting locales only to never see them again. His family was always moving, running away from an entity they hated to one that would deliver them to salvation. As Idaho grew older, he grew more cynical to the idea. Watching the suffering of his family to chase a pipe dream coveted by his father, and seeing his eldest siblings being utterly consumed by it. Ironically, he was at the

216

center of the cosmic prophecy, a role shared with his older brother. Wyoming wanted the role so badly, trying to win some-sort of latent appraisal of himself as a worthy person. In the end, his dream died along with him. Idaho, while disliking Wyoming, felt saddened by his brother's death. It was an inevitable thing. Wyoming was going to die violently sooner or later and it was better he died before hurting more people.

He chalked it up to karma, reaping what you sow. The Loupcroix legacy would be of self-destruction; caught in a desperate fantasy spouted by the regime of a genocidal madman from the words of an unknown author. Nothing good came of such ideas, only more broken lives.

His forehead was burning. A strong tingling sensation raked across his frontal lobes. A horrible scream echoed from above. Idaho clutched his head and gritted his teeth as his temples tightened, like a bad migraine. As the pain intensified, a menagerie of visions drilled though his mind.

A dead sun, a black light upon the world. The cold one who was an abomination amongst its kind. The king of the wastes, a being of terrible beauty. He will penetrate the world in a blaze of light across the sky. Dimensional disruption will continue the invasion of this reality.

Come on...we have to go home...we need to go...

The pain stopped as soon as it started. Panting heavily, Idaho dry-heaved over the side of the cot. He would have nightmares when he was younger from the myths Montana would tell him, but nothing like this. He felt a pit open in his stomach. Maybe there was real power in what Montana created. Rust Springs was in grave danger.

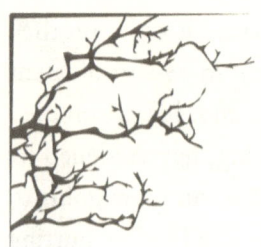

Chapter 52

Ash awoke to the sound of flowing water. The cold on his bare skin and soreness in his muscles struck his nerves. He smelled and tasted blood in his mouth. Tossed leaves covered his naked form. Ash frantically stood and wiped his face. Crusted blood was all over his chin and jaw. Looking down he saw scratch marks and dirt covering his arms, legs, and abdomen. He shivered as he tried to remember how he got to the springs. A thick fog settled over the woods and the rust-colored waters of the river.

The light he saw. Ash recalled; heart racing from the memory. He also was reminded of the pain he felt afterwards. It was the same pain as when he came home alone, and had that disturbing dream of the men at the train depot. He could not shake the feeling that those past experiences were connected to his current predicament. The blood was unpleasant, but not entirely unwelcome by him. It coated his hands and crusted underneath his nails. A morbid thought passed through his mind.

Did he kill someone and not remember?

Ash hoped this was not the case. His nose wasn't broken. Maybe he was injured some other way? The scratches were superficial, not capable of producing much blood. He gritted his teeth as the possibility of murder seemed more apparent. With no clothes, how was he going to get back home? Fear of the uncertainty settled in his soul.

Ash walked down stream. He knew there was a small campground with telephones. He could get help; call Jasper. Attila would be a better option, as Ash did not trust Jasper at the moment.

He was sure there was something twisted going on inside that house. The vibes surrounding the property set his hair on end.

He couldn't go back there again. Not until he figured out what was wrong with him. He tripped over something heavy and solid.

"Shit!"

He fell on his face. He could see the outline of a body and some antlers through the mist. Upon closer inspection, he could see it was a dead deer. Its throat had been torn and its brown fur was marred with angry red lacerations. What could have done that to an animal? He'd never seen anything like it before, even during his stint as roadkill cleanup. While his rational mind was offering different explanations, something deeper inside told Ash this was by his hand. *Outrunning the buck, he clawed the creature. In pain and fear, it ran upstream until he grabbed it by the throat with his teeth. The graceful animal died from its wounds. He was disoriented and tired after his ordeal. Water would quench his thirst. He wrinkled his nose at the stream; it smelled foul and impure. That's when it dawned on him, the veil lifting on his mind. His body was wrong; his eyes were not his own. His body was malformed and strange to him, causing him mental anguish. It was as if his human conscience broke through when he saw his shadowy reflection in the water, reviled by the horror of what he had become.*

Ash stood still, shell-shocked by his resurging memories. Revulsion mixed with desire, as he licked his bloody lips. Reality was crashing all around him. Who was he? What was he? Did he even know anymore? He closed his eyes and screamed. It was that echoing unhinged sound. Ash's spine cracked, making him fall to his hands and knees.

It's starting again. In horror, his body changed. Tears were in his eyes; he could only focus on the pain the transformation was causing him. Ash eventually faded to the recesses of his mind as something otherworldly and primitive took over.

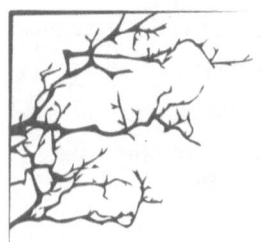

Chapter 53

Calvin Clarkson tapped away on the beige keyboard at his office computer. He was putting the final touches on his website update; a little blog post to his congregation about the necessity of unity, along with a warning about the dark times to come. He'd heard news of what occurred at The Grotto and rumors of Devon Grayhart's demise. Satan was coming through the workings of these occult-influenced groups. The Accuser was using his black magic to corrupt the minds of the cynical, the devious, and the impressionable. The end was nigh, and the Devil and his legions would bring about the prophecy as stated in Revelations.

He pressed *enter*, posting the new blog entry for the ministry's website. He leaned back in his chair. He watched the fan blades turning overhead. Calvin was reminded of the lack of air conditioning on that dry, hot night in New Mexico eight years ago.

...

Albuquerque, New Mexico, 1989.

"Thank you, Albuquerque! You have been amazing tonight!" Calvin cried out to the audience enthusiastically as they cheered. He quickly exited the stage, eager to grab a drink of water after an energetic sermon.

"Calvin?" It was his one of his many old female assistants, Cindy.

"Hi, Cindy. How did I do?" Calvin reached for the ice-cold pitcher.

"There is a woman who wishes to see you. I put her in the break room." Calvin continued to drink. He put the glass down and followed Cindy to the recreation room in the small local church.

Calvin adjusted the collar on his suit due to the stuffy heat of the room. It was mid-July and the sweltering desert climate was relentless. Calvin saw a petite Mexican woman sitting alone by herself by some ping-pong tables.

"Hello, miss? Are you the one who requested to speak with me?"

"Yes, Pastor Clarkson." the woman said tearfully. "My name is Maria Valdez. I'm here on behalf of my daughter, Crystal."

"What does Crystal need from me?"

"S-She was part of that death cult, near the border. Y-you probably saw it on the news." the woman whispered. Calvin's spirits sank. He *did* see the news report. All of those people were brutally murdered on the ranch. In the name of some pagan entity, whose worship involved human sacrifice. If there was proof of evil in this world, that cult was the smoking gun.

"Yes, I have heard of it. She was involved with the cult you say?"

Maria's tears fell down her face.

"Yes, yes. I couldn't believe it myself, when I found out. My daughter was such a sweet girl, from a good family. We've had our issues over the last three years, but I could never imagine she would turn to this..." she wailed.

Calvin, having compassion and sympathy for the grieving mother, embraced her. Her tears permeated his shirt like warm rain droplets. Calvin was at loss for words. What could he say? How could you console a parent who lost their child to demons?

...

A soft knock snapped him back into the present. Calvin straightened up as the door creaked open.

"Pastor Clarkson, we are ready to hear you speak." Kathy told him.

He arose and made the trek to the chapel area. Even now, he could perceive the blasphemous forces that threatened Rust Springs. As with Crystal Valdez, he could sense the spirits of insanity, fear, and doom surrounding Devon Grayhart before he disappeared. It was the signature of those otherworldly forces that tainted the beauty of God's creation. He would not stand for it. Calvin's congregation was waiting patiently for him. It was a packed house tonight. He took his place behind the podium.

"Good evening." he addressed them, "Back in 1989, I was traveling cross-country during a tour to share the word of God with others. I was in Albuquerque, and Cindy told me of a woman who wanted to meet me after the show. Her name was Maria Valdez, mother of Crystal Valdez. Crystal was involved with the death cult in Luna County."

Some in the crowd broke into audible whispers at the mention of the incident.

"Crystal took part in the killing and dismemberment of 30 people on that desert ranch. It was considered the most disturbing and disgusting slayings in the history of this nation. They worshiped a death god, which some anthropologists say predates the Aztecs, whose worship demands the flesh and blood of animals and humans alike. For decency's sake, I won't go into elaborate detail concerning the ceremonies. Maria asked me to meet with her daughter in prison. I agreed if it would allow them some comfort and closure in this chapter of their life. Remember, Jesus's salvation denies no one. He washed away the sins for *all* of us, amen."

The crowd resounded with an "amen" in turn.

"When I met Crystal, she was dead. Not in the physical sense, but in the spiritual. Her eyes were dull, no light what so ever. No joy, no love. I only saw darkness and pain. She was deeply disturbed as you can imagine. It took her a while to respond to me and when she did..."

Calvin paused for effect.

"It was unbelievable. She cursed me, spit at me, growling and snarling. If she wasn't restrained, I have no doubt she would have attacked me. During her tantrum, the presence of the Holy Spirit was at my back. I could also feel, contrary to its warmth and love, the cold manifestation of those demons that plagued her. I prayed, laying my hands on her. She wriggled and writhed violently, but I was able to calm her with the authority of the Spirit. I have never felt anything like that, folks, in all my years of serving the Lord. I'll never forget it."

Some of the women were tearing up.

"That day, Crystal was saved. She is still serving time, but ministering at the jail's chapel. My staff and I have met Devon Grayhart, an ex-member of the Storm-Star cult. God rest his soul. He gave off the same energy Crystal did, and he left me a very unsettling message before he died. He said the Lodge are all for bringing about a new world order and self-annihilation. This is what they believe! What's the difference between Luna and the Lodge? Very little in the way of their core teachings. These people follow false gods whose goal is destruction and desecration of all that is good in this world!" Calvin shouted the last line in righteous indignation. "And they have come to Rust Springs. Our town! Our home!"

The congregation shouted in outrage, the din reverberating their energy back to Calvin. He clutched the cherry wood podium and raised his fist.

"I, for one, will not stand for this! These occult groups are a destructive force in our society, and a proof of Satan's plan for this world. This is 1997! We could be facing the rapture come 2000! But what these wicked groups don't know is that we are the children of God. We will not be here when the years of darkness arrive, but in heaven alongside Jesus. Be vigilant, my friends, for this is our great tribulation!"

The crowd cheered with a standing ovation. The new millennium was coming soon, and they could see how modern society was leading to a great decline in morality and tradition. They were filled with encouragement from Calvin's ministry, but also a great fear of what the future had in store.

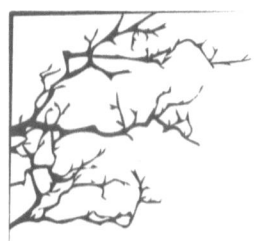

Chapter 54

Attila awoke to find the spot beside him was empty. He thought nothing of it. Daisy must have gotten up already.

"Daisy? Daze?" he called out, stretching on the bed. There was no response. Odd. His pulse quickened slightly, harboring a bad feeling. Attila knew it was likely nothing, but instinct told him otherwise. Something was off.

Once downstairs, he could see Daisy was nowhere to be found. He walked to the front window of the house. Her car was gone. Paranoia kicked in.

It was not like her to leave without informing him where she would be. The phone rang in the living room.

"Hello?" Attila answered.

"Hello, Attila." a male voice sneered.

"Who is this?"

"Attila!" Daisy shouted, sounding distant. "They are keeping me at the old farm!-"

"Daisy! What-!" Attila yelled, not liking the scared tone of her voice. His greatest fear was confirmed.

"If you want her back, come and get her." the male voice said. The call died.

"Fuck!" Attila slammed the phone receiver. He knew who was on the other line. "Dammit, Daze."

He checked the gun safe, noticing only his pistol was left. He grabbed it, not exactly sure what to do next. He had to find Ash. His strange friend hadn't called him back. It sounded like the Loupcroix were targeting them. Lucy was out of town. Radimir was in the hospital under surveillance. Grabbing the phone, he called Vasquez. The phone rang, but no answer came.

"Shit!" he exclaimed out of frustration. It looked like he was on his own. He hoped Daisy was safe, praying to a god he didn't believe in for her protection.

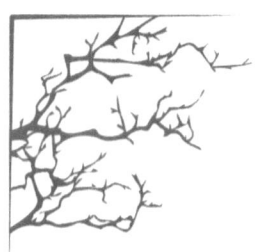

Chapter 55

"What are we doing here again? We've been monitoring this road for hours now, and I haven't seen a single car pass though here."

Stockden surveyed the snowy mist. Cooper was right. There was no one on this backwoods country road besides them. He was hungry, and tired of Cooper's constant whining.

"I don't know, Coop. Why don't you ask those crazy-shit Nazi's what they think? After all, they could be on to us." Stockden teased. He doubted his joking statement internally. They were in plain clothes and an unmarked vehicle after all. He was sure the cultists had no idea of their presence.

"Ugh, don't even joke it! I'm freaked out by all of the messed-up crap going on around here." Cooper groaned.

"Freaky stuff? Like what?"

"Ya'know me. I ain't the religious type, but Pastor Clarkson might be on to something with that supernatural stuff – "

"C'mon, Coop. You can't trust a guy like that! There're hundreds of these apocalyptic know-it-alls in full force these days. All I hear about is that Y2K bullcrap and the "end of days". Besides, the computers can't all crash simultaneously. Shoot, I hope not. I'm thinking of getting some stock in those online companies."

"It's not just him. Some people said they saw a comet a couple of nights ago and the Northern Lights. There ain't no auroras in Ohio."

"Astrological abnormalities? I wouldn't put much into it."

"And the murders." Cooper continued. "They've died down some, but there is a whole lot of wild theories about what's been killing people around here."

"Tell me more." Stockden said sarcastically. Cooper was oblivious to the tone.

"Anderson, who runs the café, says it's some sort of experiment from Hangar 59 on the air base – maybe an extraterrestrial. To Gloria Shatner, who lost her daughter, it's the Michigan Dogman."

"How would a monster come from Michigan to Ohio? Kind of a long walk." Stockden asked.

"The weirdest theory comes from Mr. Chow, who runs the Chinese restaurant downtown. He's real skittish about the comet..."

"Oh?"

"Yeah. Anderson told me that Chow was saying something about a "great calamity" and would shout a Chinese phrase every so often. Sometimes in the middle of the dining room."

"Crazy." Stockden admitted.

"Yeah, this town has lost its mind. People are afraid to go out at night. Well, except for the streetwalkers of course."

"If their johns are scared, I don't see how they're making that much money. But, I guess it's like they say: desperate bastards will do anything for pussy." Stockden snickered. Cooper laughed with him at the vulgar statement.

BLAM! BLAM!

Two shotgun blasts in short succession quieted Cooper's laughter, blowing holes in his chest and head. Stockden reached for his gun as his friend's blood and brain matter splattered across his face. He rolled out of the car, his face landing near a pair of boots. He barely lifted his head when he was shot three times in the back. The sharp pain prevented him from drawing a breath as his attackers talked to each other.

"Damn, Wash, you got him good!" one man said.

"Heh, well, it's like flushing." the shooter said, "You're the dog that startled the prey. I'm the hunter that takes the shot."

"I – uh – shot the other pig though."

"Whatever, bitch." the man called Wash growled. "Check the cruiser for anything important. I'll dump the bodies. We gotta get Idaho next."

The man grabbed Stockden by his jacket. The blood from his chest was warm against his cold skin. Being moved was agony to his wounded body. Stockden let out a shallow gasp.

"Still alive, huh?" the man asked him. "Don't worry, you'll join your friend soon."

Stockden groaned as he was carried a little ways away from the car, and dropped unceremoniously behind some dry shrubs. He grunted at the pain of being dropped on the ground. His eyesight was getting blurry and tunneled. He was knocking on death's door, bleeding out. Cooper's corpse was placed on top of him. He could barely see the destroyed face of his dead partner. A cool breeze rustled the brush as he breathed his last breath.

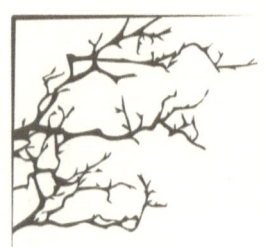

Chapter 56

Attila could only look to the dismal horizon as he drove into the outskirts of Rust Springs. Panic settled heavily in his stomach, envisioning Daisy's fate. He pulled over on an isolated forested road on the outer limits of the city. He clutched the steering wheel, knuckles whitening from his tight grip. She had to be at the compound; it was the only conclusion that made sense. The cult killed Devon, and now they would be after her in retaliation. Why did he stop?

He had an inkling where she would be, but he was not sure of himself and his ability to fight for her. He hoped Vasquez got his message. He would help; more likely scold him for running off half-cocked like this. Attila stepped out of the car, considering his next steps. His club was in shambles, his staff in the hospital and the love of his life was gone.

"Damn! Damn! Damn!" Attila cried as he banged his fist on the hood of his car. He did not notice the rustling of brush until he heard the low snarl. Attila looked towards the direction of the noise. A large animal revealed itself.

Its liver-piebald body was large and gangly. Strange crystalline spines poked out its body, and the fangs gleamed like diamonds. Attila choked on his scream as the creature charged. The beast barked as it rushed, nearly sliding into the BMW. Attila dodged, losing his footing and falling on to the cold ground. The creature skulked towards him, resting a large paw between Attila's splayed legs. The man could only utter a whimper at his impending death.

The beast paused, as its lanky frame quaked. With a shriek, it retreated a couple of paces to collapse and convulse on the ground. Attila was fixated on the awful display, as the body morphed before him. Fur receded and the muzzle shortened, while canine legs transformed into human forearms. His face quickly changed to a frozen horror when the creature's body began to twist and writhe unnaturally. Attila gawked at the insane transformation as the dog's form stretched, bled, and broke at sharp angles. Filthy fur was shed and wounds knitted together.

"Ash?"

He was starting to see the young man underneath the creature's form. A half-human scream erupted from the now nude and sickly-looking Ash. Attila, ignoring his instincts to run, crawled towards his friend.

"Ash!" he cried as fingers dug into disrupted earth, not knowing what to do. Delirious, Ash swiped at him when Attila tried to touch him.

"Ash! Ash, please - calm down!" Attila grabbed Ash in a bear-hug. The younger man struggled, but eventually stilled as he became more aware of his surroundings.

"Ash?" Attila didn't know what to make of the surreal situation. Ash did not respond; stuck in his position and choking on air. Attila rummaged through his car, finding a raggedy blanket to provide Ash some modesty and warmth. He carried him into the backseat of the car. Ash lied there in a comatose trance, unresponsive to Attila's touch. Attila gazed over the pale body. Bruises and scars created patchwork all over him.

"Poor kid." Attila bit his lower lip. He was sorry for whatever Ash was going through. All he wanted to do was help him. Ash's breathing steadied. His eyes opened.

"Attila?" Ash gasped. The nightclub owner perked up.

"Yeah, it's me, kid. How are you doing?"

"What happened? I'm sore all over..."

"You tell me. I saw a monster one minute and your naked butt the next."

"Ah." Memories trickled back to Ash. "I ...I'm a ... All I can get are glimpses of its killing, but it's like it's not me...Oh God!" Ash jolted upright, blanket falling to his hips. He was in danger. "I gotta get out!" He tried to grasp the door handle, but Attila grabbed him.

"Calm the hell down!" Attila pulled Ash against him. "Believe me; I'm fucking freaked out, but we are not gonna get anywhere unless we stop to connect the dots."

"You don't understand!" Ash screamed, on the verge of tears.

"Then make me, Ash! Give me something!"

"I'm a killer...a fucking murderer! I don't know how, but I am. I thought they were dreams but they're real – and I don't know how to stop! I have no control!" Ash cried, his slim frame shaking from fearful frustration. Attila glanced outside the window. Snowfall drifted softly on the dreary dead cornfields.

"Do you think...Jasper is a part of this?"

Ash sniffed.

"Maybe? Why?"

"Reason with me here. Your physical quirks, his mysterious illness...now that I think about it, he never mentioned any family to me or the interest in looking for them."

"He told me everyone else is dead, except mom. I don't know where she went."

"Do you remember anything about her at all?"

"Little things here and there. Like her hair and her voice."

"Did she ever do anything abnormal? I know you were young..."

"The only thing strange I remember was her abandonment. I remember the house being a mess, like someone tore it apart. I was scared of the growling too."

"Growling?"

"Yeah, like I thought something attacked mom at first and killed her. I remember being scared to leave my closet. Social workers told me an animal made it into our house, looking for food or something. Maybe it was her. Maybe she was like me..."

Attila considered Ash's account. The common factor was family, namely, Jasper.

"Jasper's been quiet lately. What has he been up to?" Attila asked Ash.

"He's either been bed ridden or going on errands late at night. I've been noticing; the next day, a body turns up. When that last killing occurred, I saw Raini and Stormi– with another dog – and the pain. Last night was different; there was a strange blue light in the basement. Then the pain, and now I am here. I think I killed a deer last night too..."

"That's a lot. You didn't suspect something fishy?" Ash shook his head, looking forlorn. Attila bit his tongue.

"Sorry, kid. I'm just worried about Daisy."

"Where is she?"

"I don't know. She left sometime late last night. Been trying to find her."

A visible tremor coursed through Attila's body as he remembered the attack. Snow flurries blew into the car, providing a cold mist.

"Here, wear this." Attila passed a grey sweatshirt and pants to Ash. "It's cold out here."

Ash put them on gingerly. The outfit was baggy on him, meant to fit Attila's larger frame.

"Everything is at the house with Jasper."

Reluctance crossed Ash's features. Attila took notice.

"You don't want to go."

"I don't trust him."

Attila stepped out and got into the driver's seat.

"What do you wanna do, man?"

Ash re-covered himself and hunched forward in the seat.

"No, I'm tired of not getting answers and I'm tired of running. I have to face this. I have to confront Jasper." Attila started the car and headed for the farmlands that lied on the outskirts of Rust Springs.

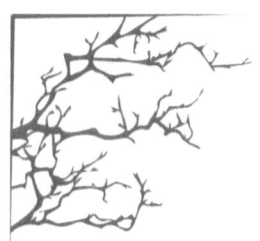

Chapter 57

Idaho wriggled his wrists against the cool steel cuffs. They were uncomfortable, and irritated his skin.

"Here, I brought you some cocoa." the female officer passed a hot paper cup. Idaho mumbled a small thanks upon receiving the drink. The contents were warm in his hands, as the snow fell steadily to the ground. The scene took him back to a cherished memory held as a young boy: Christmas in Seattle. The splendor of the city's holiday lights captured his imagination as a child. What he adored most of all, was seeing the Space Needle lit in a splendorous way; piercing the sky as it shone brighter than the stars. Wyoming and Colorado were with him along with father and mother. Dad gave them hot chocolate from a coffee shop.

Idaho brought the cup to his lips. He took of a sip of the delicious warmth. The cocoa was not as rich as he had hoped, and burned his tongue slightly.

Going into the city was a rare event for the family. Dad hated the environment of a bustling metropolis, and disliked the increased presence of minorities. Still, he managed for this one night, before they moved into the inner wilderness of Washington state. Idaho never knew another home again, due to the constant traveling and moving.

"You sure you don't want to go back inside? It's pretty damn cold, if I don't say so myself." The policewoman zipped up her coat.

"Nah, it's better than being locked up." Idaho took another sip. The officer looked slightly sheepish, as if forgetting; he had been in the cell most of the time.

"I-I understand."

Idaho ignored her, lost in his memories inside the confines of the parking lot. The concrete he sat upon dampened the back of his windbreaker. It was cold and uncomfortable, but he needed some breathing room. There was a section of the lot that was blocked off. It was where Traynor died, according to whispers from his brothers and the news around the station. The various law enforcement vehicles were covered in a coating of fine snow. They would likely be off chasing the Lodge soon.

"They're gonna raid the place, aren't they?" he asked aloud.

"Excuse me?" the officer questioned.

"The compound? It's today right?"

"I can't answer that, sir."

"Thank Vasquez for me, will ya? I know he's busy but thank him for letting me come out here. I was going crazy in there–"

A loud engine roared over his voice. The wind blew stronger as snow fell heavier. Tires squealed as the padlocked chain-linked gate burst open; headlights glowing bright as search lights. The flash of gunfire erupted over Idaho's head, hitting the wall behind him. A thump resounded where the policewoman once stood. Ducking, Idaho looked over his shoulder. Blood stained brilliantly across the fresh snow, as the woman lay dead on the ground. A car door clicked open and he saw Oregon. He snatched up Idaho and placed him inside the truck.

"Shut the door! Let's move!" Washington yelled beside him. Sitting up in the small back seat, Idaho saw Oregon wielding a rifle; climbing into the front of the Suburban. Washington pulled off before Oregon could even shut the passenger door.

"What the fuck are you guys doing?" Idaho was both angry and despaired that he was back in the custody of his crazed family.

"What does it look like we are doing, little brother?" Washington inquired back. "You have a role to fulfill."

"You're not serious?"

"Deadly. No turning back now."

The blue Suburban was roaring down Main Street. Zero visibility was on the horizon. A storm was eminent. Thunder cracked through the sky after bold, blue veins of lightning. The wails of sirens were not too far behind.

"Wash, this ain't good..." Oregon protested, "The cops and the feds are gonna have us surrounded."

"Like it matters." Washington responded, "After today, nothing will."

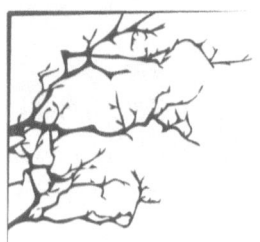

Chapter 58

Attila parked his car off the road a few yards from the house in order to avoid alerting others to their presence. Ash stepped out barefoot on the snow.

"Man, I would hate for you to get frost bite." Attila said.

"I can handle it." Ash replied. "The cold doesn't bother me."

The two men trekked the old country road, stopping when they could see the old farmhouse. No one was loitering outside, not even the dogs. The house was dark; no lights illuminating the interior. The hair on the back of Ash's neck stood up. He could sense it. An underlying familiarity to the house, or more precise, what he could detect inside it. The feeling of coming home. His rational mind was confused and scared by these sentiments, but something primal inside embraced it. It gave him peace, something he never had in his life. He moved forward, thankful he had clothes on. Ash was only vaguely aware of Attila's protests to stay put. It was dangerous, but he did not care. He knew it would all be revealed to him, once he crossed the snow-dusted lawn.

The screen door on the porch creaked open. The wood floor was wet from the snow. He was hesitant to open the door to the house, unsure what lay in wait for him on the other side. A shuffling sound from indoors caught his attention. It sounded like bare feet. He pushed the door open with such a force to make it slam against the wall. He could hear wall hangings rattle from the impact. Ash's nerves were buzzing. He grabbed an umbrella from the hall tree, as a means of self-defense. Eyes scanning the room for threats; he crept towards the basement. A crash from downstairs made him pause for a second. The blue light appeared again, radiating from underneath the door. Ash was surprised the door was unlocked, deadbolts unsecured. He creaked the door open. It was pitch black, save for a sapphire glow, pulsating like a beacon in the dark sea. Clawed hands accosted him. They were pale and spotted; nails filthy and yellow. Ash struggled in the grip, trying to pry the hands off of him. He managed to get free only to lose his balance and fall down the stairs. Sliding on the steps, Ash wheezed as he hit the concrete floor; bruising his ribs. His eyes tried to adjust to the darkness, making out two human shapes. One was hunched and the other was familiar to him.

"Nice of you to join us, Ash." Jasper snarled.

Stormi and a hunched spotted figure huddled together in the dim light. It looked dirty with scraggly hair. Its skin was stained with bruise-like markings. Human, yet long nails and a mouth full of fangs, denoted otherwise. It peered at him with cold, animal eyes.

The urge to attack rose within Ash although he had no means to do so. He was weak and injured. He settled for snarling, regressing to the back of his mind, due to the fear and shock.

"I see our blood has a pull on you." Jasper sat the fang on the wood workbench, the sapphire blue fang pulsing softly.

"Too bad your mother, Naomi, couldn't make the reunion. At least I have her wretched spawn."

"What? Mom?" Ash gasped through growls.

"You don't know, boy?" Jasper asked, "She was one of us, like your cousins."

Ash blankly stared at Raini and Stormi. The second figure moved towards Ash, making unnatural and twitchy movements. Ash cringed with fear when he saw the figure in the light. It was indeed human but mutated. The skin was pale with black spots staining it. The hair was black and messy. The hands and nails were bestial, like the ones that grabbed him. The spine was hunched in a way that mimicked a beast, something meant to crawl on four legs. Worst of all was the amber eyes, wild and mournful at the same time. A silver tag glinted around its neck, a dog tag. Ash wished it was a sick joke, but he looked upon this atrocity and knew the truth.

This twisted thing was his kin, his flesh and blood.

"Pretty isn't she? She wasn't the day her and her brother were born. Crooked bastards. They took the life of their own mother. I could never forgive them for that. I could have snuffed the life out of them you know. But I-I couldn't do it." Jasper looked crazed as he explained their backstory; hair stringy and eyes wild. "They took everything I cared about from me! But, they will served their purpose!"

The twins cowered at the angry outburst. Ash was clueless of what his uncle was referencing. Instead, he focused on the strange jagged stone sitting on the work table. It was fairly long, its blue tone reminding Ash of a deep ocean. Looking closer, he could see something wet and slimy pooling around the gem and trailing off the table. It pulsated slightly, as if it was alive and breathing.

"But I planned and waited, learning about our history from your grandfather." Jasper explained, showing off the sharp blue crystal. "The sheer cosmic irony that would lead me to gaining this fang from that misguided vagabond, no less."

Ash was unsure what was going on, sensing himself receding again. The light grew, building a heavy pressure in the air.

"Cut from the same cloth, you manifested soon enough. I had to lie and clean your filthy body in the aftermath."

Jasper pulled up his sleeves, pulling out a linoleum knife.

"Feed into my pain, my sorrow, my hate...my love."

Blood streamed from him, flowing quickly down his arms. At the same time, bone and flesh ruptured from the fangs. Stormi crawled towards Jasper; Ash repulsed by the sight of her form. The agony he was experiencing now befell his mother, losing herself in the trappings of the Jagerhund genetics. The veiny sinews consumed Stormi, who whined in pain and fear. It was not long before she became part of the flesh mass. The fleshy abomination latched to Jasper at the spine, piercing him.

Ash's body began to transform again in reaction to the horror, teeth and nails lengthening to fangs and claws. What was in his blood was ablaze, ready to strike. All he could hear was Stormi's yelps and Jasper's mad laughter.

Jasper took off his long-sleeved sweater. The grey striped fabric lifted to reveal extensive scaring over his body. Jasper turned around, showing his back to Ash. Spots, not unlike the ones present on Stormi and Raini, but with differing colors. Scabs and burn marks obscured some of the markings, which tapered downwards to the waist.

"See this? This is the stigma the Jagerhund line bears!" Jasper spat, venom in his voice.

Stormi growled, her voice wavering as its pitch lowered. Her body quivered as she morphed, body enlarging and bones snapping and reforming. Fur spread evenly and a tail sprouted. Stormi's jaws unhinged abnormally, and uttered a sharp cry. The gem's strange growths attached themselves to her and Jasper. The prehensile appendages bounded Stormi and pulled her towards the glistening flesh mass, combining the two together. Tears formed in Ash's eyes as he heard her shrieks of agony, as her body was torn and consumed and absorbed by his uncle. Raini paced in the dark corner of the basement. Jasper's resolve was steel.

"I shall bring an end to our disastrous bloodline. We lie outside the laws of nature – we shouldn't exist!" Jasper roared, mutating slowly into a two-headed monster. Raini raced toward the step. The cerulean light dimmed after Stormi was consumed, casting the underground room into deeper darkness. Ash closed his eyes as the change overtook him. His senses heightened; consciousness fading into a primordial pool.

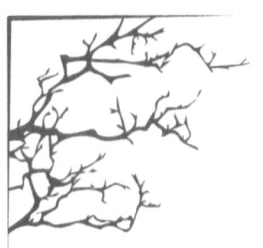

Chapter 59

Attila, 9mm in hand, silently strode across the snowy lawn. He cursed himself for not following Ash inside the house. At the time, he was afraid of the foreboding presence coming from the property; god-smacked that Ash would walk willingly into such a place. Yet here he was, creeping up the porch steps. He could hear an awful commotion; yelling and screaming. Attila considered his best means of entry as he advanced. Something in the basement was going nuts. Leaning against the front door, he could hear ghastly, ungodly noises inside.

The front door was as good as any, he guessed. The door creaked open. Inside the foyer, Attila heard a cacophony of snarling and ripping coming from the open basement. He sneaked down the hallway, peering into the basement abyss. A foul stench wafted to his nostrils, filling him with fear. Attila covered his mouth and nose with his dark duster, trying to avoid the need to vomit. The dreadful miasma was more pronounced than outside, making Attila gag. He cringed at the howls and screams.

"*Fuck. I can't...*" Attila told himself. He was reluctant to proceed any further. He couldn't do it. He couldn't face what was down there. Primal fear consumed him.

"*Still not too late to back out.*" his inner voice told him, "*This isn't your fight.*"

He lowered his weapon. In what seemed like a spilt second, he made his decision. Ash wasn't blood. He hadn't even known the kid a month. Still, Ash grew on him as an employee. As far as he was concerned, he was family. Besides, he had a bone to pick with Jasper about his deception. Daisy and Ash were depending on him.

If he couldn't help them, who would?

Gripping his glock, he descended the dark pit with as much courage as he could muster. Black oblivion gave into dark, sapphire-blue color as he carefully crept down the creaky stairs.

Ash convulsed on the floor. The young man's body looked awful in the dim light. His friend looked foreign to him; a half-formed mass.

Attila could hear Jasper say something; however the pained animal screams and loud thrashing muffled his voice.

"What the hell?"

Stepping closer, he could see a decrepit, hunched figure at the top of the stairs. It only remotely looked human to Attila, who could only stare dumbly as the thing lumbered down the stairs.

He stopped midway when he saw outlines of bestial figures locked in violent struggle. He could not see who was who. He saw a jagged, blue gem on a workbench. They were surrounded by a slimy substance that writhed and crawled around it. The sick smell was overbearing here; truly the source of the foul stench.

"Give in, Ash! Our demise is nigh! Don't fight fate!" a monstrous voice growled.

A thin string brushed Attila across his face. He pulled, hoping for a light source. When the bright bulb lit the room, Attila's hope dissolved into mortified regret. Regret tinged with the same fear from the parking garage.

"Attila! You-!" someone growled, enraged at the unwanted intrusion. It sounded like Jasper, if barely. Attila couldn't recognize his own friend. Expecting to see the man, he instead saw a two-headed monstrous imposter. The mongrel thing terrified him; shrinking back to the stairs.

Rawwwr!!!

Something leapt at Attila from the side; his peripheral vision catching the movement from the right. He fired a shot at Raini, hitting him in the chest. The dog made a garbled sound; deterred from attacking for a second time. Ash took the opening and leapt towards Raini's exposed throat. The fangs found their target, crimson droplets drenching Ash and the ground below. Raini lashed out wildly, clawing to get his attacker off this neck. The beast roared in pain and anger. Attila, encouraged to help his friend, fired another shot at Raini. The dog was hit in the left eye. He was stunned; not expecting to have good aim with his shaking hands.

Attila was knocked over by Jasper, snarling in his face. He tried to shake him off, but Jasper's grip was like a vice. The man's, if he could be called that now, face morphed into a disgusting shape. Curled horns ripped through his skull as talons ruptured through his nail beds, piercing into Attila's skin. His spotted hide was gangly, yet large and strong, with scrappy, spotted fur. His *other head* twisted wildly, snapping at empty air. Jasper looked like a true hellhound. Attila closed his eyes. This was it? Dying by the hand of a former friend, a man he thought he knew? He could feel Jasper's hot breath, and hear the terrible noises coming from Ash and Raini.

Below he could see Ash, stuck in a half-animal form, combating a grotesquely augmented yet weakened Raini. The spotted dog Attila had become familiar with over the years was now a long and bipedal humanoid; raking Ash with lengthy nails listlessly. Blood splattered against the wooden walls, which were covered in unknown diagrams and patterns. Raini shrieked as Ash tore into him violently, ending his miserable existence.

Jasper gave an annoyed snarl, releasing Attila while slapping his nephew away. The tentacles reached out and attached to Raini's corpse, pulling it toward Jasper. The dog was disintegrated as he merged with his father. It was hard to believe that Jasper, the kind soul Attila remembered, was now this viscous monster. Ash was strong, but no match against his uncle. Heart wrenching screams echoed as Jasper's larger form ripped into him.

Ash slipped on the fluids and blood, causing him to lose footing. Jasper rose his mangled paw to push Ash to the floor. On his back, Ash was vulnerable to the assault by his deranged uncle.

The tendrils of the pulsating gem embedded themselves into Jasper, augmenting his power. Staying to the wall, Attila crept towards the workbench. The light of the gem was blinding. He tentatively reached out for the fang. It burned, but left no mark. The current flowed through him, filling him with unfamiliar strength. If it wasn't so alien and frightening to him, it would have been somewhat pleasurable.

Seeing Ash getting pummeled sent him into a berserk rage. With a great cry, he charged Jasper and pierced the demonic beast's side with the fang. The light bulb shattered overhead due to the influx of the strange energy. Jasper groaned, rearing up on his hind legs. Ash rose and clamped down on Jasper's neck, clawing at his abdomen. Flames reputed around Jasper, causing Ash to back off. The ethereal fire burned Jasper and the remains of his children. Nothing was left of them. The fang dissolved to dust, killing the fire. Ash crouched on the ground, panting heavily.

Ash slowly reverted to human form. The process deeply unsettled Attila, turning his back to the sight. He crawled back towards the nearest wall, searching for some concrete comfort. He quaked as the leftover adrenaline and confusion took control. The unreality of the situation consumed him.

"Shit, fuck!" he cried as he dug his fingers into his scalp. A groan came from the far end of the room.

"Ash?" he called, remembering his friend. His hands searched for Ash, unable to see with his eyes. Attila had given up on finding his gun. The desire to find the kid and leave was his only objective. A brush of soft, wet hair against his palm told him he had achieved his goal.

"Ash?" he grabbed the body. Bare skin told him the young man had reverted to human form.

"Hmm?" Ash mumbled.

"Hey, hey. Are you okay?"

"Yeah, just a little bruised I think." Ash whispered. Attila heard a soft gasp.

"W-What-Where's Jasper?" Ash's panic rose in his voice. Attila patted him on the back gently, trying to console his companion through his own dread.

"He's dead. At least I think he is. Honestly, I have no idea what the fuck happened here."

"That makes two of us." Attila helped Ash to his feet.

Upstairs, Ash found his clothes discarded on the floor. He quickly cleaned himself of the blood and found an outfit to wear, packing up his belongings. He took a second to rinse the blood out of his mouth. There was nothing here for him. There never was. False hopes and empty promises of a family he will never have. He sighed, slinging his duffle bag across his back. Ash was numb to the whole experience even though his belly seemed full of worms. It was as if his entire being was a traitor against him, his turncoat genetics enslaving him to a body of an abomination. In the hallway, he saw the door to Jasper's room. A surge of anger fired his nerves. He had to know what the old bastard was hiding. He dropped his bag and rushed down the hallway. The lock broke as he kicked in the door with surprising force.

The room was ravaged as if a tornado tore through it. Papers were all over the floor, those same strange patterns etched on their surface. Some blood-stained washcloths were piled on the left side of the bed. Ash inspected closer. He found several crimson-coated razor blades littered on the floor and bedside table. Drops of blood on the linens and pillows. Ash was reminded of the various scars that marred Jasper's withered form. The evidence pointed to self-harm, coupled with Jasper's statements to him; self-loathing. On the nightstand was a photograph encapsulated in a wooden frame. Jasper, who looked younger and healthier, was posed with a woman in front of the Liberty Bell. The woman, who looked around Jasper's age, was plain looking, but pretty with her bright smile. A twinge of sympathy weighed on Ash's heart. Through his fear and anger, he could grasp his uncle's agony spawned from the loss of his love; something for which he felt responsible.

Ash saw a worn leather journal sitting on the bed. It was an archaic thing; yellowed pages and all. It seemed to be journals and published material by the Lodge. Ash poured over the materials. There was something written neatly in German on a yellowed page; dated May 1930:

~...~

Schwarze Sonne, Dunkler Stern
Großer himmlischer Drache
Der Tod
Gefürchtet von seinen eigenen Artgenossen
Die Verwandten des Fenrirs
Wächter des Himmels-Tores
Du schmückst die Erde abermals
Zwischen tollwütiger Freude und rasender Angst.
Das Tier wird zum Menschen
und der Mensch wird wieder zum Tier.
Du siehst den Nidhoggr
Schwarzer Drache, der auf der Welt nagt.
Hört den Ruf in dieses Reich!
Das Licht deiner dunklen Strahlen
Erfülle mich mit dem lichtvollen Geist
Leuchte auf meinem Geist

Erleuchte mich auf deine Weise
Die Hunde des Abgrunds rufen die Verwandten von Fenrir
Der Nidhoggr-Drache
der die Welt verschlingt
Feuer und Eis in der schwarzen Nacht
Ich stehe zu den Riesen der Schöpfung

~...~

Ash couldn't understand it, except from a few words he recognized from German class in high school. On the flip-side of the page, there was a scrawled, hastily-written translation on the back:

~...~

Black Sun, Dark Star
Grand Celestial Dragon
The Dead One
Feared by his own kind
Kin of the Fenrir
Guardian of the Gate of Heaven
You grace the Earth once more
Between Rabid ecstasy and maddening fear. Beast becomes man and
man becomes beast once more.
You will see the Nidhoggr
Black dragon who chews on the world
Harken the call into this realm!
The light of your dark rays
Fill me with the light-bearing spirit
Shine upon my mind
Enlighten me in your ways
The hounds of the abyss are calling Fenrir's kin
The Nidhogg Dragon
He who devours the world
Cosmic fire and ice
I stand with the giants of creation

~...~

The text chilled him to his bones. The lore between this journal and the Storm-Star cult are aligned. One of the pages contained a barbaric print, with descriptions of what looked like a bloodletting ceremony. Descriptions of fasting and recipes for hallucinogenic substances were also included.

He flipped to the very back of the journal looking for the most recent entry:

~...~

November 11, 1992

I had come to the Blue Ridge Mountains in my native Virginia to see my father. It's been years, and I wasn't sure if we were still on good terms. Mom's death and Naomi running away strained our relationship, not that we really had one. We're still worlds apart.
He told me the truth about mother and our family. I was furious and still am. How dare he defile her!
"That is the curse of the Jagerhund line." Daddy Cain told me.
It was revealed to me I was responsible for my beloved's death. I killed her...No! We killed her. I can't forget the sin of my children. I remembered the night mother became deathly ill. It was shortly after she had Naomi. It started with a flu-like illness that worsened over the years. It was if her body was killing itself from the inside.
I gripped his leathery throat. His face was ice cold. He gripped my arm with considerable force. His face changed, flashing fangs and bestial eyes. I finally saw his true self.
He warned me about underestimating him and I believed him. He said he loved my mother and wouldn't hurt her intentionally. If he truly loved her, he wouldn't have married her. He found this journal in the cabinet. Ancient family knowledge; apparently, my only inheritance (he didn't have much to give). I was disgusted by the revelation, so I wanted to leave. Cain attacked me.

The old man was deranged, growling and scratching at me. I fell backwards on top of him and the struggling ceased. I was bleeding; he cut my face with his long nails. Cain seized on the floor and fell still. I didn't connect the dots at first, but I figured out he had a heart attack. I couldn't revive him.

The medics and police arrived on the scene asking all sort of questions, carting my father off the property. Funny thing was: I didn't feel anything. Numb in an emotional sense. When someone dies, you should hurt right? Not for me. I did the honorable thing, and stayed long enough to bury Cain next to mother in the family plot.

I got back to Ohio, the twins were waiting for me. They loafed around in their animal forms. I arranged for Attila to feed them while I was away. I keep them in their hound skins. I preferred it that way. They're blood, but they aren't human to me. They don't deserve that distinction.

I didn't deserve it.

I loathe myself above them though.

It was then, I realized the age of the book due to paper being worn and yellow. The earliest dates extended into 1800s. Most of it was German, which I don't understand the language. I flipped through the pages, searching for an English text. I got my wish from an entry from father. "I've found love at last. Her father is the local butcher. She is my mate. I know it! She doesn't know about my heritage and never will. Mother doesn't want me to tell anyone. Father was a sick man and my sister is too. She still flies into fits. I can't let her meet them. We have a reputation in this town already. I wouldn't want her to suffer that..."

But you married her anyway. She died anyway!

Naomi...she was probably miles away by now, hopefully living a stable life. Or she was dead or locked away somewhere. I hope she doesn't have children in tow. I have to track down the rest of the family. I have to find them and stop them from tainting the world further with their filthy blood.

~...~

Ash's mind was blank. There was no way he could've guessed Jasper figured out the secret to the Jagerhund bloodline. There was a side of his uncle he didn't know, cold and callous. Maybe his mother was right about leaving. Life would be much better without them.

"Yo, Ash! We gotta go!" he heard Attila from downstairs. Ash ignored him. The pages were filled with innocuous notes. Surprisingly, there were references to schedules, revolving around the Lodge's drug trade activities. Flipping to the end, Ash saw those foreign markings described with reports translated from German. An entry from seven years ago mentioned his mother.

~...~

"I had no idea that our family had a bizarre secret, as I have learned from my late father. Our family has been plagued by peculiar psychiatric and physiological conditions. Odd growths, deformities, erratic behavior...often leading to early deaths and commitments to mental wards. I guess I made it out pretty good. Dad hid his well. Naomi, though..."

"She was sort of wild. At a younger age, it could be contributed to tantrums or growing pains. It became more pronounced when she was older. Seemingly fine, her moods would suddenly change. Sometimes, she would growl or bite. She ran away as a teenager, haven't seen her since. I'm unsure what her activities have been since her abrupt departure so many years ago, but I'm certain it is the same you feel now."

~...~

The notes became more deranged afterwards, mentioning a "fang" to open "aeons":

From my research, I found them! The fangs came to me in a vision. It was instinctual. Now proper contained channeling of energy is possible. If I can access the "aeon" from which my line came, we can finally be free.

Intermingled between some of the pages, were clippings from a website: www.storm-star.com[1]

Ash considered Attila's accounts of Daisy's disappearance and the incident at the liquor store on the night of the fire. Attila described the Ripper as human, or at least humanoid, savaging its prey in a way that connoted something inhuman. The journal's imagery piqued Ash's interest, inspiring him to read it again. There was a strange allure when he touched the leather binding. To him, it was a sense of foreboding curiosity; the type that precedes discovering a terrible secret. The arcane symbols were identical to the ones in the basement, every curve and angle spelling out an unknown spiraling message. He sat on the living room sofa and he continued to review the materials. Most of it was German, but the notes that were in English were vague and laconic.

"Angle sigils around the fang, creating a cosmogram."

"Continue invocation upon dimensional rupture."

Between two of the pages was a folded piece of paper. Ash took it; carefully unfolding. It was a webpage print-out titled: "Origins of the People". The pixelated image "Diagram 1" showed an old sketch of a large black orb accompanied by a crude-looking skeletal creature. Below was some text:

"The plains of Folkvagnr remain closed to this world until the fangs pierce the veil between aeons. The fang will let the Storm-Star reveal itself to all: the worthy and unworthy. The Fenris-kin heralds its arrival. Its presence will renew the earth, cleansing it of the human filth for the white race to propagate and prosper forever."

Ash looked at the bottom of the page and saw the URL was http://www.storm-starlodge.com/prophecy. Something clicked inside of Ash's brain, seeing the connections. Jasper's goal of murdering him and the Lodge's objectives weren't the same, but

---

1. http://www.storm-star.com

come from the mythos of this book. They made contact with things beyond this world.

"Dammit, man! We gotta go! Now!" Attila yelled below. Ash, with the book in hand, ran to grab his bag. He quickly descended the stairs, meeting a pacing Attila.

"What took you so long?"

"I found this in Jasper's room." Ash flashed the book. Attila snatched it and flipped through the pages, pausing when he found a page from the Storm-Star website.

"What?" Attila, astonished that Jasper would have material from an organization he claimed to revile; staring incredulously at the find. Some sketches fell out on the floor, covered in strange symbols which seemed to illicit memories from him.

He passed the material to Attila.

"Look familiar?"

Attila skimmed over the journal and webpage with his eyes. "Other than the similarity to the shit we saw in the basement, I don't see your point."

"It's the same setup. I think Jasper wasn't entirely insane. That creature he summoned and w-what I am... it's all connected. Do you see this fang and the skeleton creature?"

Attila nodded slowly.

"Also, I think the fang, ya'know that weird stone, is the same thing that Wyoming accused Devon of stealing and looked like the same one Jasper had." Ash explained.

"Shit." Attila muttered as he followed the logic. "You think Jasper was the murderer?"

"Could be." Ash cut off; as he remembered that night those two men by the tracks were killed.

"I'm guilty too." he said internally.

"Well, maybe we can find a way to end all of this and find Daisy in the process." Attila said. He shook his head. "No. This is too crazy. Ash, everything is too crazy – these people are crazy."

"I get it! I'm fucked up over this shit too!" Ash yelled.

"I'm sorry –"

"I'm not even human!" Ash shouted over Attila. He balled his fists. "I-If there is a way to figure this crap out, we should try it. I want to understand!"

The two men remained quiet for a moment, the wintery winds howling outside.

"Okay, kid. What should we do?" he inquired. The ember of Attila's cigarette glowed like a beacon in the dim room. Ash rose to his feet.

"We need to get a hold of those fangs." he told his companion.

"I was wondering why he wanted to borrow my occult books..."

"Weird, huh? I also found some bloody razors-"

"Well, that would explain the scars..." Attila sounded remorseful. He pocketed the old journal and headed out; Ash in tow. The sky was grey with thick clouds, and snow was falling heavier.

"A storm's coming." Attila noted.

"Where are we going to go?"

"Not to the cops, that's for damn sure. I mean, how are we going to explain this crap to the law. We need to go back to my place, get some things and find Daisy."

"What happened to her anyway?" Ash asked.

"Damn, I forgot to tell you. Well, I'll explain it when we get down the road."

The BMW was covered in a blanket of snow and ice. Attila unlocked the car and started it while Ash hopped in. Slamming the doors shut, they raced on the road to Anchorage Farms.

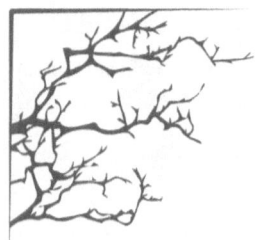

Chapter 60

C haos erupted in the station. The body of Officer Caroline Witter was dragged from the snowy, bloody pavement into the station. Government agents were gathering their tactical equipment and forces together; ready to strike.

"Idaho Loupcroix is gone. Whoever was driving that Suburban was involved." An agent paced out the route the criminal family took out of the parking lot. Luckily, burnt rubber highlighted the way boldly.

"We've got to follow them now! Has anyone heard from Stockden and Cooper?" Deane asked.

"I've been trying to contact them for a while now, but they are not responding." an officer chimed. Vasquez prayed to God the two were alright. They were good cops, and there shouldn't be any more bloodshed today.

"That's no good." Vasquez said. "The Loupcroix are on to us."

"They're a paranoid bunch. It's been hard to conduct surveillance because of it." the FBI agent noted.

"Get to the vehicles! We're ready to roll!" Carbine shouted over the noise. Immediately, personnel exited.

So much for a peaceful resolution. Directly killing a police officer and kidnapping a suspect escalated the situation. With Stockden and Cooper non-responsive, he feared the worse.

"Vasquez!" Carbine called, "We need you on the scene. Get in my car." Vasquez followed the senior agent, anxious about what was about to transpire. Snow was pelting him outside. The thick clouds

were black, and the air was misty. The ominous rumbling of thunder
could be heard in the distance.

"In this weather, sir?" Vasquez questioned Carbine cautiously.
The weather for this time of year is unprecedented and unusual.
In all of his years he lived in Ohio, Vasquez could not remember
a thundersnow occurring. A simultaneous thunderstorm and
snowstorm could prove an obstacle or an advantage, if they could
navigate in it effectively. "Also, considering what the Lodge believed,
I doubt they will go peacefully."

"Too late. The Loupcroix demonstrated their contempt for the
authority of the law and those who enforce it. It's time to act –
before someone else gets injured or killed." Carbine told him. "The
ATF and DEA are on their way, considering the activities of the
Storm-Star group."

"Understood." Vasquez answered. He sighed as he entered the
black van. There was nothing that could be helped. It was destined
that the Loupcroix got into a confrontation with who they hated the
most: the U.S. Government. Leaving the familiarity of downtown
Rust Springs, Vasquez embarked with his colleagues into unfamiliar
territory.

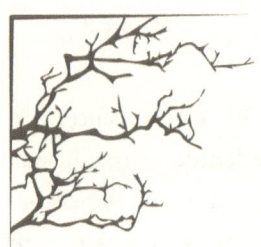

Chapter 61

"We have to turn left here." Attila turned around a bend on the lonely road to the compound. It wasn't long before Anchorage Farms was in view. He slowed the car.

"What are you doing?" Ash fingered the switchblade in his pocket.

"Think about it. They are expecting us. I'm guessing they have patrols around the area." Attila explained, backing up the car. He diverted off the road and into the mouth of a wooded area.

"We'll start here." Attila parked and cut the ignition.

"Start?"

"Daisy is in there. We're gonna have to hike it." Attila grabbed his pistol, visibly unpleased by his only weapon of choice. "I wish I had a little more firepower, but I gotta make due. You good?"

"I guess. Don't have much of an option now." Ash pulled out his switchblade. The snow crunched underneath their feet as they moved cautiously through the dead woods.

"Wouldn't be surprised if they had boobie-traps." Attila commented.

"Yeah." Ash looked around; paranoid of potential traps under the snowy earth. They came to a perimeter, a tall military-grade fence of sorts. Through the chain link, he could see a pair of guards leaving the area. They waited a beat to approach.

"I got a pair of wire cutters back in the car. I'll be back." Attila said. Ash stood nervously by the fence, constantly checking his surroundings. The sound of a truck quickly got his attention as he retreated back into the woods.

"Let's go! Let's go! They're here!" a male voice said in the distance. Sure enough, a rusty orange truck drove by the fence carrying several armed men.

"Did they see you?" Attila's sudden question made Ash jump in his skin.

"Shit! You scared the fuck out of me!" Ash whispered, trying to keep his voice down.

"Well did they?"

"No!"

"Good. Let's get to work."

Attila got to work on the fence, cutting out a hole big enough to get through. They slipped through; careful not to catch their clothing on anything.

"What now?" Ash asked.

"We follow that truck."

The dirt tracks sure enough led to a clear overlook where the compound complex was. There was hardly any movement, save for guards rushing about.

"Where do you think she is?" Ash asked again. Attila bit his lip.

"I don't know. We'll have to-"

"Freeze!" a guard yelled, "One more step and I'll shoot!"

Ash and Attila put their hands up. The switchblade dropped from Ash's hand, landing on the snowy ground. The man's rifle was trained on them.

"Don't move! Who are you and what are you doing here?" the guard continued.

"Easy, man." Attila kept his arms raised. His gaze turned to Ash, giving a knowing look. The guard came closer to Attila to pat him down.

"You stay still, buddy." the guard pointed at Ash. Attila took advantage of the guard's position and swiftly kicked him. Once knocked down, Attila accosted the guard. Ash quickly picked up his blade. Attila dominated his opponent and pulled out his gun. A well-placed pistol whip knocked the man out cold.

"Solved our gun issue." Attila held out his pistol to Ash, while confiscating the guard's rifle.

"Ever shoot one of these?" Attila asked.

"Once. A long time ago." Bitter memories swelled inside Ash. He retracted the switchblade, placing it in his pocket as he took the gun. The weapon was dense and cold in his hand.

"Good enough."

Descending the incline, they had little issue getting to the center of the compound. Hardly anyone was by the barn; the residents preferring to stay inside the trailers or making a barrier near the entrance to the farm. They took cover behind the faded old barn; its heavily weathered white paint peeling off and crusting like a fine dusting of snow. Sirens filled the air.

"Looks like the cops are here. Federals as well." Ash said.

"That's great. What Rust Springs needs is a little stand-off." Ash could sense Attila was anxious to find Daisy and leave. Snow gently fell and dark storm clouds loomed overhead. A grim voice filled his head.

"Did you hear that?" Ash asked.

"Hear what?"

A gunshot and yelling got their attention. It sounded like it came from the front, past the growth of trees surrounding the dirt road leading into the compound.

Ash could barely hear people from inside the barn walls. It made him tense and there was a similar ominous presence to the one in the basement. Winds kicked up and the snowfall was coming harder. Lightning cracked, sounding more like the sky snapping in two. *Screams, blood, fire.* He remembered the words from the journal: "The Fenris-kin was loose."

"Do you feel that?" Ash's voice trembled from strain.

"...Yeah..." Attila sounded spooked. The barn shook from impact, a loud roar coming from within.

"What the fuck?" Attila yelled, "Did a fucking bomb go off in there?"

The winds were deafening and the snow was blinding now. When Attila looked around, Ash was obscured by swirling flurries. Ash found his switchblade inside one of his pockets on his worn pair of jeans. The confiscated pistol was heavy in his hand. A gun and a blade. It wasn't enough to face the Lodge, but it was better than nothing.

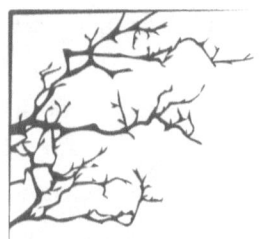

Chapter 62

I daho could only look as the gates to the compound opened to him; a place he had no desire to be. The guards allowed them passage and quickly closed and barricaded the gates. Washington drove on the gravel up to the house, which served as their personal living quarters.

"Spread the word to put the place on lock down." Washington ordered Oregon. "I suspect the government bastards aren't too far behind. Arm ourselves and prepare to fight."

Oregon ran out to the trailers that housed the other members.

"Come now, Ida. You need to see Montana."

"No! I want no part in this!" Idaho protested.

"The way I see it, you don't have much of a choice." Washington pulled him out of the back seat. "This is the day we've been waiting for. All of that effort, planning and bloodshed leading up to this moment. You've seen the power Montana has. He can make this happen."

Idaho noticed the atmosphere around the land was oppressive; suffocating even. It was as if thick smog was choking the life out of him. The sensation filled him with panic. Something was deeply wrong here.

"Please, no!" he begged frantically, "You can't!"

"We must." Washington replied calmly, keeping a firm grip on Idaho's wriggling form.

Idaho tried to drag his feet, catching snow and mud. With every step they took towards the barn, the worse he felt. He heard an echoing, repetitive crunching sound; as if a great beast was devouring something eagerly. An oppressive rotting odor attacked his nostrils, making him retch.

"Jesus, you don't smell that?"

"What? It smells like wet earth-"

"Or that sound? What the hell is that?"

"I don't hear anything."

"Don't fuck with me –!"

"I'm serious, Ida. I don't hear or smell a damn thing. It's just nerves."

"Please, Wash." Idaho pleaded, "Something bad is going to happen."

His whines fell on deaf ears, as Washington forced him to keep pace. The sturdy barn doors opened, revealing Montana at the front of the pews. Colorado accompanied him; looking disappointed when she saw Idaho. The cosmogram was complete; stretching from a central focal point and spreading outwards on the floor, seats, and walls. In the center of the smaller red fang shards, lay the purple fang. They glowed steadily.

"Looks like the fangs are channeling the energy well enough, even without the extra support from the blue one we lost." Colorado commented.

"Good." Montana responded. "My improvisations are working, but we need to focus. Without the other fang, it'll take more effort to bridge the aeon of Folkvagnr to this one."

Idaho was trembling with fear, his insides were like wriggling snakes. His eyesight was blurry as he gazed at Montana. He sensed the malicious energy emanating from his older brother. The maddening chewing was staunched with a crisp crack, like the crushing of thick glass. A low, reverberating groaning rattled his bones. Idaho could not determine what the sounds were coming from. He looked about wildly, fearing the noises were inside his own head. The overhead light flickered briefly.

"It's happening." Montana said. The elder brother gave him a wild look of a man over the edge. "This world is broken, its illusions shattered. We stand here in the zero hour, fulfilling a destiny in the making for thousands of years."

Montana walked towards his youngest brother. Idaho closed his eyes as the terrible presence approached. Montana looked into his eyes as if trying to penetrate his mind.

"You were always a perceptive kid. You're the perfect vessel for the Fenris-kin." Montana gently caressed his youngest brother's face with his fingertips.

"I hate to interrupt, but we got a whole lot of G-men bearing down on us!" Oregon shouted from the doors. Behind him, red-blue police headlights blinked brightly.

"Seal off the doors, prepare a perimeter and get the children inside the bunker." Montana commanded. "Wash, Ori...I'm counting on you to lead the men and women into battle if need be."

The two men exited the church; leaving Montana, Colorado and Idaho to complete the ritual. Montana chanted in that odd tongue, causing the fangs to radiate hues of amethyst and ruby; their strange energy moving outwards towards Idaho.

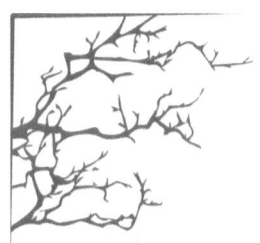

Chapter 63

Calvin Clarkson was deep in prayer inside the confines of his church afterhours. He always felt safer inside the building rather than his private home. This was the house of God; dedicated to the Lord and where he was closer to God because of it. He was in terrible agony sitting on the cushioned pew. The presence of the Devil had come to torment him again; this time with dreadful assaults on his spirit. He had to stay strong in faith, but there were doubts in Calvin's mind.

The presence was worse than the one all those years ago in New Mexico. This demon was so powerful. The doors near the podium platform opened. It was George, a middle-aged volunteer at the ministry who helped with website maintenance.

"I'm gonna get on home, Pastor Calvin." George addressed him, "Did you see the weather outside? Crazy, huh?" Calvin kept praying, shifting with discomfort.

"Did you need me to do anything else before I go?" George asked again.

"Please sit with me, George." Calvin said finally. George obeyed, sliding into the pew. Calvin lifted his head and stared out at one of the wall paintings. Depicted on the canvas was a half-naked man, superimposed over images of heaven and hell. The man was striving to move towards the blue sky and silver clouds, above where angels were waiting. From below, demons grasped for his feet with their clawed fiery hands.

"This is the eternal struggle of man, no?" Calvin questioned. "Disavowing his earthly nature for that of divine salvation. Yet, here we sit – in the throws of a dark age where the enemy will prevail, and the Beast will rule until the return of Christ." He paused, giving a frustrated sigh. "I often wonder how God could keep loving us after we go astray. The sheer patience and love...and here we are, throwing away our precious spiritual nature to abominations – perverted abominations causing rabid ecstasy in the mind of the mad and evil and utter terror in the hearts of the good and sane."

George paused for a moment, considering his next words. "Uh, yes, well there are those people who are trapped by Satan's power, but it's that reason why we are here: to bring the word of God to those so they may be delivered. That is our mission; your mission that you have for our ministry."

"Yes, George but I fear there are people who have accessed a deeper level of depravity in this world. Far beyond any run-of-the-mill occult group or depressed kid. The hate-cult called the "Storm-Star"...I sense it's utter oblivion on our doorstep."

"What are you talking about? I know you're upset about the Lodge – we all are – but I doubt –"

"No!" Calvin gripped George's upper arms intensely. "You cannot be like the disciple Thomas, harboring doubt in your heart in spite of the evidence. Must you touch the horrors before you believe them?" George was flustered by the sudden physical contact. Calvin looked truly distressed, his grip tightening painfully. "You cannot know the horror of true evil...and I pray that you never do."

"Please calm yourself, Calvin." George patted his pastor's arm gently. "Do you wish to pray before I go? Will that make you feel better?"

A flicker of realization crossed the church leader's features. His eyes blinked and his grip slackened, retreating to his personal space. Calvin, apprehensive, cast his eyes downward.

"Y-you may leave, I'll close. Thank you and be safe." Calvin whispered.

George made his way to the wine-colored carpeted walkway leading to the main exit and entrance of the church. He attributed Calvin's odd behavior to the stressful week he had been having concerning the cult. George knew Calvin had a big heart and was concerned about the well-being of his community and country. The charity emanating from the ministry; from help hotlines to donations and information resources, made George proud about dedicating his time and skills in service to it. A nagging, guilt pestered him. He hoped the man would be okay by himself in the storm. He was concerned about driving through the mess himself, fearing zero-visibility conditions. Bitter winter weather greeted George on the other side as he stepped on the sidewalk, walking briskly to his car. He could not wait; he had a sick child to take care of at home. He shared a quick prayer for himself and Pastor Clarkson.

Inside, Calvin continued to pray, hoping to encounter a holy ray of light – something that would erase the shadows from Rust Springs. In this titanic maelstrom, it would be nothing short of a miracle.

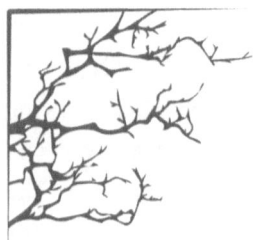

Chapter 64

The barrier of law enforcement vehicles obstructed Vasquez's view of the compound in a sea of red and blue. Carbine barked orders from the back of the van, communications equipment crackling out information to field agents. They armed themselves and donned protective gear with winter camouflage, ready for potential violence that may break out. The procedure was methodical, despite the chaotic weather around them.

"I want snipers posted around the perimeter, and stake out some men on the Loupcroix property. I need eyes in the sky..." Carbine commanded, writing notes on a pad. Vasquez climbed out of the vehicle to get a better look of the situation. He walked towards the front entrance of the compound, dodging people as they ran past. A reinforced gate with two guards standing behind it was positioned before a police vehicle. They were dressed in mixed army fatigues and civilian clothing, carrying assault rifles in front of their bodies. They remained fairly stoic, considering what was at their doorstep.

"Do we have a negotiator?" Vasquez heard someone behind him ask. "We have arrest warrants we need to serve."

"We have someone en route." an unknown voice responded. Amidst the convergence, Vasquez recalled the material he and Mullen reviewed concerning the Storm-Star belief system. It's printed pamphlets and website warned of an inevitable conflict between the deceitful and antagonistic federal government and followers of the Storm-Star itself. It was clear who would be the victor in the end, if the mythology were to be believed. Vasquez's spirit sank as his mind came to a frightening conclusion.

Were Carbine and the agencies falling into Montana Loupcroix's trap? It didn't seem outside of the realm of plausibility. With all of the anti-cult resources he had read from the department, Vasquez was aware that cult leaders who push an apocalyptic view have no qualms about violence or death if the end justifies the means. It was a dim, desperate mentality and its outcomes are written in blood for the annals of history.

He went to approach Carbine to offer a warning against using force to approach the Loupcroix. On the road, a car approached the encampment from the winter mist. Pulling aside Carbine's van, a man stepped out and introduced himself.

"Hello, I am the negotiator -."

"Ah, yes." Carbine greeted the man with a firm handshake, "Let's get you acquainted with the situation." He looked around. "Where's Vasquez? – Oh, here he is." he said upon seeing the detective.

Vasquez dipped his head as he came closer.

"Agent Michaels, this is Detective Antonio Vasquez with Rust Springs PD. He has been conducting most of the investigation on this case." Carbine informed the bespectacled man.

"A pleasure but a shame under these circumstances." Michaels rubbed his hands together. "Boy, is the weather miserable or what?"

"The sentiment is shared." Carbine stated. "Concerning the matter at hand, Vasquez has insight into the philosophy of the Storm-Star cult which could prove useful in opening communication with them – "

"Sir, I have a suggestion to make." Vasquez interjected.

"Go ahead."

"Montana Loupcroix seems hell-bent on a conflict between the government, and those he considers unworthy to inherit this "new world" they wish to bring into existence. It's important to remember they do not trust us, and will easily resort to violence as they see fit. The fact of the Loupcroix siblings' involvement in murder, robbery, and other terroristic activities, proves we have to be on guard. It would not surprise me if this was their intention all along."

Carbine and Michaels were quieted for a moment by the information offered them.

"I will keep that in mind, Detective Vasquez." Michaels grabbed a bullhorn from the van. "I was afraid we might be dealing with individuals with a doomsday mindset."

"That aside, they believe in two entities; the one by which they derived their namesake, the Storm-Star, and one that accompanies its destined arrival, the Fenris-kin." Vasquez explained. "They desire the destruction of this world into a new reality they call, Folkvagnr, wherein the white race will rule. Allegedly, Montana Loupcroix and Idaho Loupcroix will bring this prophecy to fruition."

"Ah, I am familiar with groups of this nature. Apocalyptic visions and views of racial superiority are a common theme. What's more telling is this Montana and Idaho are heralded as messiahs of some sort."

"You'd be correct on that notion."

"Then, it would seem pertinent that I speak with those two men."

Both Carbine and Vasquez escorted Michaels to the compound gates. The guards watched them with vigilant interest, as they advanced on the snowy grounds.

"Hello, My name is Agent Wilford Michaels. I would like to speak with whomever is in charge."

"What makes you think we'll wanna talk, asshole?"

"Apologies for my assumption, but I just want to talk."

"Screw you! You're with the Feds. Why should we trust you?"

"Please, sir. I don't want any trouble, only peace. I want to talk to Montana Loupcroix."

The two men looked stunned; one of them breaking out the radio.

"There's a Fed here wanting to talk to Mr. Loupcroix."

"-*click*-Let him in.-*click*-"

The guard looked at Michaels.

"Come with me, but surrender your weapon."

Michaels gave his pistol to the guard.

"Like I said, we don't know ya. Besides, you seem too chummy with the government pigs." the guard retorted, shifting his weapon.

"I only wish to promote an open dialog between our people and your people. We don't want trouble any more than you do."

The guard took out a two-way radio, grunting something into the receiver. He waited a second for a response. It chirped into his ear upon being given. The gates creaked open. Michaels followed the guard inside the compound gates. The wire on him gave some small comfort as he entered the lion's den.

"You and you alone are allowed to come in unarmed to say your piece." the guard informed them. Michaels removed a pistol from his coat. He walked a couple of feet inside the compound with two other guards following behind him. The gates closed once more as lightning flashed overhead. Carbine and Vasquez retreated to their barricade. The FBI agent pulled out his own radio.

"Are you positioned?" he asked.

"Yes, we have a good vantage point from here. But..."

"What?"

"We've spotted two unidentified figures breaching the security fence around the compound."

One of the guards was received a distress signal from the radio he was holding.

"We've been compromised! Fire!"

Shots rang and Michaels was hit in the chest.

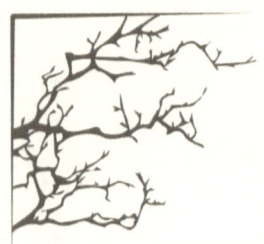

Chapter 65

Ash's heart raced as armed guards patrolled the property, their flashlights shining on the shimmering snow. Hopefully, the Lodge won't find their footprints. He tried to cover them the best he could, while they navigated the compound. His denim-clad legs were freezing while Attila surveyed the land. Finding Daisy was the top priority and they were deep in enemy territory.

The authorities were here already here. Something must have happened to warrant this surveillance. He crept around a corner of a trailer, only to be stopped by Attila. Guards were taking a man into the barn. The reverberating in his bones again; the same from Jasper's basement but more pronounced. The fangs were there, placed in a neat circle around Montana. The hair on the back of his neck stood up on end. He sensed two energies in the air around him. One was a howling, ravenous power bent on consuming everything it could encase in its maws. The other was a staggering oppression, one that caused immeasurable dread in his soul. A great repulsion set in, as if his very being was in upheaval against it.

"God...d-do you feel it too?" Attila's wavering words were almost lost in the strong gust of wind and snow. The storm was worsening, making Ash question their sanity in this whole affair. The telltale light was coming from the barn, but it was darker.

"Fuck, fuck, it's here!" Attila was on the verge of a panic attack. Ash could not blame the man. He sensed the same foreboding presence, but they needed to be quiet.

Shit! Ash led Attila to the other side of the trailer to avoid detection. Flashlights beamed around the corner. Ash and Attila trudged away from the makeshift structure. They needed to get to the barn. Attila placed his hand in front of Ash's path. Through the snow, a guard was wandering the property. Attila crept forward; Ash in step with him. They were close to the guard now, within arm's reach. Attila pounced.

A gunshot rang through the air when he attacked the man, clear as a bell, from within the barn. The guard was distracted for a moment, giving Attila the chance to push him down. The men struggled in the snow for a moment. Attila took the man's weapon and knocked him out with a well-aimed butt to the face. Yelling and screaming could be heard, along with an eerie, otherworldly wail. Ash's nerves were on fire when he heard the noise; his being informing him of the danger. Attila panted; looking around wildly. The dark light beamed brighter as they were consumed by lightning and snow.

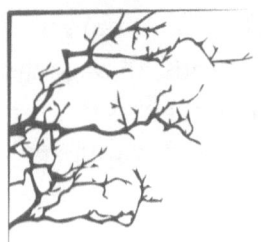

Chapter 66

"Get the guns!"

"Lock it down!"

Daisy was vaguely aware of the commotion. She tried to stretch, finding her arms tied to a wooden chair. The rough rope cut her wrists.

Opening her eyes, she saw she was in a house, more specifically, the kitchen. It was dark; windows drawn shut. She heard gunfire and harsh howling wind.

Daisy scanned for anything that could get her loose. She dare not make a sound, unsure if any Loupcroix or their lackeys were about.

She eyed a knife on the counter next to some pots and pans. Daisy shuffled the chair with her weight, propelling it forward.

"Damn..." she strained against her bonds. The legs on the abused chair became wobbly through her struggling. She lost balance before she could get to the counter.

The chair broke apart, freeing her. The ropes slackened and she immediately slipped out of them. She jogged clumsily in the dark to the front door; the light between the boards on the windows as her only guide. Her legs were still sore from being immobile for a long time. Blizzard wind greeted her face with snow and icy air. She could hardly see five feet in front of her. Thunder cracked overhead. Screams and gunfire were barely audible. She caught something in the corner of her eye. A hand was hanging on to the porch, blood dripping on the white paint. Someone was injured or worse.

"Help me!"

Daisy saw a heavily armed and padded body. It didn't look like a compound member.

"What's going on?" Daisy asked loudly, her voice lost in the wind. She approached closer. "Are you alright? Oh god-!"

The man, a SWAT police officer, had a missing left arm. The nasty wound on his side was strangely cauterized in some places.

"Help, help..." the man cried weakly, getting hoarse.

"Hang on. We need to get out of here." She was saddened she couldn't do more to help. She violently held on to him. The officer screamed in pain.

"Don't let it take me!" he cried. He was abruptly silent. Daisy lifted her head out of the snow. She regretted that she had eyes when she saw the attacker.

Starry eyes and fangs of crystal devoured its human prey in front of her. Daisy could not make a sound if she wanted to. She was transfixed on the horrible sight; staring blankly at the bloodstained maw before her. The pain of her dislocated shoulder snapped her out of it.

The creature reared its terrible head, having eaten the man whole. It flashed out of view, disappearing. A ghostly howl rose over the din of the thundersnow.

Daisy was alone; the unforgiving cold and the pain in her shoulders overtaking her. Snow melted under her tears, as she wished to have Attila's warmth at her side.

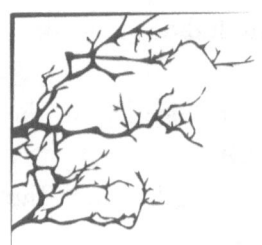

Chapter 67

"What the hell is going on in there!" Carbine roared into the radio. A full-blown blizzard was in effect now, adding more to the chaos and confusion. The compound guards started shooting into the outer barricade. Vasquez shuffled around federal agents and RSPD officers as they held their ground and took cover; drawing their weapons and firing back. The two guards backed off, spraying bullets to deter anyone from coming closer to the compound. An ATF agent next to Vasquez fired his rifle. He ducked behind a police cruiser, readying his own weapon. He could not imagine the accuracy under these conditions. The shooting stopped as suddenly as it began.

"Hold fire! Hold fire!" Carbine yelled. Someone cried out an affirmation of compliance, as everyone held their breath and bullets. Blood-curling screams and shouts rang out from the Loupcroix property followed by gunfire. But, that was not what made Vasquez's blood run cold.

A distant howl, unlike anything he had heard before, sounded in the distance.

"Team 1, come in!" Carbine commanded. "Have you breached the perimeter? Team 2, can you get a visual on Michaels and the Loupcroix family?"

"This is Team 2. Negative, sir. Team 1 is not responding, and I cannot get a slight on any target. Michaels is not responding; feared dead." a voice churned out over the static, "Wait – Michaels' wire is live..."

Carbine tuned into listen, but only heard ear-piercing white noise from the other side. The retched sound was punctuated by infrequent low chanting in an unrecognizable language. The combined audio gave him chills.

"Team 1! Team 1 coming in over!" a panicked voice charged.

"Team 1, what is your status?" Carbine asked urgently.

"We're pinned down – trapped! Two of my men have been injured and one is dead. We need back up now!"

"What is the situation?"

"I'm unsure, sir. The visibility is shit and cult members are either attacking us or getting killed – my men are spooked."

"What do you mean? – Explain."

"We saw two unknown men, one a black male and a young, possibly, white male. They got one of the cultists and – Oh god—-!"

Team 1's voice was abruptly clipped with a frightened yelp before going dead. Carbine changed the frequency dial grimly.

"Team 3! Get ready to roll out. We have to secure the area. If this gets any hotter, we will have to employ military intervention."

Another group of agents walked cautiously to the front; postures low and weapons raised.

"This is getting out of control." Vasquez thought. Ash and Attila were in there too. He worried for their safety. Against his better judgment, he left Carbine's side and ran to the gate. Using an armored vehicle, the FBI and ATF bashed the front gates of the compound inward. Men on foot trailed the rear, as it made its way down the snowy path with Vasquez in tow, as he followed the agents into the kill zone.

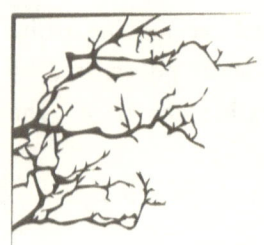

Chapter 68

Attila stumbled blindly through the snow towards the house. The storm was furious; Attila hadn't seen anything like it. It wasn't conventional Ohio winter weather for sure. He couldn't tell where he was going or where Ash was. Gunfire and faint cries and shouts were muted around the snowy field. He tripped over something, almost falling over. He looked down to see a bloody, dismembered arm. Fear shot through him when he saw the body lying near it, red hair spilling on white.

"Daisy!" he called for her, rushing to her side. She was cold, lips turning blue. Her arms were held out at a weird angle. Attila was dismayed and angered at the sight of her broken figure.

"Daisy..." He gently cradled her in his arms. He had to get her out of here. Gunfire rang in the air, followed by a ghostly howl that sent chills down Attila's back. He carried Daisy and moved closer to where the house was. He cursed the biting wind. He stopped dead in his tracks before he reached the steps.

In the corner of his eyes, there was a large skeletal animal glowing bright green with fangs of obsidian. Attila estimated it was the size of a moose. Burning rags of flesh hung from its body as it sniffed the air. It dissolved in the wind like ash, giving an earth-shattering howl in its wake. Attila fell to his knees. On the snow, he covered his face, crying in fear. He was so scared; his nails were digging into his flesh so hard to cause blood to bead from the marks. Anything to keep from seeing that horrible thing. A migraine brewed in his skull and his mouth was dry. A great darkness fell on him. Time slowed and his strength was sapped.

Blam!

Attila cringed as a shotgun blasted close by, followed by the sound of a bone-shattering crunch. In the corner of his eye, he swore he saw a giant skeletal appendage pass in and out of the thick whiteout.

...

The unit moved swiftly and methodically as they searched for threats. Vasquez kept up, trying to keep his vision clear through the storm. Splotches of blood stained the pure snow a stark crimson, while chewed body parts and viscera were brutally strewn across the area.

During his time in Cincinnati, he was used to seeing bloody scenes from the aftermath of drive-bys to serial killer victims. Rust Springs was on a whole other level despite the peaceful, rural surroundings. Between the Rust Springs Ripper and the cult, he couldn't choose which was worse. There were burn spots around the gore as well. Upon closer inspection, Vasquez saw the spots were distinct indentations, like a claw print. He was curious, but he was unsure of what caused them.

Firepower exploded in the direction of the boarded-up house, battering the agents in a spray of bullets. Team 3 engaged but the two men already on the move, taking shelter inside the house. The unit leader silently signaled to surround the entrances. He took four other agents to the porch steps to break down the door. Finding success, they bustled inside. A tall man clad in a leather jacket and jeans escaped through one the upstairs windows onto the roof.

"Over here!" Vasquez called out to the unit members outside. The man, with an angry scowl, aimed his pistol at him.

"Please let it hit." The detective prayed internally; unconfident about his aim in the snow. He pulled the trigger, the sound of the expelled bullet leaving the barrel. The man, taking a hit in the abdomen, staggered on the roof. The suspect slipped on some ice

and fell to the ground a few feet below. Vasquez rushed to his side. The man was in visible agony, clutching his wound tightly with his reddened fingers, and setting his teeth in a grimace.

"What's your name?" Vasquez asked urgently. The man sneered and spat out some blood defiantly.

"Doesn't m-matter. I'm the l-last person you're ever going to s-see." The man's breath fogged in the icy air.

"Where's Idaho Loupcroix? Have you seen Asher Jagerhund or Attila Gadsden?" Vasquez knew the man did not have much time. The man laughed spitefully as blood trickled down his chin.

"Heh, I-Idaho is with Montana - As for those other t-two, no, I h-haven't- " Washington choked between wet coughs. The blood on his white shirt was spreading.

"Hang on! We'll get help – "

"S-shit-pig. I-I've made p-peace that I won't come out of this alive. T-The S-Storm-Star will carry our p-people to Folkvagnr - "

Washington violently coughed. A mist of warm blood droplets sprayed Vasquez's face.

"A-And the kin on F-Fenris — will tear at your corpse!"

With a series of wheezing and bloody coughs, Washington fell quiet as the death rattle took his voice. Team 3 reconvened around his dead body. Vasquez rose as he searched the growing darkness for Ash and Attila.

"What the hell was that?"

The unit leader walked up to Vasquez. He shifted his feet uneasily on the snow. The rest of the team stopped in their tracks. The leader looked over the dead man.

"I was forced to engage." Vasquez said.

The unit leader sighed, searching around for any other threats. He gave the signal that the area was cleared. He was prepared to give updates to Carbine. Before he could, a swell of dark energy engulfed them.

...

Ash slowly advanced towards the barn, noticing the burnt and demolished front end. The energy coming off the place was mesmerizing. He growled, baring his teeth in malicious excitement. The melted snow uncovered scorched grass and gravel; the embers on the wood strangely fresh despite the storm. It was as if a fireball tore through the building. It was dim inside the damaged structure; the only light source was a rich wine color emitting a glow from the fangs in the center of the interior. An inky, black shadow coiled around a central figure in the middle. Ash could detect the scent of two humans; one dead and one intermingled with another smell. The scent was indescribable, but menacing.

"This is the one they all fear, its own kind shirk before it." a distorted voice said. It was that of a man, if the said man were speaking with the sound of a million tongues. Ash watched as the environment withered around him, transforming into a different space. He took pause, unsure of how to proceed. The ground beneath him took the form of a night sky filled with luminous stars. Overhead, serpentine plasma soared at neck-breaking speeds. Drifting into the celestial void was a large reptilian creature. Its black body glowed with a ghastly brilliance. Ash adverted his eyes from the eldritch being.

"The Storm-Star...progenitor of Folkvagnr. Do you see its majesty? Can you even comprehend, worthless one? I have taken union with it – divinity defined! I forsake everything: my body, this traitorous nation, and the deplorable reality that shouldn't exist! This is the true way – the beginning and end of it all!"

The voice cackled in an abysmal cacophony, the hymn of a mad man. Ash froze in place, burying his face in his hands. The terror experienced by his other half made him want to claw his face, but something resisted the impulse. The true abyss and the fruit it bore for those who sought it for whatever insane reason. It cared not for their intentions. It only cared to spread outside of its plane of existence, that deep pit of oblivion. This would not be the first attempt. It spread its influence across time, manifesting itself through dark endeavors of men.

The all-to-familiar ache in Ash's body returned. He was on the verge of transforming into his bestial self. This time, however, it was welcomed. Compared to the unyielding mental agony, the physical pain convinced Ash he was alive and real. The strange comfort brought the reassurance of tangibility in this bleak aeon surrounding him. Unlike his previous transformations, this one was more grandiose as it tore the fabric of his being into a more formidable visage. Ash lost consciousness in between the stretching, breaking, and tearing of his body.

"I can sense the Surmara - you're one of it's kin?"

In his new body, Ash was mutated beyond recognition. The energy of the Storm-Star grew exponentially, as it struggled to manifest in this plane of existence. The black eye of the storm was now open, absorbing everything around it. The maw of oblivion was gaping wide, as it was poised to strike the final blow on this young aeon. Ash lashed out defiantly with his limbs and sank his many teeth into the fleshy form the Storm-Star surrounded itself around. His primal side cursed him for his betrayal, but his more human side spurred on his actions. The abomination in front of him must not exist. The Storm-Star and its host uttered an enraged scream, writhing in pain as Ash's fangs found their mark. The taste of blood and toxic, inky ichor pooled in his mouth. Time stood still and darkness fell across the land. The clash between Ash and an ancient, timeless entity hit a crescendo.

Something tore through Ash, splitting him. He emitted a silent scream. His body was coming apart, separating into tiny, molecular bits. The great serpent coiled in on itself, fatally wounded as the storm died. Ash couldn't sense Montana anymore. He flew though a supersonic tunnel, stars streaking past his eyes. It wasn't long before he became blind as well, removing his remaining senses. A flash of white disabled his consciousness as he traveled into oblivion.

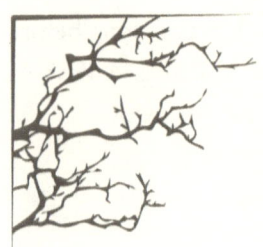

Chapter 69

The darkness broke as suddenly as it came. The storm died off; thunder ceasing to roar and the wind stopping to a faint howl. A veil had been lifted from Vasquez's eyes and the elephant stepped off his chest. He could breathe easier and see clearer.

Around him, the tactical team looked bewildered by the experience. Some searched the skies, looking for a sign the occurrence was real. The corpse of Washington Loupcroix lay frozen and partially covered by snow; his eyes staring up unblinkingly. The night was clearer and visibility improved greatly with the storm gone. More importantly, the foreboding presence was gone.

"Everyone accounted for?" the unit leader addressed everyone. Some nodded and some gave a verbal affirmation of their status.

"Team 3, come in!" Carbine's voice glitched into existence. "What's your status?"

"Everyone is fine and accounted for. We had a confrontation with one of the Loupcroix siblings, Washington. Vasquez used deadly force against him when he resisted - " the commander used his radio to confer with Carbine.

"Vasquez is with you? He was supposed to stay out of the hot zone."

"He understands. I confronted him about this issue. He believes some individuals connected with this case may still be on the property."

"Yes, well, proceed with caution. We don't know what is going on – we lost air visual." Carbine said gruffly, beyond annoyed at Vasquez for not obeying orders.

The team made their rounds as they searched the compound. Satisfied with the empty house, they navigated to the series of trailers that littered the property. Some were living quarters, filled with beds and personal effects. Some were filled with weapons, explosives and rations. One trailer had been partially destroyed as if firebombed. Vasquez investigated what looked like a greenhouse of some sort. The roof was devoid of any snow and the odor emanating from the structure roused Vasquez's suspicions. Impressive groves of marijuana plants were being grown inside the warm structure. His mind recalled the alleged reports of drug dealing, along with the evidence found inside Traynor's safe. It would make sense that a group operating off the grid would make ends meet through illegal means. These days, drugs were high in demand.

Another curious location was an ugly, stained trailer. Vasquez treaded lightly around it, noticing broken glass and containers. It had a faint ethanol smell to it. The door hung open off its hinges. Hypodermic needles were littered all over the trash-lined floor. This was probably Devon's trailer from the lab evidence. Based on his sister's reports, he was producing meth for the Lodge until their falling out.

"Hey! I got something here!" Vasquez approached the camouflaged earth structure. Vasquez recognized it as a bunker of some sort, no doubt, with locking mechanisms on the other side of the doors. The team tried to break down the doors, only to hear the cry of an infant inside.

"There are children in there." someone noticed. Vasquez's gut clenched. The situation became more tenuous; they had to be careful lest they harm innocents.

"Hello, is anyone in there?" Vasquez did not get a response. "My name is Detective Antonio Vasquez with the Rust Springs Police. I have FBI and ATF agents here that would like for you to come out peacefully."

"Bullshit! We're not leaving!"

A male voice rang inside the metallic reinforced structure. Vasquez could see tiny air holes in the door.

"Sir, what is your name?" Vasquez asked.

"Oregon Loupcroix." the man said. Vasquez sighed, considering his next words carefully.

"Mr. Loupcroix, we are not here to harm you or anyone else. All me and my colleagues want is for you to come out so you can leave..."

"I ain't fucking leaving!" Oregon was rattled by something. "Not with that thing outside!"

"What do you mean, Mr. Loupcroix? What thing?"

"The Fenris-kin! Montana brought it from the sky!"

A tremor passed through Vasquez. His body remembered something his mind did not catch. He did see...something – in the strange darkness that settled over him. The crystalline body whose fangs flashed in the night, its maw stained with the blood of unwitting prey. He shook his head.

No, it had to be an illusion, a brief madness of some sort overtaking him in a moment of weakness. He wished it was a delusion, but he knew in his bones it was not. Vasquez looked around, seeing the other agents looking tense and ready for action. In their eyes, he could tell they knew too. Even the bodies scattered across the snowy field spelled out the presence of something much larger than a siege gone bad.

"Sir, I am not sure what happened here, but I assure you it's passed – "

"You fucking liar!" Oregon snarled. Vasquez caught the whimpering noises of the children in the bunker. "You didn't see what I saw – it's eyes! They never blinked; always watching and waiting – that thing will never rest! Have you seen its belly – full of the stars and galaxies it's consumed!" The rant was interrupted by a sharp banging sound, like something hitting the metal walls inside. "How could we live with that out there? Knowing it's out there!"

"Oregon!" Vasquez yelled, "Don't do anything - "

A shotgun blast boomed inside of the bunker, followed by screams and more gunfire. Vasquez retreated several paces back. He took his own weapon out, prepared for the worst. The din quieted. Some children and women were crying. After a few moments, the steel doors grinded open. Four women and a couple of children walked out towards the armed men who escorted them towards the compound entrance. They looked shell-shocked, some streaked with blood and tears. Bringing up the rear was a woman holding a revolver, clutching her bleeding left arm. Her dirty, brown hair was wild and unkempt, as she stumbled towards them. The agents commanded her to drop her weapon. She did listlessly. Vasquez caught her before she fell on the ground. He could tell she was in intense pain, eyeing the bullet hole through her arm.

"It's okay, ma'am, we will get you to a hospital." he reassured her.

"I shot my husband...I don't care where you put me." Another agent came to carry her away.

Vasquez trotted to the bunker entrance. The team leader led him down some steps into the rustic, yet reinforced fortress. The body of a man, assumed to be Oregon Loupcroix, was slumped against the railing. Two gunshot wounds to the chest. His eyes were just as wide and crazed as he sounded a few moments earlier. Shelves of food and ammo lined the walls, while weapons lay locked in boxes. The bodies of a woman and two children lay on the floor in a pool of blood. The woman was on top of the children face down, as if she was trying to protect them. Vasquez clenched his fists in anger at the unnecessary waste of life. The radio crackled to life again.

"Carbine requests Vasquez's presence at the barn."

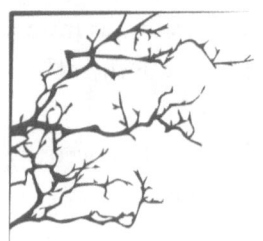

Chapter 70

"**D**amn thing's blown to hell." Carbine murmured, surveying the burnt remains of the wooden structure. He stood in what was once the archway of the barn turned worship-hall. The charred wood twisted outwards. Some of the pews were demolished as well, splintered and black. Jagged claw marks tore the dusty wood floor. Foreign symbols covered parts of the floor and walls. Near the back of the barn was an utter mess.

On the altar was the body of an emaciated man. His ravaged body possessed burnt out holes for eyes. There was a black inky substance oozing from his mouth, ears and nose. It was also caked under his long, cracked fingernails. The man was most likely to be Montana Loupcroix, the ever-evasive leader of the Lodge. Carbine looked closer at the body. What drove the cult leader to this dramatic conclusion? More importantly, who or what could have done this to him?

Looking to his right, he found another corpse being photographed by a forensics specialist. It was a female with her face twisted in utter agony. The most grotesque feature on her body was her clawed out eyes, done by her own hands no less. If that didn't do her in, it was the wounds to her throat and wrists; bleeding and open from a blade lying nearby.

"Good God..." he murmured at the ghastly scene. What did she witness to do such a thing to herself?

"Special Agent Carbine!" an ATF agent chimed, "We found someone!" The two men were dragging a tall black man, who looked dazed and unresponsive. "He was outside the farm house, buried in the snow with a female. He was lying there in a ball muttering something." Based on the damp clothing, Carbine estimated he was there for a while.

"Get the man a blanket! He's freezing for Christ's sake!" Carbine barked. One of the agents searched for something warm to cover the man with.

"What's your name, son?" Carbine was more interested in what the man knew than his physical state.

"Attila..." the man slurred, slumping on the pew.

"Attila Gadsden? Your detective friend, Vasquez, has been looking all over for you. Mind telling me what you are doing here, Mr. Gadsden?"

Attila blinked, deeply considering the question.

"Daisy...Daze..."

"Daisy? Is that what you said?"

Attila swung his head towards the FBI agent at the mention of the name.

"Daisy? Where is she?"

Must've been the woman they found with him.

"I'm sure she's safe, son. Is that why you were here?"

Attila looked more agitated as Carbine asked questions. He picked at one of his long dreads with his nail, gripping his knee with his other hand.

"They took her. I had to get her back..."

"Who took her?" Carbine's ears pricked up at the new information. "Was it the Lodge?"

"Yeah and I found her, but I saw...that monster..." Attila shuddered. Carbine didn't know how to respond to the statement. Since he arrived in Rust Springs, he'd been bombarded by all sorts of wild stories concerning the Rust Springs Ripper, murders, crazy Neo-Nazis and odd creatures roaming the night. With the sudden darkness falling on them an hour ago, Carbine was more likely to

believe weird meteorological phenomenon in that regard. He was
not so sure about the nature of the deaths on the property and
what he heard over the radio. The skeptic in him said it was silly to
believe in creatures like unicorns and leprechauns. Still, it was hard
for Carbine to figure out a rational answer.

"What monster, Mr. Gadsden? Did you see the darkness too?"

Attila continued to mumble erratically. The agents returned with
a blanket, throwing it over his shoulders. He did not seem to notice.

"Could someone please escort Mr. Gadsden off the premises?
We will need to question him at a later time." Carbine would not be
able to get anything more out of the shell-shocked man. An agent
stood aside Attila, as he took the man away from the scene.

Carbine was curious to where the other person of interest,
believed to be Asher Jagerhund, was located. Attila made no mention
of his associate, only Daisy Grayhart. The investigation carried on as
normal. Disturbingly, barrels of cyanide and explosive materials were
found in a shed on the eastern side of the encampment. Weapons
and drugs were accounted for, along with bizarre literature and
audio-visual recordings produced by the cult. Carbine glimpsed at
some of the brochures, filled with jargon and symbols lost to him.
On the computer desk, numerous CDs, video tapes, and floppy disks
related to the cult's activities and records were stacked around the
desk's surface; the floor as well. Upstairs, a good cache of money
was found in a false wall. The cult could have done a lot of damage
with what they found. Poisoning the local water supply, blowing up
infrastructures or occupied buildings were distinct possibilities.

The sun was rising outside, signaling a new day and bringing
much needed light. The sun also revealed the most disturbing feature
of the expansive crime scene: the bodies. Carbine did not recall
seeing any animals on the premises. Yet, he observed his men lying
ravaged and lifeless on the ground. He looked upon one corpse, its
innards carved and burnt while the head was missing. The headless

neck was cauterized as well. He bit the inside of his cheek in frustration, not knowing what could have done this. Footsteps crunched in the slushy snow behind him.

"You wished to see me?" Vasquez asked softly.

"Took your sweet time getting here." Carbine mildly scoffed.

"I apologize, but by the time I got to the barn, you were gone." Vasquez politely replied. Carbine noticed a slight irritated tone in his voice.

"I have to keep track of what is going on around here. I met your friend, Attila Gadsden."

"How is he?"

"Fine but he's obviously witnessed something traumatic."

"What about Ash? Daisy Grayhart?"

"No sign of him. Mr. Gadsden did not mention him either in our conversation. Ms. Grayhart was found unconscious next to Mr. Gadsden and has been rushed to the nearest medical center for treatment." Carbine told the detective.

"Why -what? Did the Lodge have anything to do with it?"

Carbine shook his head.

"We don't have all the details yet, Vasquez. It's a possibility; considering the connection with her brother to the cult, as you well know."

"I'm worried about Ash. We should investigate his house; it's on Yellow River Road."

"Possibly. He could be there for all we know. No sign of Idaho Loupcroix so far, even though he was abducted from the station and taken here. Your men found the bodies of Officers Stockden and Cooper off the road there. Must have happened before the abduction."

"Do you know of any other location he could have been stashed in?"

"Not to our knowledge."

Vasquez scratched his head in frustration; a whole bunch of dead bodies and missing people. He hated the fact more shit was pushed on his plate than he could even clear. To top it all off, nothing added up.

"I suppose I'm done here?" Vasquez said.

Carbine didn't respond, deciding instead to jot down some notes. There was nothing he could do at the moment, but record these events and whatever insane conclusions resulted from the raid. There was something odd about the scene inside the barn. Whatever got Montana Loupcroix, decimated him. The body was split in half, like a torn sheet of paper. Entrails leaked out like silly string from his torso. The condition of the barn suggested some sort of explosion, but the state of the bodies within was a different story. There was a sharp, odd-shaped purple gemstone surrounded by smaller tooth-like red ones lying next to the bodies. Yellow tags staked out their locations. Unusual items, considered sacred by the Lodge. They looked like gemstones, but their luster and shape were unlike anything Carbine had seen.

"I'll see you back at the station." Carbine resigned. The two men parted ways in search of their own answers.

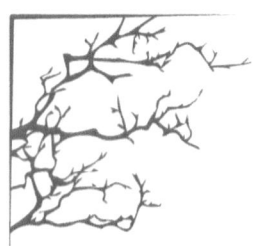

Chapter 71

Calvin Clarkson sat in his office watching the news events unfold on the television screen before him. Crying women and children. Stretchers were carrying out dead bodies by the dozen while the officers on the scene blocked reporters. Boxes of evidence carried out and placed in trucks to be transported off the scene.

He did not sleep at all last night, not with that terrible aura hanging around. He prayed for salvation throughout the night. It would seem they were answered; the presence gone. As he knew with cults, the destruction from their aftermath is devastating. It was Luna County all over again; shaking his head at the similarities. No matter their beliefs or intentions, they still worshiped those false gods and idols.

In this ungodly age, it was no surprise these new age cults would be taking root in society. It only empowered him to keep fortifying and enlarging his ministry. His research and personal experiences with the occult, only confirmed his convictions. There was a real evil in the world; demonic influences corrupting and defecting men to the darkness.

"Pastor Calvin?" Kathy chimed over his introspection. "It's time to prepare for the afternoon service."

"Go ahead, Kathy dear, I need a few moments to prepare myself." Calvin was still glued to the screen. Kathy looked at the TV as well.

"A shame." she commented sadly. "It's all over the news, even on the national level."

Calvin grumbled in agreement. The news changed to a female commentator, discussing the rise of these extremist groups.

"Are you going to comment on these events to the congregation tonight? Or on the news?"

"I'm compelled by God, in my heart, to do so. It's difficult to comment on the case, but I will discuss the threat of real evil in this world." Calvin rubbed his temples.

"Well, I won't keep you." Kathy told him, exiting the office to leave him alone again.

He turned the television off, choosing to get up and peruse the various media he had produced over the years. Books, films, and audiotapes on spiritual resources, Satanism and the occult. He did not always believe such things to be a threat or even real, until he saw the evidence. If not the daycare scandals and the proliferation of new age ideals, it was the personal experiences gained from interviews and counseling from torn, depressed families. He did research into some of these odd cults and the people who preach their tenants, such as the metal band *Eldritch Enema*. After publishing a few books and appearing at conferences for concerned Christians, he became someone in the evangelical community. With his fiery flair in ministry and knowledge of media, he skyrocketed to stardom.

Clarkson prided himself in his accomplishments, taking out a book titled, "*Dictionary of the Diabolical: An A to Z Guide on New Age and Occult Systems*", which was published four years ago. He skimmed the pages, reviewing the information that took him years to compile. Met with positive reception from his acolytes and some negative from the skeptics and detractors, it propelled him to expert status. Tapping into the paranoid pulse of American society, he was able to gain authority in the world. Not to mention, sizable profits from his endeavors.

Calvin chuckled to himself, putting the book back in its place. It was all for a good cause and if he happened to be benefiting, who would deny him? Although tired, he was ready to go forth and preach about the necessity of spiritual fortitude, his answers to the

Storm-Star catastrophe and what the faithful expect in the last of days.

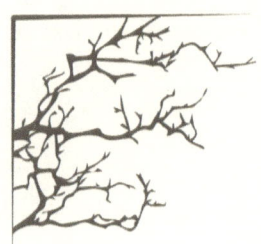

Chapter 72

Raymond Mason was briefed on the details of the case; trying to remember what notes he had taken. He was on his way to interview a person of interest to the case, dodging colleagues in the busy hallways.

The special agent found the interview room and opened the door. A tall black man sat up in the seat across the table, eyes droopy as his dreadlocked hair hung in his face.

"Mr. Gadsden?"

The man was unresponsive.

"Mr. Gadsden?" Mason called again, a little louder. The man stirred, raising his head and blinking in the bright overhead lights.

"Huh, uh...where's – where's Daisy?" he asked. Mason flipped through his notes, the name familiar to him.

"Yes, Ms. Grayhart. She, to my knowledge, is at St. Agnes Memorial. She suffered some injuries."

"What? I-Is she okay?"

"I'm not sure at the moment but I believe she was stable at the time they extracted her."

Attila fell silent; shocked. The news was hard to swallow.

"Mr. Gadsden, I would like to ask you a few questions concerning the incident at the Loupcroix property."

"Yeah, I-uh-" Attila stammered.

"Why were you on the Loupcroix property this morning in the possession of a firearm?"

"Where? I was trying to find Daisy. I knew she was there."

"Why?"

"Because of Devon. They killed him and she wanted to settle the score."

Mason remembered something about this, putting it down in pen.

"Yes, Detective Vasquez informed us of his findings. Is that why you showed up armed?"

"Yeah, I mean, I wasn't planning on killing anyone. It was for protection. Those fucking bastards are dangerous."

Mason took notes.

"Hold on! Where's Ash?" Attila interjected.

"Jagerhund, I presume?"

"Yeah, we lost track of each other during the storm."

"We conducted a search of the Jagerhund residence and we found some...disturbing things."

Attila clutched his head, as if in pain.

"Oh god-Dammit!"

"What's wrong?"

"The basement - "

Attila gave a small, shaky chuckle. "Heh, heh...not sure. Blood, blood everywhere."

"We couldn't find anything except for some blood and burned materials. The place was a mess though."

"It was Jasper! He was the Ripper!"

"The Rust Springs Ripper?" Raymond asked, astonished. "And Jasper is?"

"My friend, Ash's uncle. He was the one doing all the killings."

Mason took more notes, trying to keep track of the outrageous statements.

"So what happened in the basement?"

Attila gave him a thousand-yard stare.

"You wouldn't believe me." he choked. The tone in his voice made Mason uneasy. There was something off.

"Let's see." Mason replied. Attila paused. To Mason, the man looked unsure of what to say next.

"I, uh, got Ash and we went to the house."

"Why?"

"Ash said he needed to confront Jasper about something. We drove down and Ash went in first. I told him to stay. There was something weird about the house; freaked me out."

"Like?"

"An odd, twisted presence. It made fucked-up sense once I got the balls to go inside." he continued, "Some fucked up shit downstairs..."

"Go on."

"You know what?" Attila stalled. "It's too crazy."

"Mr. Gadsden, please."

"Well, Ash and Jasper were monsters or something. A bunch of flesh was...pulsing – and the smell and screams – "

Attila shut down, mumbling something about "fangs". An uncomfortable silence passed before Mason cleared his throat.

"Let's go back to Daisy. What happened at the Loupcroix compound?"

Attila sighed deeply.

"I-I don't remember much. The storm I remember and I, ya'know lost Ash, and made my way around the barn, but I blacked out."

"Did you see or hear anything?"

"A howl." His posture tensed.

"Howl?"

Attila didn't answer. Tears formed in his eyes. He began to shake.

"I saw...I saw..."

Mason waited with bated breath, giving Attila space to work through whatever experience the man had.

"The dead one." Attila whispered.

"What?"

"The cold one; the one its kind fears."

"Are you referring to a person or-?"

"He consumes all."

Mason matched Attila's words to the bloodbath at the raid. Something had brutally and viciously killed some agents. It was "impossible", others described, something outside of human capability.

Attila dry heaved, loudly and abruptly.

"Jesus!" Mason jumped a little in his seat.

"I can't! I can't! Where is she?"

"Can I get some help in here?" Mason asked. Two officers came in and removed Attila from the room. The nightclub owner struggled feebly for a bit in their grasp, fighting invisible forces.

"Well, that was productive." Mason whispered sarcastically to himself as Attila was dragged out. While he was sympathetic towards Attila, the interview failed to give him any new revelations. The testimony was just ramblings out of a traumatized mind. He was not sure what to make of what he heard. Strange murders, cults, and obtuse objects of worship that plagued this Midwestern town. His superior, Carbine, was not as elaborate with the details either. Mason exited the room only to run into the devil himself.

"Special Agent Carbine. Wasn't expecting to see you here."

"Yeah? Well, don't be too surprised. I've been trolling all around this damn place for leads." Carbine snorted.

Mason was not sure what to make of the situation as well. The different factions to the case seemed outrageous and fantastical, like a bizarre horror story he had walked into.

"Got anything new to share?" his superior asked him.

"Yes and no. Gadsden claims Jasper Jagerhund was a shapeshifting serial killer, and his significant other was taken by some monster summoned by the Lodge."

"Did he say anything about this Ash character?"

"Yes. An employee and friend...another shapeshifter."

Carbine chuckled, a sound absent of mirth. "Well, we're not any closer to a concrete story for public records but we have a vague idea of what the Ripper's and the Storm-Star's goals were."

"It would seem..."

"Have you heard of the Luna County case?"

"Yes, I'm familiar with it."

"Well, the cult there believed in an old, pre-Aztec death deity who is popular in Mexico among the derelict elements of that country." Carbine explained. "While different in theory, they made use of similar symbols found in the Storm-Star materials and the Jagerhund property." Carbine walked over to the table and picked up the folder. "Not to mention the gemstones, or I guess "fangs" as they are called, we recovered. We'll send them to Langley for further analysis."

Mason followed Carbine out of the room. The station was still buzzing with activity, filled with the women and children of the cult.

"I wasn't there, sir, but did you experience an enveloping...darkness of sorts." Mason asked.

"Like the thundersnow?"

"No, like - Gadsden was describing it to me-like a suffocating oblivion of sorts...he described voices, like an entity of a terrible nature was there." Mason elaborated. Carbine stopped and looked at him, scrutinizing sternly.

"I didn't see or hear anything, Mason. Are you sure it wasn't a hallucination on his part?"

"I don't know. Then again, what could have torn up our men apart like that?"

"It's something we're looking into."

"Gadsden also mentioned the evidence of higher powers, due to his experiences." Mason divulged. Carbine shrugged and walked off.

"Mason, depending on what we find, I'm not ruling it out."

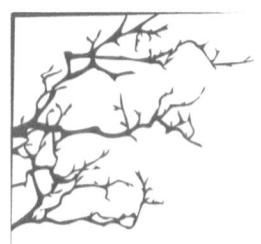

Chapter 73

5 months later
   Somewhere in Northern Michigan

ELMER AND RICHARD DROVE along the highway listening to the radio after an unsuccessful hunting excursion.

"Something terrible happened here in Rust Springs and the FBI, ATF, and police are being tight-lipped on the whole matter." Calvin Clarkson cried on the air. Richard was slightly familiar with the case details. He turned up the radio's volume.

"I can't even get in contact with involved parties, hard as my team tries. Like it never even happened. Well, I think we are all owed the truth - "

Richard was looking forward to going home. He had to get ready for work in the morning, and wished to leave their failed weekend behind. The woods were creepy this time of night. Coupled with the isolation, Richard rather not contemplate on what was lurking out there.

"World's crazy." Elmer lowered the volume. Richard could only sigh.

"I'm gonna change the channel on the radio, ok?" Elmer informed him.

"Go ahead. Not the best thing to listen to now anyway." he said, "Turn it to sports or something." Richard briefly took his eyes off the road. A split second later, he saw a pale nude body flash in the headlights.

"Whoa! – Shit!" Richard yelled as his truck collided with the poor soul in the road. A loud thump resonated over the hood. Richard slammed on the breaks, skidding on the still icy road.

"What the hell happened?" Elmer wiggled around, reaching for his seatbelt. Richard was already unbuckling himself and exiting the truck. He raced to the naked body laying a few feet away from him.

"Please don't be dead." Richard chanted inside his head. He fell on his knees when he reached the body, melting snow soaking his jeans.

He looked over the body of the young man who was bloody, scarred, and bruised. Blood seeped through matted, shaggy hair.

"Oh, god." Richard, with shaky hands, checked for a pulse on the cold, clammy skin. It was there, but it was faint. Over the loud roar of the truck, he could also hear ragged breathing.

"Elmer! Get out here!" Richard hoped they could save the young man. Elmer lumbered to his side.

"Help me lift him. Keep him stable."

The two hunters placed the injured man in the back seat of the truck, careful not to agitate any possible internal injuries.

"How far is it to the closest town from here?"

"A good half-hour."

"Dammit." Richard slammed the door shut. "I hope we can make it."

They hopped back in the truck, not bothering to fasten themselves in, as they sped down the road.

"How's he doing?" Richard asked. A good ten minutes had passed.

Elmer looked behind.

"Same, more or less. Where the hell did he come from?"

"It's freezing out here. I wouldn't be surprised if he has hypothermia. Or frostbite."

"Maybe it's drugs. I'm surprised he could walk across the road in this weather. I mean, who else would walk around these woods butt naked unless they're on something?"

Richard felt bad for the strange youngster. This was someone's son...and he had hit him. Was his family looking for him? Based on the crusty beard and long nails, he could tell the man has been on his own for a while. He looked no different than some of the bums he had seen on the streets.

"Wonder what's his story."

"Who knows? Kind of reminds me - "

A snarl erupted from the emaciated body of the young man as he sprung to life, attacking Elmer. Richard opened his mouth, only to have blood splatter on his lips. Elmer's eyes bugged out of his skill as his jugular was ripped open.

The truck ran off the road and into a steep embankment. Richard was jarred by the impact, the driver's airbag burning his face as it was deployed. Nothingness greeted him.

He groaned, breaking the surface to consciousness. It was snowing now, white flakes falling from the starless sky. He was sore all over and a sharp pain told him that his left arm was broken.

Outside of the cracked window, Richard could see a four-legged beast hobbling away. He thought it was a wolf at first, based on the posture and conformity of the body. However, the large sharp protrusions denoted an unnatural creature. Richard shut his eyes, tired and lured by an inviting siren of sleep. A mournful, bestial cry echoed over the woods.

...

May 1999 Rust Springs

DAISY WALKED INTO THE big master bedroom. Attila slept peacefully as she opened the curtains. When he slept, Daisy was reassured he was in a better place. He was progressing well in the therapy. With each new day came new challenges; however, and there was no telling what this day would bring.

"Attila?" Daisy pulled open the curtains, letting the late morning light in. Her fiancé grumbled, turning on his back.

"What-what time is it?"

"Ten after eleven."

"Well, it's Sunday."

"Thank god, huh?"

"Yup, the bar would still be open for Metal Mondays."

Attila sighed. The insurance pulled through, and The Grotto was re-opened after repairs were completed. The bar gave him a sense of purpose and kept him occupied, but it was a daily struggle. Medication helped but the bar was tainted with the memories of Ash and their fateful meeting.

Daisy had incurred some trauma from the experience, but it was different. It was like a bad dream. She hardly remembered the raid at Anchorage Farms. For that, she was grateful. Attila could remember every agonizing detail, and she hated herself for every moment she made him experience.

"C'mon I'll get some breakfast going." she offered.

Once downstairs, she fixed some eggs and pancakes. Attila, seated on the couch, turned on the TV.

There was a great shout from the boob-tube. An angry man waving a rifle and standing off against police.

"A man, allegedly affiliated with the disbanded Storm-Star Lodge, engaged police in a standoff at a local bank."

Attila was fixated on the television screen. A news clip from Minnesota about a "Dogman" haunting the wilderness of Princeton was the current report.

"I was out driving from a friend's house and I saw it along the road." a frantic young woman told the reporter. "I thought it was a big dog or something, but it rose up on two legs-like a man!"

The clips turned to a scene of state troopers and police dogs searching the woods alongside the road. Daisy swallowed. She knew what that meant. Ash was still out there, tormented by the bloodline Jasper tried to sever from the world.

"Ash..." Attila murmured.

Daisy set down her tea.

"'Tila? What are you talking about?"

"Ash was a..."

She had heard from Attila's sessions about Ash and Jasper becoming monsters of sorts. She didn't believe it; it was too fantastical. It made her guilt-ridden that she couldn't comprehend what he had experienced. She couldn't remember much herself on what happened that day.

"Attila, what are you talking about?"

Her fiancé jogged back upstairs.

"I want to go to the farm!" Attila yelled to her downstairs.

"The farm? Why the hell would you-"

Daisy stopped herself. She should follow the therapist's recommendations, and go with him to the site. Maybe it'll help him find closure.

The drive to Anchorage Farms, or what was left of it, was uneventful and not entirely unpleasant. Anxiety crept upon Daisy the closer they got. She hoped Attila would benefit from the experience. The property was lush with the vibrancy of spring. All of the structures the Loupcroix had were removed or demolished. Nature had grown over most of the remains of the buildings. Vibrant wildflowers bloomed everywhere; she'd never seen anything like it. The dread and horrors of the compound was lost in a sea of life and color.

There was a little modest memorial over the vacant dirt lot where the Lodge once stood. It was a thoughtful, if not generic dedication, to the memories for those who died on that day in November 1997.

"Do you remember?" Attila asked her, walking hand-in-hand. She shook her head.

"No. I still don't."

Her charge on the Loupcroix was the only thing she remembered. She didn't recall what Attila told her: being held captive, finding her injured in the snow and seeing monsters.

The wind kicked up, blowing cool air over her. She closed her eyes.

The howl...

She opened her eyes wide as she gasped.

"You've seen it too." Attila said. "The demon from the stars."

Daisy looked at him, all those missing memories crashing into her like a tsunami. The fear, the cold, the death and Attila's warm body holding her. Tears formed and Attila held her.

"I'm sorry. I'm sorry I didn't believe you." she sobbed.

"Shhhh. It's okay." He told her. It was funny; she was expecting to console him while it turned out the exact opposite.

"I-I don't know..." she stammered.

"Ash is alive." Attila said numbly.

"Yeah." Daisy said.

"We have to go find him."

Daisy didn't say a word as they drove home. They had packing to do tonight.

Don't miss out!

Visit the website below and you can sign up to receive emails whenever I.N. Morgan publishes a new book. There's no charge and no obligation.

https://books2read.com/r/B-A-NNAH-PRIX

BOOKS 2 READ

Connecting independent readers to independent writers.

About the Author

Being a writer was a dream I had since I was eight years old, when I spent my time writing stories in a journal my parents had bought me. Birthed in spectacular fantasy, my work grew darker over the years into genres such as horror and neo-noir. Visit Heavy Rush Media LLC for more of my works and updates!

Read more at https://www.heavyrushmediallc.com/about-me.